CITY OF HATE

TIMOTHY S. MILLER

CITY OF HATE

-a novel-

TIMOTHY S. MILLER

Printed in the United States of America

First Edition, 2020

ISBN 978-0-9985554-4-7
GMGB02

Cover design by Darin Bradley
Cover art by Clint Sawyer
Interior layout and design by Aaron Leis

Goliad Media is a production house based in Denton, TX,
showcasing art, literature, music, and mixed media.
We dream of empty places.

goliadmedia.net

For Christie and Bella

"Nothing, absolutely nothing happens in God's world by mistake."

Alcoholics Anonymous, 3rd Edition, Page 449

"Things do not happen. Things are made to happen."

John F. Kennedy

1

I KNOW HE'S DEAD because part of his skull is missing.
I know he's dead because the room smells like blood.
I know he's dead because a sudden sadness overwhelms me.
I forget if Bob's someone I know, or perhaps I've stumbled onto the death of a stranger.
The only time I feel this way is when there's a death in the family. Bob isn't really family. Then again, he is.
I'm dizzy. My gut's burning up. My head's about to disconnect from my spine. I forget things I've known forever. I have pain in new places. Old scars start to fester, turning into new wounds.
This is what happens when I need to face up to something. I compartmentalize it. I forget it. I move on with my life as though what I'm going through at this very moment isn't happening at all.
His eyes are glazed over. No one's home. Not anymore. He'll never see light again through those eyes. They're empty. He's hollow. He's a shell. If I hold him up to my ear, I'll hear the waves of a thousand oceans.
I'm tempted to take the gun, to pry it out of Bob's hand. It doesn't belong there. If I take the gun, will it feel like a gun or will it feel like something else?

But none of this matters, because I don't take the gun.

Instead, I run out of his apartment, down the stairs, and vomit in a pile of leaves. I rid myself of the dim room, the dank air, the bloody prologue before decay, the reek of soiled clothes and I'm running to my car, speeding off down the block and the Dallas skyline's getting smaller and smaller. The only thing I know for sure is that I need to get away. I'm not comfortable here.

This city turned on me.

Driving down Ross toward my apartment—the evening bringing darkness—everyone I see wants nothing to do with me. Drivers. Passengers. Pedestrians. Mechanics working on their cars. Women— their hair all dolled up, nails done—leaving the salon.

Or they're immediately hostile.

They want nothing to do with me; they want to tear me apart.

I'm afraid.

I'm opened up—exposed—face to face with death.

I feel nothing at all.

Death found Bob quick and swift. It gave him little warning— not a creep but a pounce. He hadn't struggled. He hadn't fought it one bit, hadn't—at any moment—begged for mercy or forgiveness. There wasn't a trace of any of that. No trace of light. Only darkness. The tried-and-true viciousness of death.

I ignore stop signs.

Which means I've made it two blocks before a cop pulls me over.

I watch the reds and blues mixing into oblivion—grip the steering wheel until it feels like it's going to break off in my lap, rotate my eyes from the rearview mirror to the windshield, from the rearview mirror to the windshield—until every scenario that I can possibly go through has been ridden into eternity.

He gets out of the car. He walks toward me with his flashlight, his hand on his gun. He does all of these things slowly—almost floating—the wind scooping his boots off the pavement, sitting him at the side of my car.

He asks me why I'm in such a hurry that I would so brazenly disregard the law of the land and the safety of others.

I tell him I discovered my best friend dead in his apartment. Although it was staged to look like a suicide, I have a sneaking suspicion that it's cold-blooded murder.

That isn't true. I tell him nothing. When he asks me why I'm in such a hurry, I tell him that I need to piss. I'm in a hurry to get home so I can take care of business. I say nothing about finding Bob dead in his apartment. I can't tell you why. I wish I knew.

What are you running from, son?

Is this a hypothetical question? When running my plates, had he produced a history of flight—incident after incident—where reality was aversion, drinking myself into oblivion, when avoidance of everything went into overdrive? Incident after incident where alienation became me, when even marriage to the most beautifulwonderfuldreamy woman imaginable couldn't tear me away from my self-destructive tendencies.

What am I running from?

———◆———

At least I would have the brains about me to confide in someone I could trust—maybe like Gerald—someone who could give me good advice as to what I should do next.

Again, the big answer is no.

Instead, I drive to Lemon's apartment.

He just got out of a twenty-eight-day stay at rehab because he got busted for exposing himself in Tietze Park in front of an entire Girl Scout troop. The judge said he could go to jail or rehab. He chose rehab. Lemon can't stay sober to save his soul. A thirty-five-year-old man who never grew up. He's one step away from moving back into his mother's house. And I'm going to ask him for help.

These kinds of decisions don't make sense. I'm out of control, making random decisions without fear of consequence. I'm living my life by total chance. Heads: I do something rational. Tails: I do something irrational. Tails every time.

———◆———

I knock on Lemon's door. The barrage of lights being turned off and then on again, the routine of blinds being peeked through—these rituals of the paranoid, flawlessly perfected and carried out—until the nerves settle down and the door opens to a crack.

For the longest time, he just stands there—his long hair in his face, stringy and hopelessly unwashed—looking at me through the crack in the door, uncertain of whether he'll let me in or not.

"I know," he says. "I haven't been to a meeting. I'm depressed—"

"Shut up, Lemon," I say. "That's not why I'm here."

There's this moment of silence when he looks at me—stunned, the kind of look reserved for the dead—like I'm not who he thinks I am.

He closes the door. Removes the chain. He opens the door again.

He's in serious trouble, Lemon. It's like looking at Bob all over again, but with a pulse. Barely. He hasn't eaten. He hasn't showered. He needs to be locked up.

"I'm suicidal," Lemon says.

He motions me inside, motions me to take a seat.

"I've been thinking about blowing my brains out all afternoon and you treat me like I'm a piece of shit."

"Why do you want to kill yourself?"

"Uh," Lemon says, "because I have so much going for me? I'm depressed. How was I supposed to know they were Girl Scouts?"

"The uniforms?"

"So they were dressed alike. But that's not all. I'm depressed because I'm under a goddamn microscope. They come into my apartment and tell me I need to clean up after myself. It's like I'm in kindergarten. Cocksucking caseworkers."

"I need your help."

Lemon's apartment is a mess. There's shit everywhere. Lemon Pickens doesn't give a rat's ass that cleanliness is next to Godliness.

I move an empty pizza box off of the couch so I can sit down. "Your caseworkers have a point. It wouldn't hurt to clean up a bit."

"Back off," Lemon says.

"And if you're trying to make a good impression with the court, you might consider taking the framed picture of Lee Harvey Oswald off the top of your television."

"I'm sentimental," Lemon says. "What can I say?"

"Do you have any cigarettes?"

"I thought you quit?"

"Just give me a cigarette."

"Jesus, what's wrong with you?"

"I'm in trouble."

"Then why'd you come over here?" He walks over to the television, pulls a cigarette from the pack, sticks one in his mouth.

"I need to talk to someone."

"What's in the envelope?" Lemon says, handing me a cigarette. He finds his lighter in his back pocket—takes it out—chucks it at me.

"Bob's dead," I say, letting out a mouth of smoke, slowly calming, slowly coming around, slowly letting go of whatever it is that had wrapped itself around me.

"No shit?" He takes a long pull from his cigarette and collapses into the corner of his couch, puts his feet up on the coffee table and waits for details.

"I hadn't seen him for a couple of days. So I went over to his apartment after I got off work."

"And?"

"He was dead. The top of his skull blown off."

I say this as though there's nothing unsettling about walking in on your buddy with his brains splattered against the wall. I say this with the calm assurance of someone who's in total denial.

"Gruesome. What'd the cops say?"

"I didn't call them."

"Didn't call them?"

"Bob had stumbled onto something. One of his coworkers was missing. Bob thought it might be connected to an affair she was having with his boss."

"So why not go to the cops?"

"Because what if Bob was right? What if Celia's disappearance was foul play? What if whoever killed Bob decides I'm next. Maybe they think I know too much."

"We've got to pursue this. I have resources. I'm well connected. I know people."

"Let's not overthink this one. Let's do this one—"

"One day at a goddamn time. I'm sick of one day at a time. We've got a goddamn mystery to solve."

"Calm down," I say. "I'm about to show you something, but you've got to keep your mouth shut. You can't tell anyone."

"Jesus," he says. "You took them from the crime scene. Pictures of her."

"How do you know?"

"I watch television."

"I totally underestimated you," I say, opening the envelope. I lay them out in front of him.

"Can I keep one of those?" he says.

———————

"I'm not wearing any panties," Maggie says.

"Can I call you back?"

"Jeez," she says.

"I promise I'll call right back. I have to take Charlie for a walk."

"Victor gets home in the next hour or so," she says. "So hurry."

"I'll hurry."

———————

She starts right where she left off.

"I'm not wearing any panties."

"Oh?"

"Don't you want to know what I'm doing?"

"Yes."

"I'm lying here in my bed, touching myself."

"Nice."

"I'm touching my pussy. You've got me so wet. I want you inside of me. Are you jacking off yet?"

"Not yet."

"Take off your pants."

"They're off."

"Now touch your cock. Think about shoving it inside me."

"Ok—"

"Think about fucking me. Are you licking my nipples?"

"Yes."

"I've got to go. Victor just pulled up. I'll see you at work."

I hang up the phone. I'm numb. As much as I care about Maggie, I can't focus. It's not too late to call the police, not too late to turn myself in and tell them all I know.

But the pressure of the unknown won't let me do it. I'm not comfortable with what might happen. As long as I'm on the run, I can control what happens to me. I may be too far to turn back.

I've been running for a long time.

I don't know what else to do.

———◆———

I could tell the cops that I don't know much about Celia. Just what Bob told me. Bob was smitten with her. Or she had something on him. One of the two.

I wonder if he killed her.

Were they sleeping together?

If they were, more than likely it was one of those things that happened when she was drunk. She was definitely the kind of woman who tossed down a drink or two. I've heard the stories. When drinking, Celia dropped all her inhibitions. Even though they were just friends, they probably slept together—a night of drunken passion—and then she probably slept with him a few more times out of guilt.

And, of course, the inevitable. Bob became emotionally involved.

He finds out that she's sleeping with their boss and feelings of jealousy slip into his thoughts. Pretty soon, Bob's following her, stalking her outside of her apartment, calling her at random.

He peeks through her apartment window. He waits until the wee hours of the morning, when he knows people have gone to bed, won't be walking their dogs, won't walk by the forty-year-old man perched between a couple of bushes, getting his rocks off by the slight chance that he'll see Celia in her underwear.

He justifies it to himself because they're friends. It comes from his desire to know more about her. It's not about the sex. It's not voyeurism for the sake of voyeurism. He wants to see how she lives her life when her guard is down.

Peeking through her apartment window isn't enough. Maybe Bob gets the desire to see her in the flesh, without the hindrance of a pane of glass. He'll find himself inside her apartment when she's out one evening—easy enough because she leaves a key under her doormat—rummaging through her panty drawers. Holds them up to his face. Jacks off in the middle of her bed. Thumbs through her journal. Logs onto her computer. Reads her emails. Searches for clues that would expose what she really wants in a man.

She comes home with Gavin.

They're both drunk out of their minds.

Slurring their words.

Laughing.

When they stumble into Celia's bedroom—missing half of their clothes—Bob bridles his rage in an effort to remain hidden. Bursting out of the closet and ripping a hole in Gavin's face would get him fired. It would upset Celia. All chances of them having a life together would be flushed down the drain.

So he endures the pain—clicking away at his camera, hidden away in the closet—in order to save his future.

It isn't easy, but Bob prevails.

With Celia ignoring him at work—giving him the old brush-off—those pictures snapped from the back of her closet burn a hole in his proverbial pocket. This is his way out. He slides those pictures in a manila envelope and places them in Gavin Thompson's mailbox with instructions on where to send the cash. Unless old Gavin wants his beautiful wife to receive a set of copies.

There's always the chance that Bob and Celia are in on this together. After sleeping together for several months—in their late-night, cigarette-after-sex conversations—they concoct a plan to extort money from Gavin Thompson in an effort to give hypocrisy its day in court. After all, Gavin's a sleazebag.

Running a foundation that preaches ultra conservative values while spending his evening at the local topless bar, preaching ultra conservative values while fucking every assistant that comes his way, whatever he gets, Gavin Thompson deserves. On top of that, Gavin Thompson is running for Governor.

I'll be honest, this wasn't the first thing that crossed my mind. It's not that I forgot—it just wasn't important to me. When your best friend's brains are splattered on the wall behind him, you're not really thinking about Gavin Thompson's recent foray into politics.

At the same time, it's not like I can ignore it. If you turn on the television—on pretty much any channel—you'll hear old Gavin Thompson talking about the importance of his family. You'll hear him talk about his relationship with God. You'll hear him talk about the recent slide of the nation away from what this nation was founded on—the desire to serve God with all of your heart, soul, and strength. If he has his way, he's going to bring it back.

It's hard to watch this scumbag go on and on about country, God, and family, when you have pictures of him getting his cock sucked by a woman who clearly isn't his wife. It's hard to watch this scumbag go on and on about the nation's decline in family values when he's eating his assistant out like he's at a Texas chili cook-off.

And if Celia and Bob can give this hypocrite his just reward, then so be it.

Celia and Bob agree that having sex with Gavin—in an effort to give him his due—won't get in the way of their relationship. It's one of those things they can overcome. The end justifies the means. No telling what kind of money they can get for those pictures.

So one evening, after Gavin's many pleas for her to have a drink with him, Celia gives the performance of a lifetime. Celia takes him back to her apartment—making sure he's drunk—and Bob hides in the back of her closet, clicking pictures that will get them both out of debt. This is their way out of a life of nine-to-five workdays, boredom, drudgery, their way out of a life they both hate and despise.

Regardless whether Bob was in on the blackmail or not, his jealousy gets the best of him. And his guilt. While stalking Celia—sleeping with her, or not sleeping with her—he's dating a woman who thinks he hung the moon. Bob met Rachel in AA. But regardless how much she loves him, he's unsatisfied. They've lost their connection. Whatever they had in the beginning—that longing to make each other complete—is gone.

He's torn.

He's infatuated with Celia.

But he loves Rachel.

So what does Celia have that Rachel doesn't?

Maybe it's all sexual. Maybe it's because she doesn't want him. Maybe it's the thrill of the chase. He's spent his whole life searching for the things that elude him—that up-and-down continuum—where regardless of how much he searches, he always ends up empty.

That's what I'll tell them.

Celia Povicov visits me in my dreams and tells me to find her. She tells me that only I can find her and bring her safely home. She takes me by the hand and leads me through a door—perhaps the door to her apartment—and in the darkness, I get the feeling that we're having sex. Groping each other. Tongues. Hands. Fingers. Tongues. The lights come on and she's a dead body in the morgue. I'm on top of her. She's dead. And naked. She opens her eyes. And says, *Find me.* She opens her eyes, stiff and cold, and says, *Find me.*

2

DEBRA WILSON DOESN'T HAVE our best interest in mind. But she's received some God-awfully-long instructions telling us how to prepare for a virulent outbreak of streptococcus bacteria. It's one of the many ways that she can flex her managerial muscle. Forcing us to show up an hour early—when we would rather be at home sleeping soundly in our warm beds—she'll take us through a series of drills, preparing us for the highly unlikely scenario that a pandemic will hit and every customer will become an inherent threat to our safety and well-being.

We've endured these threats before.

Sessions on reacting to the advent of the possible—but highly unlikely—robbery of Lone Star Bank. She'll read from her cue card as though she's teaching her Kindergarten Sunday School class the story of the Great Flood. The underlying meaning of her whole presentation is that if anything bad happens, we deserve it. We should consider ourselves lucky that we have a job in the first place.

Never mind Debra Wilson securing a job as branch manager based wholly on her father being the president of the southwest region. With the kind of facial tics Debra Wilson exhibits on a daily basis, she wouldn't have made it through the first interview.

In her mid-to-early forties, Debra exudes a sense of managerial authority without skill, competence, or intelligence. Her ability to string words together to form complete sentences is on the verge of miraculous.

Nevertheless, Debra Wilson's our boss. She's our authority figure. And she'll exhibit her sense of dominance in as many different ways as possible.

Her first of many suggestions—should we get word of the arrival of the mother of all pandemics—is to smile. Smiling makes the fear go away. "Smiling is God's gift to us," she says. "We can repay him by giving it back." She grins from ear to ear as an example—her eyebrows rising and falling into a tic—and instructs us to follow her example. She rates our smiles on a scale of one to ten.

I'm not sure whether to include the tic in my smile or not. I get a six.

Maggie makes gun motions with her finger. She sticks them in her mouth and pulls the imaginary trigger. Her head falls forward. Her arms fall to her sides. She slumps down in her chair.

Debra ignores Maggie's sudden death, or she's distracted by her own sense of purpose, as she pulls a surgical mask over her face—snaps the elastic around her head—and gives us a demonstration on how to breathe normally, despite wearing surgical masks. It may seem strange at first, but she assures us that we'll quickly adjust.

"Any questions?" Debra says.

I look away from her. I avoid eye contact. I don't have any questions.

"Help yourself to more coffee and donuts if you wish," she says.

Maggie's still dead.

She's not moving.

The dead don't help themselves to more coffee and donuts.

———◆———

Maggie's hungry.

Starving.

It's been so long since she's eaten, she has no idea what she's missing. It's been eons since she's felt full. Entire worlds have come into existence and blinked out into extinction since she's had her needs met. The idea of plenty is foreign to her. Satisfaction is so far removed, that even the idea of hunger escapes her. She doesn't know that she's hungry. The concept of need is altogether lost on her.

It's unnerving.

One day soon—unless she finds something to fill her up—she'll disappear.

Only I will miss her.

Her son will be too young to understand. Maggie's mom will become his surrogate parent, and he'll forget his mother altogether, except for occasional glimpses of her hollow shell in his dreams. Any concept of what Maggie Smith used to be—her relation to him in any finite way—will be lost to his memory.

Her husband, Victor, will be too busy to notice his wife's disappearance. He's an actor. Which means he's unemployed. Which means he works contract for a promotions agency. Which means he hands out cans of Copenhagen to fans at NASCAR races, Mistic and Zima at concerts at Reunion Arena, free T-shirts at Mavericks' games, if you take the time to fill out a credit card application. Which means he travels a lot. Which means Victor's so wrapped up in himself, he won't miss her. He'll be content—having more time to think about himself—no longer having to tolerate her musings on love.

She'll appear to him as a mirage on occasion. Driving down a lost and lonely highway in the blackness of lost evenings—rain beating down from the sky—he'll glimpse the silhouette of a hitchhiker stuck out in the rain. He'll pass her by. He'll think to himself that he should have stopped and picked her up, this lost and lonely fugitive. She looked vaguely familiar.

———◆———

"I'm leaving Victor," she says.

"Just like that?" I say.

I look for any kind of emotion, look at her deep in the face to see if it matches what she's saying.

17

"I've been thinking about this for a while."

Nothing registers. Her face is blank. Empty. It doesn't have anything to say.

"I didn't think that was an option."

She looks at me as if she's under attack. She studies my words, rolls them around in her head, moves her eyes away from me. She studies the empty lobby. She looks at her hands. She runs her hands through her hair.

"What am I supposed to do?"

"Have you said anything to Victor?"

"I told him I was thinking about it."

"What did he say?"

"Good luck."

"He said that?"

"That's Victor for you."

"Are you ok?"

"No," she says. She says this nonchalantly, without a moment's thought. "But I will be. I don't relish the thought of being a single mother, but I can do it."

"If there's anything I can do," I say.

"You're sweet," she says. "You're a great friend."

———◆———

Debra tells me that I have a phone call. She tells me that I can take it in the break room.

It's Lemon.

"Read the front-page."

"Slow down," I say.

"The front-page. Of the newspaper. Read the front-page."

"I'm at work."

"I know you're at work. You still need to read the front-page."

"I don't have a paper."

"Private detective killed in cold blood in front of ten-year-old daughter."

"Quit jacking with me."

"I'm not. Listen to this. Forty-five-year-old private investigator, Billy Joe Harris, was found dead in his private residence after his daughter made a frantic phone call to 911. Investigators believe foul play was involved."

"That's enough," I say.

"First Bob, then Billy Joe Harris."

"Stop," I say.

"You're next," Lemon says. "You'd better get out of there."

I'm sick to my stomach. I hang up the phone and walk back out to my station, go through the motions with my next customer, and I can't get Lemon's voice out of my head. *You're next, Hal. You're next.*

"Are you ok?" says Maggie. She looks right through me. There's no keeping this from her. I'm not ok; I'm in danger. She knows.

"I'm fine."

———◆———

I punch him in the throat—crushing his larynx—because he wears too much cologne.

He's the guy who almost takes your breath in the garage elevator when you're taking it to the first floor. It permeates the air and sticks to your clothes. It's like he's trying to cover up the fact that he smokes or something, but it isn't that. He doesn't smoke. He's one of those health conscious pricks who works out for two hours before he makes it to work, gets manicures and pedicures, gets a massage once or twice a week, gets his suits and shirts tailor made, never wears the same tie twice.

One of those guys who talks about how much he spends each year on his membership at the Dallas Country Club, how much he spent on the diamond broach he gave to the girl who he's been seeing for less than two months, and the three-hundred-thousand dollars he spent on a loft uptown that he pretty much uses only a couple times a week when he's too drunk to drive home. The same place where he gets three-hundred-dollar escorts to give him blowjobs because he wouldn't dare get caught having them pull up to his home in Highland Park.

His newest model luxury blah blah blah is parked in a space for compact cars. There's absolutely no getting into my car.

He has parked way too close.

This dick with his *Thompson for Family Values* bumper sticker doesn't give a goddamn whether I have to climb in through the passenger side or not. He doesn't care about me, you, or anybody else other than himself. He doesn't give a fuck about family values.

All the bumper stickers in the goddamn world won't make him start thinking about anything other than himself.

So when he wheels his newest model luxury blah blah blah in the spot right next to mine—whether his car fits there or not—his mind is not focused on whether I will be able to get into my car after a long day at work.

I have no choice but to climb in through the passenger side.

I have barely opened the door, when, as Fate has it, he walks through the elevator and out to his car, swinging his sleek black leather—I'm better than you because I have money—briefcase.

I feel like breaking every bone in his body.

He comes into the bank on Fridays, five minutes before it's time for us to go home, pulls out an envelope stuffed with transactions, and takes his sweet-ass time.

Every Friday.

When I take Maggie over to the Starbucks across from the bank, and he happens to be there, he'll make constant comments about the shape of Maggie's ass. Wouldn't it be nice to stick my dick in that. He says it loud enough for us to hear. He snickers. He laughs. He even goes so far as to ask her for her phone number. When she blows him off as nicely as she possibly can, he calls her a cunt under his breath.

That's our history. This sack-of-shit of a human being.

"Oh, did I park too close?"

"Just a tad."

"Sorry about that."

"This space is for compact cars."

"So suddenly you're the parking space police?"

"I'm just saying."

"I hope you didn't scratch this baby. I wouldn't want to carve you a new one."

"I've had a long day."

"What's wrong, buddy? Is that cunt holding out on you?"

I punch him in the throat. Straight. Hard.

The wind squeals out of him. His eyes tear up. He goes for his throat like he can stop the pain by covering himself up.

I catch him in the nose, as fast and as square as possible.

When his nose snaps—a nice clean pop—blood squirts out of his nose and onto his white pressed shirt.

I should feel sorry for him—all sprawled out and helpless on the concrete floor—but I don't.

It looks as though I've shot him at point-blank range.

Blood pools up on the front of his shirt as though he has a hole the size of a small planet right in the center of his chest.

That's what your nose does when you break it. It bleeds a lot.

He's collapsed in a patch of oil.

I step on his face and grind it into his hair.

I want him to remember this.

Every time he gets the urge to say something nasty about a total stranger—call her a cunt, talk about sticking his nasty dick into her—I want him to remember the smell of motor oil, the harsh-nerve-rubbing pain of a broken nose and the pleasure of breathing before having your larynx crushed by the swift blow of justice.

Maybe he'll think twice before parking his oversized luxury car in a compact car parking space.

I break the taillights of his luxurious car with the tip of my well-worn, scuffed dress shoes.

I call him a prick.

I get into my car through the passenger door.

I drive away.

I've barely broken a sweat.

———◆———

When the two plainclothes detectives at the top of my stairs start flashing their badges and asking all of their pointed questions, a hot rush of panic settles into the base of my skull. When you're innocent, you're not supposed to have a panic attack before the two detectives ask if they can come into your apartment, before they even have time to identify themselves. You're not supposed to sweat like this, to have these kinds of palpitations, the sudden urge to admit you did it, that you killed them all. The innocent don't behave this way.

"Mr. Hal Scott?" says one of the detectives, Cohen, or something like that.

"Yes," I say.

"Can we talk to you?"

"Sure," I say.

"Do you know what this is about?"

"Bob?"

"What about Bob?" says Cohen. He leans forward. He doesn't need me to tell him anything but he's going to wait around until I do. He isn't nervous. He isn't in a hurry. He won't be leaving until I cooperate.

What do I do here? I'm not used to being interrogated. I'm not used to being under suspicion. But then again, I am. I'm not only under suspicion, but guilty. Guilty. Everybody knows it. But I'll deny it. Even if I've done it right in front of you. Even if I have the gun in my hand, I'll say, *This isn't my gun. This isn't me. This isn't my hand.*

I'm not in the mood to go to jail. I could do without an intense question-and-answer session, fingers in my face, *Where were you at so and so time* and *Don't you know that the only people who don't call the cops are people who are guilty?*

"What about Bob?"

"He killed himself?"

"When did you find out about your friend's death? He was your friend, correct?"

"Yes," I say. "He was a good friend. I found out this afternoon. My friend Gerald called."

"We're sorry about your friend, but we're here to ask you a few questions about the death of Billy Joe Harris."

"Billy Joe Harris?"

"You do know him, don't you?"

"No, I mean I saw him once, but I don't really know him. I certainly didn't know him well enough to kill him."

"Whoa, slow down, pardner. Who said anything about you killing Billy Joe Harris? We want to ask a few questions."

I need a drink.

Everything about me needs a drink.

There's only one way for me to numb the feeling overtaking me at this exact moment. A Jack and Coke. It's been over a year since I've had a drink. I need one now more than ever.

"Can I get you something to drink?"

"We're fine. Feel free to get yourself something."

"I think I will."

I grab myself a Dr. Pepper. Pour it in a glass of ice. Watch the glass get cold. Watch it bead up.

"Mind if I smoke?"

"It's your apartment."

"Right," I say. "Do one of you have a cigarette I can bum? I'm out."

They look at each other. They look at me. They're playing my game. They're onto me. They're close to breaking me. Soon I'll be leading them to the body. Case closed. Onward and upward.

The one catch is this. I don't know where the body is. I don't know what body they're talking about.

Jacobs reaches into his shirt pocket and retrieves a pack of Marlboro Reds. He slides a cigarette from the pack and slowly hands it to me. So far, he hasn't uttered a word. But he doesn't have to. He'll let Cohen do the talking, while he interrogates me in silence.

"Thanks," I say. "You have a light?"

"Are you sure you smoke?" says Cohen, pulling a lighter out of his pants' pocket.

"I'm trying to quit," I say. "You actually caught me when I'm between quitting and smoking."

"You're smoking now," Cohen says.

"Yes," I say, letting out a mouth of smoke. "I guess I am."

"What were you doing at Billy Joe Harris Investigations four days ago?" Cohen says.

"My friend Bob and I—"

"The one who committed suicide?"

"Yes. That Bob."

"Hmmm . . ." says Cohen.

"A guy screwed him over. Took him for some money in a Canadian Lottery scam. Bob wanted to find out more about the guy. Bob wanted his money back."

"How much money?" Cohen says.

"I'm not certain."

"Continue."

"That's it."

"Well, Hal, there's a little more to the story. Remember Thelma Granger?" says Cohen.

"Never heard of her."

"She knows you. She got your license plate when you left his office. After your friend pummeled Mr. Harris into a pulp. Miss Granger was in his waiting area. Her poodle is missing."

"Bob didn't exactly pummel Mr. Harris into a pulp."

"That's how Thelma saw it. We would ask Mr. Harris, but he's wearing a toe-tag in the city morgue. And Bob isn't much help. So what happened between Bob and Mr. Harris?"

"He refused to give Bob his money back."

"So Bob beat him to a pulp."

"If that's what you say."

"No sir. That's not what I'm saying. I'm asking you what happened."

"Maybe Bob overreacted."

"That's all we need for now. You're not planning on taking a trip anytime soon, are you?"

"No."

"If you should change your mind, how about you give me a call first?"

Cohen hands me a business card.

"I'll do that," I say.

———◆———

"Are you ok?" Maggie calls me five seconds after they leave.

"I'm fine."

"I don't like it when you lie to me."

"I'm not lying."

"Bullshit you're not lying. I can hear it in your voice. I know you better than you think."

"I'll be fine."

"So what is it?" Maggie says.

"I told you, Mag—everything's fine."

"Whatever," she says.

She knows I'm not telling her the truth. She also knows that there's nothing she can do about it. The only thing she can do is tell me that she's here for me.

"I'm here for you."

"I know. I know," I say.

"Really," Maggie says.

"I know."

———◆———

Gerald's the one you've read about in the papers. You've seen his mug plastered all over the television, the one who shot his brother-in-law in the head during one of his blackouts, that one. Spent time in prison. A lot of time. Did ten or twelve years. He looks like he would kill you if you looked at him the wrong way.

But he wouldn't. Not Gerald. Not who he is now.

Gerald would do anything in the world for you. He doesn't have a streak of meanness in him. Try telling that to his brother-in-law, I guess. You could. He survived. The bullet jammed in his skull, and he lived to tell about it. He's not interested in how Gerald turned his life around.

"Come here often?" Gerald says, scooting up to the bar.

I'm having an iced tea at The Dixie House. It's a laidback home cooking kind of place with a large oak bar settled in the middle of the room, the kind with a bartender who will talk with you about anything, with two televisions blasting sports above his head. It's a popular place. Patrons are always plentiful, enjoying their evening meals: chicken fried steak and mashed potatoes, okra, broccoli rice casserole, fried corn, peach cobbler, apple pie.

Gerald laughs at his own joke.

I laugh too.

But it feels forced. A lot has happened. I have so much going on. Gerald has so much going on. It's not an easy time for any of us.

"How're you holding up?" Gerald says.

"I feel like I'm going crazy."

"I know Bob was your friend. He was my friend, too. His death doesn't change any of that. But you're ok. I didn't say *going* to be ok. You're ok. You need to know that."

"I don't feel ok."

"I said nothing about your feelings. I said you're ok. That's all."

"I'm in trouble," I say.

"What kind of trouble?"

"Some cops came by my place today. They're asking a lot of questions."

"You don't have anything to hide," he says.

"I was there," I say. "I found him dead in his apartment."

"And you didn't say anything?"

"Right."

"You should have called me."

"I should have done a lot of things. They think I'm guilty."

"We're all guilty of something."

I'm not certain where he's going with this one. All guilty of something. Maybe. But not guilty of the kind of thing they're trying to pin on me. I haven't harmed anyone; that's for sure.

"Are you sure?" Gerald says.

He's reading my mind. He's questioning whether I've harmed anyone. I'm overwhelmed with the kinds of harm I've caused.

"Huh."

"Are you sure they think you're guilty of something? Don't get yourself worked up over something that isn't true."

"But they're asking me questions."

"That's what cops do. Don't stress out over something that's completely standard fare. Go with the flow, Hal. Go with the flow."

"I don't think he did it."

"He had been drinking. He was heavily in debt."

"Yeah, I know. But it doesn't make sense."

"Suicide never makes sense. Death, for that matter. Or drinking, after all of that time sober. None of it makes sense. But Hal?"

"Yeah?"

"It doesn't have to make sense. Sometimes it just is."

"He's left-handed. The gun was in his right hand. If you're left-handed, you don't shoot yourself in the mouth with your right hand."

"Hmmm," Gerald says.

"Did you know about the missing woman?"

"Missing woman?"

"He worked with her. She was sleeping with his boss. And then she disappeared. We went to see a private detective about it."

"Can't say that I knew anything about that."

"Yeah. We went to see this Billy Joe Harris guy. And he turns up dead."

"He's dead, too?"

"Yes. There's more," I say. I slide the manila envelope across the table.

He opens the envelope and spreads the pictures out in front of him.

He raises his eyebrows.

"Jesus," he says. "You didn't."

"I don't know why. I just did."

"So this is the missing girl?"

"Yes."

"Looks like blackmail," Gerald says.

"Yes," I say. "It looks that way."

"It got him killed," Gerald says.

It sure did.

3

WORD GETS OUT QUICKLY about the Virgin Mother's image appearing under the triple underpass right next to the Grassy Knoll. It's all over the television. These pilgrims making their way in droves, walking down the Grassy Knoll from their cars, scooting down the sidewalk and under the bridge. They push through in tight but orderly lines, surrounded on both sides by graffiti, and then, on the right wall, a little more than halfway to the other side—the appearance of the Virgin Mother. She's a moldy shadow with splotches of light, a patch of algae in the shape of Mary the Mother of Jesus.

Not that this is a new phenomenon. I hear about them everywhere. The face of Jesus appearing on a flour tortilla. The Virgin Mother appearing suddenly on a grilled cheese sandwich.

Regardless of its lack of originality, the moldy image of the Virgin Mother—so close to the site of JFK's assassination—brings a multitude of believers to pay their respects and to ponder its meaning.

God has finally forgiven Dallas for killing America's beloved president. If God can forgive Dallas, then America can forgive Dallas, too.

The media's turning it into a circus, a frenzy, playing the devil's advocate on one side, and on the other, believing each and every word. They're trying to place this huge significance on why the Virgin has appeared only five hundred yards from the sight of the tragic assassination of John Fitzgerald Kennedy. The headlines: "INFAMOUS CITY FORGIVEN, CITY OF HATE NO MORE, VIRGIN VISITS DALLAS."

"It's ridiculous. Period," says Lemon.

We're sitting on the Grassy Knoll, watching the pilgrims.

"They refuse to believe in government conspiracies, but they'll stand in line for hours to see a patch of mold. Unbelievable."

"Aren't you curious? What's that about contempt prior to investigation?"

"You couldn't pay me to stand in line with these people. They say I'm crazy because I believe that a spaceship crashed at Roswell, because I say that Timothy McVeigh was secret black ops recruited by Clinton to blow up the Murrah Federal building in an effort to frame the militia movement, because I say that Oswald was a Patsy. I'm the crazy one."

"Hey," I say. "Lower your voice."

"Lower my voice? They don't care what I'm saying. They're too busy hoping a patch of mold will heal them of their afflictions."

I know why these people are here. I won't be joining them anytime soon, but it's definitely something I understand. We're all looking for a way to fill that God-shaped hole. I'm certainly not going to get all crazy because someone else wants to spend their time that way. They can do what they need to do.

"Gullible assholes," Lemon says.

"Whoa," I say. "Aren't you being a little hypocritical? Let them believe what they want to believe."

"If they extend the same courtesy."

"Who is this *they* you keep referring to? If *they* extend the same courtesy. These aren't the bullies of your childhood. We don't even know these people."

"Bullshit. I deal with them every day. These are the same people who turn up their noses when I try to sell them a magazine. Like I'm the one that's crazy. The Virgin Mary. I don't have a right to judge, my ass. These people have been waiting their whole lives to be judged by me. I'm certainly not going to fail them now."

"You're funny. You conspiracy people—"

"Don't you *conspiracy people* me. We don't all belong to the same fan club. We're just truth seekers."

"As are they," I say.

"Idiots," Lemon says. "The whole concept is an oxymoron. Virgin birth. Give me a goddamn break."

I wonder why Lemon's afraid. With all this anger spewing out of him, he's got to be afraid of something.

Maybe he's afraid of losing himself as a result of this miraculous visitation. It could change everything he's known up to this very moment. What will happen to his world now that the Virgin Mother has arrived?

Hobos who were more than likely CIA. The Umbrella Man. The Babushka Lady. Jack Ruby. Oswald. Oswald's Russian Double. The Mob. The Magic Bullet. On and on until you're blue in the face.

All this could change. All that Lemon has ever known. Intrigue. Tales of double-crossing heroes and villains. Good and Evil. Puppet governments. Pro-Castro Cubans. Anti-Castro Cubans. Russian spies. Suddenly overshadowed by something miraculous.

What about Lemon? When the Dealey Plaza's known as a place of miracles, as opposed to a place of conspiracy, what happens to Lemon's world then? Does it slowly unravel? Does everything he's ever known fade into oblivion? When you're the self-proclaimed bastard son of Lee Harvey Oswald, conspiracies are all that you have. With your whole world at stake, it would be a shame to let some fairy tale miracle—some fairy tale visit from a fairy tale Virgin—get in the way.

———◆———

I'm waiting for Lemon. We're at Conspiracy Books. His mother's bookstore. Only blocks away from Dealey Plaza. Only blocks away from where John F. Kennedy was assassinated. He wants to pick up his paycheck.

The main room's filled with more books than you can imagine. And outside of the main room, endless hallways lined with books lead to other rooms. Arrows pointing toward the Revisionist History section. Arrows pointing toward the Area 51 section. Rows upon rows of books about the imminent world domination of aliens from another planet. Rows upon rows of books of government cover-ups. Hallways leading to more hallways, leading to more tiny rooms until I'm lost amidst monuments to conspiracy after conspiracy, until I can't find my way back.

I stumble onto the occasional patron perched on one knee or huddled in the corner or seated in one of the half-dozen hard-backed chairs scattered sporadically around the store—pushing his glasses back on the ridge of his nose—thumbing through magazine after magazine, searching for the eternal riches of the universe.

A couple doing their homework at a table in the corner. A young man with a backpack, bent on discovering the secrets embedded in the corners of the dollar bill. A middle-aged woman reading a book on palm reading in the Psychic Phenomenon section.

Conversations about shadow governments, Freemasons, and the Illuminati. Conversations rising from the stacks about everything that nobody is telling us. No wonder we're afraid. No wonder we're all tied in knots.

I'm browsing. Reading titles. Flipping through books. Looking at pictures on the wall—black and white mementos—of people who seem familiar, pictures of people who I don't recognize.

"You buy into any of this?" says a girl with a hoop through her nose. She's behind the counter. Sitting on a stool. Reading a paperback book about alien abductions. She has four or five studs in her ear. A stud through an eyebrow. Tattoos up and down both arms: purple, red, blue, green. Fairies with florescent wings. Rainbows. A unicorn. An alien. She's wearing a *Who Shot J.R.?* T-shirt.

"Buy into what?"

"You know," she says. "This." She waves her arms around the store.

"I don't know—"

"Sure you do."

"I'd like to think I'm open-minded."

"Wishful thinking," she says. "We're not a bunch of wackos. We're looking for answers. These books are blueprints, my brother, blueprints."

"Blueprints?"

"Directions. This is how we bring the revolution back. Point your finger at us all you want, but stay out of our way."

"Jeez," I say. "Tough crowd."

"I tell the truth, brother. I tell the truth."

———◆———

We're at Lemon's mother's house in Oak Cliff—one block off Davis, on Bishop—one block away from the famed Texas Theater. His mother needs some boxes brought down from the attic.

Being there—in the house Lemon grew up in—gives me the creeps. They live in filth. They don't care about keeping things neat and orderly.

Shelves upon shelves of books. Records. Knickknacks. Stacks of books in the corner. Books on the coffee table. Stacks of books in the bathroom.

And cats. Cats everywhere. There must be fifteen to twenty cats. The house smells like cats.

———◆———

While Mary watches *The Days of Wine and Roses* on her VCR, smokes her Kool cigarettes, and eats Cheetos out of the bag, we're in the attic. It's hot. Dusty. Sunlight the color of mildew slips in through the small windows, spilling droplets of sunlight around our feet like memory. If it splashes on us—it'll seep through our skin, mix with our blood—we'll have sudden revelations of Mary's life. All of the memories that are trapped in these boxes will move into us and the boxes will be empty.

This is their life, sealed in plastic. Pieces of them in books yellowed by age, books smelling of cigarettes and coffee, books that cough up dust when opened. Pieces of them in little trinkets of Dallas, frozen in time.

I find a picture of a scantily clad young burlesque dancer in sequins and wings, standing next to Jack Ruby. It must be Lemon's mother.

She walks to the front of the stage as light as she can be. She almost flies. Jazz plays in the background—a live band, horns, the thud of drums, the *tsss tsss tsss* of a hi-hat—while patrons send cigarette smoke into the air, drinking their beers, giving their catcalls.

She ignores them. She's not attracted to them. She doesn't need their attention to fill some empty space. So why does she tolerate all of this nonsense, night after night? The groping. The nasty words. Jack patting her on the ass as she slips through the curtain at the end of her act.

He's violent, Jack. It comes natural. He would as soon slap you upside the head than try to settle things with words. He sits in his office drinking whiskey until he has had more than he can stand. He spots a couple of sailors who have been drinking his wine without tipping the girls, walks over to their table and explains that the girls don't work for free. He has goddamn rent to pay around here.

They tell him to lighten up.

He grabs one by the throat and throws him down the stairs while cursing the other. And he walks back into his office and starts drinking whiskey again.

While the dancers are settling up with the house, Jack berates them for not making him more money. He might as well be selling shoes. He might as well be washing windows. Because they're sure as hell not making him any goddamn money.

Don't kid yourself, Jack's making money. He's making a shitload, marking up his cheap wine. He doesn't pay much rent. At the end of the day, Jack Ruby's coming out just fine.

They wouldn't say anything like that to Jack.

Jack is family. He takes care of them. For all of his rough-and-tumble theatrics—for all of his gruffness—Jack's a kind soul. After all, Jack pays their rent. He buys their clothes. He doesn't expect much. He just has a few rules to follow.

"You're not whores," he says. "You're my children. If you feel comfortable letting them touch you a little, that's your business, but no fucking the patrons. I'm not a goddamn pimp. My kids don't screw for money."

Of course, that's not counting Jack.

He's pretty much slept with all of them at least once. He wines them and dines them their first couple of weeks—finds them a place to stay, gets them all set up, takes them shopping—and then gets a few free blowjobs.

Once you've been there for a while that mostly ends.

But not with Mary. Or Angel. That's what they call her. That's her schtick. Don a pair of oversized wings and prance out on stage as graceful as she possibly can, in her high heels. And her pasties.

She goes off into her own little world for a while. She erases them from her memory. She searches for silence and catches it. All she can think about is the angel inside of her.

Jack won't be happy.

He's too old. It would weigh him down. He'll lose a dancer.

But it's none of his business. He's not the father.

The father. That's its own story. If she searches herself, it isn't love at all. As hard as it is to fall in love—even with someone you know intimately—it's impossible to love a stranger.

But, then again, Lee's mysteriousness is attractive.

His quiet personality.

His shyness.

His otherworldliness.

One second he's Lee. And the next, he's turned into Lee Harvey Oswald.

Rummaging through a box in the corner, Lemon's eyes light up—he's visiting another world, another time, another place. I'll wonder later if his eyes lit up or if that's something I imagined after the fact. But what I know now—much later—is that he found what he was looking for. Lemon stumbled onto something that was bigger than all of us, something that would place us all in a treacherous kind of danger.

4

DON'T THINK YOU KNOW where this is going. Keep in mind, I'm not telling you everything. I'm just telling you all that you need to know. But rest assured, this isn't going to be one of those cliffhanger *Dallas* episodes where someone dies and the next season you find out it was all a dream. This really happened. It went down just like I'm telling you. But I can't tell you all at once. Unfortunately, there are a few things I can't tell you at all.

I didn't kill Bob French.

I didn't kill Bob French.

I didn't kill Bob French.

I'm trying to convince myself. I'm practicing my speech for the interrogation. There's going to come a time when they haul me into the police station downtown and demand a statement. I'll be in a cold room with white walls, a table, and two chairs. They've looked at my phone records. They know that Gerald isn't the one who told me that Bob was dead. They know that I was there when Bob died. Or at least shortly after. They know that I discovered his body.

Someone saw me. A neighbor walking her dog. Or the nosy bitch landlord who was always telling Bob to turn his music down. *Don't you know that it's two o'clock in the morning? Turn your goddamn music down for Christ's sake.* The nosy bitch landlord who was always telling Bob to dump the ashtray that he kept on his balcony. *Don't you dare smoke inside. You're going to burn the whole goddamn place down.*

And my vomit.

I vomited in a pile of leaves at the bottom of his stairs.

The landlord's husband raked leaves early that afternoon. There was a nice pile there. I was nauseated. I remember the nausea. Vividly. Finding Bob dead like that—wasn't the easiest thing to take.

I barely made it down the stairs.

I almost vomited in Bob's living room. I almost vomited on the carpet right next to him. For some reason, I was able to control the dizziness settling over me, was able to fight the urge to vomit. I picked up the pictures. I tucked them in my pants, underneath my shirt. I stumbled down the stairs.

I wasn't thinking at that moment. I had no plan. I was doing everything by second nature. My trip down the stairs wasn't mapped out. I didn't notice my surroundings. The landlord could've been standing at the bottom of those stairs, for that matter.

I had only one item on my agenda.

To get the hell out of there.

Vomiting in a pile of leaves at the bottom of those stairs wasn't on my agenda. I would forget it altogether. Until now.

I remember it vividly.

The investigators found it. They have their sample. They'll run their tests and they've got their man. They've got their man at the scene of the crime. All they need is a motive.

There's no motive.

I had no reason whatsoever to kill Bob French. He was my friend. That's what I'll say once they've taken me downtown. I had no reason whatsoever to kill Bob French. He was my friend. I'll pause between *no reason whatsoever to kill Bob French* and *He was my friend.* I'll pause and take a breath. My lip will quiver. I may even stop and take a drink from the glass of water sitting in front of me. I'll pause, take a drink, and tell them the rest of my story. I'll tell them to investigate all they want. They can test my hands for traces of gunpowder. Interview my friends. I had no reason whatsoever to kill Bob French. He was my friend.

But they're not convinced that I'm innocent. They'll take all I've told them and they'll break it down. They'll ask me to repeat my stories. They'll want to know the last time that I talked to Bob. They'll want details of our trip to see Billy Joe. They'll have questions about the Canadian Lottery scam. They'll ask me where I was at the exact moment of Bob's death.

They're convinced I'm leaving something out.

———◆———

The meeting has already started. Someone's reading *How it Works*. A guy named Kyle. A guy with less than thirty days sober. He's still shaky, still looks all strung-out, like he's coming undone. It's not easy to see someone like this. He's dying, really. His body's begging for him to put something in it. Something that'll give him his life back. At this stage, he doesn't have much to hold on to. But he's here to survive. He's looking for answers. He's willing to do anything. He reads out of chapter five in the *Big Book* as though his life depends on it. His life *does* depend on it.

I grab myself a cup of coffee, throw a quarter in the coffee can, and find a seat in the back row by the door. Sit next to a guy with a trach in his throat. He gurgles when he breathes. It's a little disconcerting—this struggle for breath—but, at the same time, I don't have much of a choice. There aren't many seats left. So I sit here and listen to him struggle to breathe. I sit here and listen to his life rattle around in his chest. I close my eyes and meditate on this life rattle. His breathing reminds me of the sea. I'm lying on a beach somewhere, listening to the water gurgling all around me.

I'm peaceful. With my eyes closed and the sea gurgling all around me, everything stops. Everything but the sea. Everything stops but the gurgling of the sea.

A girl in front of me is sharing. Just got out of rehab. Says something about wanting to die. Ever since she had the abortion. She wants to drown herself with booze. But she doesn't have to do that anymore, she says. Slowly but surely, she's drying up. She's turning into something else. Not that the thought of death doesn't hover around her, from time to time. She often has her own funeral in her head. Everybody she's ever loved is there. Everybody she's ever hated is there. They come to her funeral because they can't *not* be there. They have to see her—have to pay their last respects—because in one way or another, she's saved their life. In her death, somehow they find life. Having her own funeral calms her down, she says. That's scary. That's why she's here.

"Keep coming back," we say. "Thanks for sharing."

Rachel's sitting in the corner. She waves at me. She looks away. Her eyes are red. Swollen. She's been crying. It's not easy on her. It never is.

A young girl named Candice is chairing the meeting. She's wearing a tight, white shirt and what looks to be a school girl's uniform.

It's hard to focus.

I can't keep myself from staring at her white shirt.

I can't keep myself from staring at her nipples poking through.

I look away. I look at Rachel again.

This probably isn't a good idea. There's nothing I can say to her. There's no way I can tell her that everything's going to be ok. I can't tell her that *one day* she'll forget about Bob. She'll just wake up, and the pain will be gone. And that'll happen sooner if she starts fucking someone else.

It works every time.

A guy named Trip is sharing. His wife left him for another woman. He has a year sober. He's thinking about drinking. Do you know how hard it is to walk in on your wife and she's slap-dab in the middle of your bed with another woman? It's not easy. He had left for the afternoon because his wife needed to study. She was back in school. Had finals coming up. Her study partner, Amy, was coming over, and they were going to study together. So he went off to the bookstore and browsed around for a couple of hours. He decided to go home early, even though his wife had told him she needed plenty of time and for him to call before he came home. He didn't see why any of that was important. He could just go to the bedroom and watch some television. He walked through the front door and they were lying on the couch—naked—eating each other out.

"Thanks for sharing," we say.

Candice looks embarrassed for him. The last part of the story was too much for her. They need to move on. She's embarrassed to the point of turning red. It's like she was the one sleeping with Trip's wife.

Most of the men in the room are turned on.

They want Trip to share again.

Instead, a woman named Rose. Old. Washed up. Shriveled. Veins for hands. Who the hell knows what she's sharing about. I've tuned her out by now. I'm in between staring at Candice's nipples and watching Rachel huddled in the corner.

"Thanks for sharing," we say.

We stand in a circle and say the Lord's Prayer, and I keep looking at Candice in her white shirt, showing nipples.

Her school girl uniform.

We say *Keep coming back, it works if you work it*, and I think of the numerous ways that I could take Candice on, and Lemon walks in. He's winded from the stairs.

"I need to stop smoking," he says.

"Nice for you to show up on time," I say.

"I missed the bus."

"That's what they all say," I say.

"Jeez, he says. "Look at the tits on her." He points at Candice in her tight, white shirt.

"You're an animal," I say. "A real pig."

"I can't help it," he says. "Natural instincts run wild."

"Yes."

"It would help if she would buy clothes that fit. I can't help it that she's wearing a shirt three sizes too small," he says.

"Hello," Rachel says.

"Hi."

"Can I talk to you?" she says.

"Sure."

"Do you think you could give me a ride home?" Lemon says.

"That's fine," I say. "Wait for me at the car."

———◆———

I walk down the stairs with Rachel after the meeting. There is a group of us, smoking. Rachel digs into her back pocket for a pack of smokes. Pats her front pocket for a lighter. I pull my lighter out and light her cigarette for her. She smokes her cigarette down like it's her last one ever. She blows the smoke in a vicious line above her head and looks off into nowhere.

She's thinking about things that happened long ago as if they happened last night. Her past is hovering all around us. She's confusing yesterday with today, and by the time she makes it to the present, it'll be tomorrow. She'll be old. She'll be lonely. She'll have all of these regrets. Her life will have passed her by, and it'll be too late.

I don't know what to say to her.

She's the one who needed to talk to me, and now I'm supposed to open up. She's the one who needed to talk to me, and now I'm supposed to read her mind and say exactly what she needs to hear.

It doesn't work that way. I'm not a mind reader. And I'm empty. I have nothing to offer her.

———◆———

It feels like it may rain. The sky could open up at any moment. It's what we need, really. It's been hot, lately. Stifling. A nice rain would cool things off, would wake things up. A myriad of life would spring open and the world would breathe again.

The landlady looks at us with suspicion, glares at us while grudgingly leading us up the stairs to Bob's apartment.

She's tired of this. People moving in, people moving out. This isn't what she signed up for. She's supposed to be retired. She should be lying on a beach somewhere sipping daiquiris out of a crystal glass, not getting a dead man's apartment ready to rent. She shouldn't be worried about getting blood out of the carpet. She shouldn't be concerned about fragments of bone embedded in the thin walls.

She should be watching television, drinking her daiquiri out of a paper cup. Instead, she has to worry about rinsing this out of her consciousness. She's stuck with the problems of people she never cared about. This isn't what she signed on for. Not at all.

She looks at me like she's seen me before. She saw me walking up the stairs to Bob's apartment the night of his death, with a gun.

"If you're going to smoke," she says, "smoke out here on the balcony. Ash in this can." She points to a coffee can below his kitchen window. "I don't want any smoking inside the apartment. It stinks enough as it is."

The thought of walking into Bob's apartment and smelling death creeps me out. It's already stuck in my head. The image of Bob with part of his skull missing. His head all bloated. His left eye pushed back unnaturally. His left cheekbone crushed from the pressure. His face all chalky white with hints of purple.

But Gerald needs our help. We're going to clean up Bob's apartment. We're going to box things up and move them to a storage unit. We're going to get the place ready to rent out.

It's the least we can do.

Gerald shouldn't have to do it by himself.

We owe him this.

The landlady pushes past us and walks down the stairs.

"Holler at me when you're done," she says, still glaring at us.

"She's pleasant," Gerald says.

"Yes," I say. "A real beauty."

"What's her problem?" Lemon says.

Bob's place is pretty much like he left it.

Clothes left lying on the bed. A few books on the nightstand. Bills on top of his television.

"They took his computer," Gerald says.

"Really—"

"Can't imagine what they think they're going to find."

"Who knows," I say.

"Porn," Lemon says. "Bob was a sick bastard."

"Shut your mouth," I say. "Judge not lest you be judged."

"Enough," Gerald says. "Start boxing things up." Gerald points to a pile of boxes in the corner. "I told Martha we would bring her a few of his things."

"How about Rachel?" I say.

"She asked for us to bring her a picture or two. Maybe one of them together."

"Right."

"But everything else," Gerald says, "goes to storage."

"Ok," I say, staring at a bookshelf in the corner.

"Why are we going to keep any of this shit?" Lemon says. "He's dead. It's not like he needs it."

"Why don't you chill out," Gerald says. "Have a little respect."

"I'm not showing any disrespect. I'm just laying it all out. He's dead, for Christ's sake."

Gerald shoots him a dirty look, and we start putting stuff in boxes. Lemon walks out onto the balcony to smoke.

"It's too bad that it had to end up this way," Gerald says. But he says it as though this was inevitable. He says it as though he knew it would end up this way all along, like he has some window into the future that shows him exactly how everything's going to turn out. Not that he can do anything about it. Forced to watch it play itself out exactly like it had played itself out in his vision, there's nothing he can do to stop it. It's an inevitable thing flinging itself through the universe.

It makes him tired. It wears him out. It weighs him down.

I'm taking books down from Bob's bookshelves. They're covered in dust. There may have been a time when Bob paid them more attention, but for the most part, they had been left to gather dust.

It feels invasive. Even going through something as indifferent as his books. It's like hanging outside someone's window. Waiting for them to disrobe. Waiting in the bushes in hopes someone doesn't spot you—camped outside someone else's bedroom window—hoping to see them in their underwear.

But, at the same time, this feels very familiar. Placing things in boxes. Holding a picture frame of Bob and Rachel smiling outside the gates of Disney World. Pictures of Rachel in a heart-shaped frame. Taking the remnants of his life and placing them in a box. Wrapping it with tape. Stacking them in a corner. Watching the boxes get higher and higher. Watching Bob's life disappear.

When I was fifteen, I watched my mother box up my brother's things. All of his toys. Wrapping them neatly in plastic and placing them in boxes. Soon after, she started drinking again.

And Sam. I helped her mother go through her stuff. We packed it in boxes and placed it in a U-Haul. Watched them drive away with it. We did it all in silence. We were filled so full with grief that we didn't have room for language. We searched ourselves for memories that we dared not share, lest they be lost.

I regret not keeping anything. I let her mother have it all. I had taken Sam from them. They knew it. There was no forgiving me. They had too much grief and no room for forgiveness. I would get nothing from them but silence. They would forget my name.

And now, with Bob, I don't want to leave empty-handed. I want to take something with me. I need something to remember him by. I won't make that mistake again.

I take his only copy of the *Big Blue Book of Alcoholics Anonymous.* I don't know why I take it. He died drunk. But I need something. Anything.

We pack all of Bob's boxes into the back of Gerald's truck and drive away in silence. Gerald doesn't say anything. Lemon doesn't say anything. I don't say anything.

A new tenant will move in. A woman. She won't know anything about Bob. She'll move in a new couch. A new bed. A new computer. She'll have her boyfriend over on the weekends. They'll fuck in Bob's old apartment. They'll smoke their after-sex cigarettes on the balcony. They'll talk of a future together. They'll talk of a life bigger than they could have imagined.

All traces of Bob will disappear—condemned to the boxes of his memory—locked in a storage shed just miles from the very place where he smoked cigarettes on the balcony—watched the smoke drift into the hot Texas air—wishing for dreams that would never come true.

Light bent through curved glass, slowed down, catching glimpses of reality and laying them down in all of their nakedness, missing only their thoughts.

Laid side to side—in order—you can fill in the blank spots. You can add your own images to tell the story.

Standing at the foot of the bed—in a thong, her bra tossed on the floor, her shoulder-length hair caught in mid-stream, as though she has just flung her hair back—when the shutter clicks. Her ribs are jutting out of skin so clear you can almost see her organs.

On all fours, panties off, a nice shot of ass and leg.

Riding an unidentifiable Gavin Thompson, caught on the way down, or on the way up. There's no way to tell.

Shot of a clearly identifiable Gavin Thompson, kissing her in the middle of the bed. They're sitting in the middle of her bed. Kissing. Caught in this embrace.

Shot of Gavin's wide shoulders, bare-assed, fucking her in short bursts.

Shot of her sucking Gavin's cock, him leaned up against the headboard. Clean-shot of her ass, legs spread.

———◆———

I take the pictures out and masturbate. I jerk off in my living-room with the pictures laid out in front of me. In my fantasies, it's my cock that she's sucking.

And while it may seem sick and wrong to masturbate to pictures of a total stranger, it's not as bad as it seems. I know her. I know all about her. I know her hopes and dreams, her past and her future. These are not just random pictures of a woman caught up in a blackmail scheme that just—by happenstance—ended up in my possession. This is Fate.

I set it in motion.

5

I CAN'T GET THE IMAGE of Bob out of my head.

I'm playing it back over and over.

It's one of those things you don't have any control over. But, if I did—let's say I had the power to make these images go away, let's say I had the power to make everything stop—as sick as it sounds, I don't know that I would.

It would be nice if I could let go and let God—if I could just push it all away into the category of things that happened in my past—but it's not as easy as that.

I need to hold on to it. Replaying these images in my head is penance for all of the things that I've done wrong. I've got all of these sins that have been adding up—stacked one by one, on top of each other—and the only way that I can begin to unstack them is by dragging myself through the images of Bob and his bloated skull. Bob and his brains spread out across the wall. Bright red pools all around him. On the chair. On the carpet. Chunks of his brains on the front of his shirt.

Each time these images run themselves through my mind, it is my penance. This is a small way that I can make penance for all the wrong that I've caused.

It's not the first time. The summer my brother died—and for many years after—I replayed the minutiae of that fateful day. Throwing the ball. My brother running out into the street. The awful thud. Anytime I was feeling guilty, I would replay that thud—that awful thud—in my head, would push the play button over and over. Thud. Thud. Thud. By the time I was through, I felt a sense of peace. Everything was going to be ok.

But it never is. It doesn't work that way. Replay this kind of stuff long enough, and it doesn't want to leave. It's stuck there. The play button has gotten jammed. There's no turning back. You've got no other choice but to find some way to cover it up.

That's when I started drinking. From the second that I poured something down my throat, I felt the relief I had been looking for my whole life. The second that I poured something down my throat, I forgot. All of those visions of my brother running across the green grass—out into the street, getting hit by the neighbor's car—and that awful thud, were gone.

But they return.

You drink them down.

One's gone, and you create another.

Sam. The screech of metal on metal. The sound of breaking glass. The screams. The blood as it flies around the car like a fine mist.

Recreating death in a drunken haze.

Make it stop.

A drink is all it takes. One drink and it goes away and you're at peace with the world. You're sailing smoothly and everything's coming up roses. The sound of metal on metal will return and a drink is all it takes. One drink and it goes away and you're at peace with the world and you're sailing smoothly and everything's coming up roses and the sound of metal on metal and a drink is all it takes and you take that one drink and it all goes away.

I'm losing my mind.

I'm going crazy.

I need a drink before I blow my brains out.

———◆———

Being stuck in your apartment—the walls closing in around you— when you're losing your mind, isn't the best idea. At least that's what

Gerald says. Whenever I tell him about one of my episodes, he has some piece of sagely advice to give. It's usually something about getting out of my apartment. Go for a long walk. Call someone. Go to a meeting. Do anything to shut the noise out. Get out of yourself. Never go inside your head alone. It's a bad neighborhood.

I should take his advice.

I should call Lemon and see how he's doing. Or, I could call Gerald and tell him what I'm going through. But I already know what he'll say. He'll tell me to go help somebody.

So I call Maggie. I get her voice mail. "This is Maggie. I can't take your call at this moment but if you'll leave your name, your phone number, and a brief message, I'll get back with you as soon as possible."

I don't leave my name. I don't leave my phone number. I don't leave a brief message. I want her to get back with me as soon as possible, but I don't want to leave a message.

Charlie's looking up at me like he's trying to tell me that the best way to get out of myself is for me to get my lazy ass up off of the couch and take him for a goddamn walk. Before he pisses all over the apartment.

———◆———

So Charlie. Instead of coming out of my skin, jumping into my car, and driving down to the Landing and throwing back Jack and Cokes—one after another—until all of the voices are gone, letting my violent impulses get the best of me and going next door and beating the shit out of the punk who plays his music so loud it makes me feel like bashing his face in while his slutty girlfriend shivers in the corner in a bra and a pair of panties, I should take Charlie for a walk.

He deserves it, Charlie. I definitely don't run him like I should, like I used to when my life was simple. I didn't have anything to lose. I didn't have anything left. I stumbled across his picture at the Lakewood Starbucks, looking more ragged and mangy than he should look, since they're looking for a home for him and all. A picture that showed him looking all scrawny and in need of attention, with a caption that said he needed a home. A dog was the last thing

I needed. Something to take care of. At the same time, it would do me good. I spent a lot of time feeling sorry for myself. I spent a lot of time locked up in my apartment. I spent a lot of time throwing down way too many Jacks and Cokes at the Landing. It was about time that I did something good for a change.

Charlie had been abused. When I picked him up from a woman with a do-rag on her head—wearing a tank top and a pair of jeans that were way too tight for her—Charlie was shivering in the corner of the backyard like somebody took a steel-toed boot to the side of his head.

I felt a surge of love for him. Any kind of sympathy for anything just wasn't in the cards for me. I didn't have anything like that in me. But it happened all the same.

It saved me. It was one of those things that kept me from going through some pretty rough times.

But regardless, I still don't want to take Charlie for a walk. But I'll do it anyway. Walking Charlie will do me some good.

———◆———

It's cool out. Walking Charlie helps. There's a slight wind blowing through the trees, and it feels like it could get cold. The branches of the large trees that hide large, old houses with nice furniture and happy families inside, could suddenly wither up and die.

But it's ok.

Seasons change.

If I stick around and don't do something crazy, I'll get a chance to watch everything bloom out again, watch everything sprout and grow all around us. If I sit back and don't panic, everything will turn out ok.

Charlie's enjoying his walk. Looking almost regal as he prances down the sidewalk—weaving and bobbing—sniffing of this, sniffing of that. He's not too fearful since there isn't much traffic down these side streets, since it isn't raining, since the sky isn't streaked with lightning.

As if we followed the hand of Fate, we're suddenly in front of Bob's apartment. Nestled behind a much larger house surrounded by trees—what looks like a garage, and a flight of steps, a balcony lined with potted plants—is the place where it all began.

Bob's sitting in a folding chair, smoking a cigarette. Rachel's standing next to him—one leg tucked behind her—leaning up against the wall. On the surface, they look like they're enjoying the night air, but something's wrong.

I can't hear what they're saying, but Bob's pacing on the balcony, waving his cigarette in the air, flicking ashes into the wind. Rachel is close to tears. As I think about walking closer so I can get an idea of what's going on, they disappear.

All that's left is an empty folding chair.

A few potted plants lining the balcony.

A gentle breeze.

A little spot in the back of my head—that little dark spot of fear—flares up out of nowhere. There's no safety. Even in an evening stroll, walking Charlie. I can walk from here to eternity. I can literally walk until my ass falls off, but everything's not going to be ok. Just when I think the worst is over, the party's just getting started.

———◆———

Maggie answers the door in an oversized T-shirt and jeans. She raises a finger to her mouth to let me know that Tyler's sleeping.

He's sprawled out on the couch. He's unaware of the frustrations, the agonies of mortals. He dreams the dreams of angels.

Maggie scoops him up and motions for me to make myself at home. She whispers that she'll be back in a moment.

Maggie's apartment is as full as mine is empty. She's a collector. Her small apartment's overflowing. But she has a place for every-thing. Mementos line her bookshelves. Little memories of her childhood. Figurines. Pictures in tiny frames. Postcards.

It's overwhelming. It's hard for me to breathe.

She must feel the same in the open vastness of my apartment.

I don't know what I'm doing here. I do. I don't.

I know what I want. I want to get out of my head. I'm tired of the images of Bob sticking a gun in his mouth and blowing a good part of his brains on the wall behind him. I'm tired of feeling like running away. I'm tired of my loneliness. I'm tired of one-night affairs. I'm tired of surfing internet porn. I'm tired of slick magazines. I'm tired of masturbating. I'm tired of the lack of substance in my life. I'm tired of relationships that lead nowhere. I'm tired of having lunch with Maggie—getting to know her on this superficial level—and then watching her leave. I'm tired of having a relationship that is relegated to superficial conversation and occasional phone sex.

Is it possible to have phone sex with a woman for six months—to work with her, to eat lunch with her every day—and not know her at all?

I know what I want. I want to make love to Maggie. I want to feel what it feels like to care about someone.

When Maggie walks down the dimly lit hallway and sits with me on the couch, it's like we've never met. Or we have—but something happened—and now we're starting over.

"Why are you here?"

"You asked me to come over."

"Do you always do what you're told?"

"I needed to see you."

"Ok," she says. She smiles. "Here I am."

"Here you are."

"Did you come over here to have sex with me?"

"I don't know . . ."

"Really?" she says. "You don't know if you came over here to have sex with me or not?"

"I'm not saying it wasn't on my mind. But that's not why I'm here."

"Then why are you here?"

"Do I have to have a reason?"

"If you could know what your reason is, what would it be?"

"I like you."

She kisses me.

Kissing Maggie takes my mind off of everything else. We are comfortable dancing with strangers. We forget that we are friends, forget that we work together.

"What about Tyler?" I say. I'm nervous, not certain how I feel about the little tyke walking in on us while I'm making out with his mother.

"Stop worrying" Maggie says. She gets up from the couch and moves the coffee table to one side of the room. "Take your clothes off."

She pulls her white T-shirt over her head. Her breasts are small, but they're beautiful. Beautiful. Firm. Perfect. She steps out of her jeans. She's wearing a pair of simple cotton panties, which are soon at her ankles. She kicks them at me, and I catch them with one hand.

"Good catch," she says. "Now, do as I said."

I take off my shirt. I take off my jeans.

"All of them."

"I'm embarrassed."

"Would me sucking your dick make the embarrassment go away?"

She crawls over on her knees—pulls my underwear down around my ankles—and without missing a beat, starts sucking me off.

I'm about to come when she stops and moves back to her spot sitting cross-legged in the middle of her living-room floor.

"Join me?"

I'm standing next to her couch with a massive erection.

"Don't worry, Hal, I'll fuck you soon enough."

I feel guilty.

I feel terrible.

I feel overwhelmingly sad that knowing her—as good as it feels to have her as a friend—is not on my mind. What I want is to turn her over the arm of her leather couch and fuck her so hard that she begs me to stop.

But Maggie Smith won't have it any other way.

"Are you going to join me or not?"

"Coming."

I sit next to her, cross my legs.

"Close your eyes," she says, taking my hands in hers.

"Ok."

"Do not—under any condition—open your eyes."

"Ok."

"Promise me."

"I promise."

"Ok," she says. She reaches over and kisses me, thrusts her tongue inside my mouth. I'm about to explode. After a moment, Maggie stops kissing me. She pulls away from me. She straightens her back, still holding my hands.

Suddenly, all of these thoughts that have been spinning around in my head are pushed out by something else. They're overshadowed by one very clear message. I start to cry. I'm overwhelmed.

It comes out of nowhere. One second I'm holding hands with Maggie—nursing a full-blown erection—and moments later the only thing keeping our hands linked is that Maggie won't let go. Tears run down my cheeks. I'm crying so much I don't know if I'll be able to keep my promise. I don't know if I'll be able to hold it all together.

My thoughts are not my own. My mind has been taken by force and is being molested without my permission. I've been taken to another place. Where that place is, I'm not certain. Lying next to Maggie in the middle of her living- room floor—feeling useless, empty, knowing that we will not make love tonight—I'm absolutely lost and found in the same moment.

"Are you ok?"

"Yes."

"Don't you want me? Now that you know me, Hal? Don't you want to fuck me? Now that you know."

I've got nothing to say to her.

6

WHOEVER SAID VIOLENCE never solved anything doesn't know what he's talking about.

Violence is the only language some people understand.

Not that I'm fluent, but I know enough to get by.

Take for instance, Mr. Personality. Mr. Sack-of-Shit of a Human Being. Mr. I Vote for Family Values.

Ever since I rearranged his face, he's been Mr. Congeniality. Opening the door for us when we walk over to Starbucks, doing his dead-level best to keep his eyes off of Maggie's ass. When he fails, he at least keeps his comments to himself.

He's a little nervous around me—slinks away when he happens to walk by me in the hall—but otherwise, you can say that our little escapade gave him an almost miraculous transformation.

It's enough of a change that Maggie notices.

"You'd think you beat his ass or something."

I just nod and say I really haven't noticed a difference, and quickly change the subject.

"There's a smirk on your face," she says. "What did you do to him?"

"Nothing," I say. "Absolutely nothing."

Try telling Maggie that the reason that you rearranged Mr. Congeniality's face is that you're in love with her and that you're trying to protect her. It sounds like some kind of macho shit. I broke his nose clean in half in an effort to protect your reputation. Try telling Maggie that the reason you rearranged Mr. Congeniality's face is because you want to spend the rest of your life with her.

It wouldn't help win her over. It would make her suspicious. She would have this sliver of doubt about my character, would wonder when that part of me—that I had pushed so deep into the darkest recesses of my soul—would reveal itself.

This violence isn't something I plan. It comes out of nowhere. It's more than needing a cigarette, it's like one second I'm totally normal, and then the next, I combust.

———◆———

I've just counted my drawer when Cynthia Thompson walks in.

Cynthia Thompson. You've seen her in *Paper City*, that slick magazine that tells you about the comings and goings of the people who matter. Standing there with her husband—raising their wine glasses—at some charity benefit, at some foundation auction, at some art gallery opening that has her husband's name tacked to it as a sponsor. They stand there with their smiles painted on, for the cameras. You've seen her blonde highlights glowing, her cleavage coming out of her sheer white Chanel gown, her string of pearls. Mrs. Future First Lady of the State of Texas.

Something isn't right. She's a woman scorned. Not that she doesn't have someone on the side; she does indeed. But it was done out of spite. Her husband has been fucking his assistant. Yes, she has given a blowjob or two. Yes, she pleasures their accountant on the nights that her husband stays late at the Foundation. She enjoys their attorney on the nights that Gavin is out of town on business. She's been unfaithful a time or two, but that's what you do when your husband is spreading his seed in women who are young enough to be your daughter.

Don't tell me that half of Dallas doesn't know what's going on. Superficial? Totally self-absorbed? Of course. But so out of touch that they don't see the gleam in her husband's eyes when that goddamn bitch of an assistant walks over to her and tells her that it's nice to see her again?

Those young lips have been slobbering all over her husband's cock. Not that it matters. Half of the women at these events have had her husband's cock in their mouth.

But walking up to her and telling her that it's nice to see her? It's goddamn humiliating. She wants to reach out and scratch her eyes out, this bitch. She wants to reach down and leave scars across her perky boobs. She wants to bring blood to her taut skin, to her fit—*I work out at the gym all day so I can fuck your husband*—body.

But she doesn't.

She hates herself for it. She despises staying with Gavin for the money. She's content to be humiliated because she enjoys driving the latest model Lexus. She enjoys living in their house in Highland Park. She enjoys fine dinners in the nicest restaurants. She enjoys her membership at three of the most luxurious clubs in Dallas. She enjoys seeing her picture in *Paper City*. She enjoys the thought of living in the Governor's Mansion.

It makes her want to cut her own wrists.

It makes her want to overdose on her Valium.

It makes her want to cut off Gavin's dick while he sleeps, and feed it to him. *I've had to suck your worthless cock for years, and now I'm going to give you a taste of your own medicine.*

This doesn't happen. Instead, she makes him endure long silences on the way home from the charity benefit that has his name tacked to it as a sponsor. She plays the role of the perfect wife to pay him back for all the misery that he has heaped upon her.

Their children are the only thing keeping her from suffocating him in his sleep. They're the only thing that keeps her from packing up her Gucci bags, taking a car to the Dallas Fort Worth International Airport, and flying to France to start her life over.

She wishes she could honor them by cutting their father's throat. They would be better off. His hypocrisy wouldn't corrupt their veins. Free from his lying and conniving, they would become the kind of citizens that make the world proud.

This won't happen. They're spoiled rotten. They'll grow up to be carbon copies of their dear old dad. Carbon copies of their dear old mom. They'll get blowjobs from their assistants. They'll spread their legs and fuck monotony so they can support this lifestyle. They'll stay in worthless marriages. They'll live their own lives of hypocrisy. They'll die—like both of their parents—unhappy, unfulfilled.

She should have killed them when they were young.

She should have saved them from their private tutors, their private schools, their extracurricular activities. She should have saved them from their addiction to name-brand clothing, ten-thousand-dollar birthday parties, Ivy League educations, and trust funds that never run dry. She should have suffocated them in their beds.

They would be better off.

But she's spineless. She doesn't have the balls.

She comes into the bank on Fridays. She always has some kind of Starbucks Latte with her, which she sets on the counter as she writes out her deposit slip with her well-manicured hands.

She always gets in my line. If for some reason it looks as though she's going to get Maggie, she'll let someone go ahead of her as she rifles through her purse.

She lumps Maggie into the category of young women who sleep with her husband. The little whore bitches.

I say Good morning.

She asks me if there's anything going on in the news, alluding to the television hanging over my head that quietly broadcasts news updates from CNN.

She calls me by name. Even if she has to glance at my nametag on occasion to make sure that she has it right.

I chat with her, ask if there is anything else I can do to be of service, Mrs. Thompson.

"Not without me going to prison," she says.

Maggie catches me looking at Cynthia's ass as she walks through the lobby and out of the double doors.

"Careful, Tiger," Maggie says.

"What are you talking about?" I say.

"Grrr," Maggie says. "Grrr."

———◆———

The day couldn't drag on any slower.

I've been standing here so long I'm about to lock my knees and pass out.

Debra has been on a tirade, going into long diatribes about how we need to maintain more drawer accuracy. If we keep losing the kind of money we're losing—by the time we count our drawers and go home for the evening—the bank will have to file for bankruptcy.

That's a load of bullshit.

If anything, ole Debra's taking a cut at the end of the day to stock up on Krispy Kremes. This woman's worthless. She doesn't know jack about managing a bank, can barely manage her facial tics that seem to act up at the most inappropriate times.

Maggie's off in her own little world today, which really shouldn't surprise me. It isn't any different than any other day, but I seem to notice it more. The silence is killing me. I'm tired of standing here—waiting for what seems like hours for a customer to come into the bank—with Maggie standing right next to me, not saying anything.

I look up at the clock across the lobby and watch the second hand crawl across the Roman numerals, as if it's low on batteries. It crawls around the gold Roman numerals as if it's about to stop entirely.

We'll be stuck here until the end of time.

We won't age another day.

I'll never get to sleep with Maggie Smith.

———◆———

Time starts again when Lemon walks into the bank, frazzled and out of his mind.

"We've got to talk," he says.

"I'm at work, Lemon."

"Take a break," he says. "This is important."

"Have a seat," I say, pointing to a chair in the lobby. "I'll see what I can do."

I ask Maggie to cover for me, tell her I'm going to take a quick break. I find Debra in the break room—dunking a donut in a cup of coffee—reading her horoscope.

"Do you mind if I take a quick break?"

"I don't pay you to smoke cigarettes."

She dunks her donut in her coffee, takes a bite, and her eyebrows break out in a tic. Her forehead spreads into a series of wrinkles—her skin dancing up and down—and she eases into a series of throat clearings. Uuuunngh. Uuuunngh. Uuuunngh. I wait until the show's over.

———◆———

"So what is it?" I say.

We're sitting on a concrete bench out front—tucked in an eave between buildings—smoking cigarettes.

"They're following me," he says. He looks around after he says it—pushing the hair out of his face—taking a drag off of his cigarette.

"Who?" I say.

"I don't know," he says. "That would make everything real goddamn easy," he says. "But it's not like I'm going to stop long enough to ask them."

"Do you see them now?"

He looks over his shoulder. He takes another drag off of his cigarette—blows a thin stream of smoke through his nose—and is silent.

"So do you see them now?"

"No," Lemon says. "I'm telling you, these guys are good. But they slip up from time to time. But they want me to see them. They want me to know that they're on to me."

"What are they on to?"

"You know. The thing . . ."

"No, I don't know."

"I can't say."

"Then how am I supposed to know?"

"Oh, you know."

While Lemon's going on about knowing what they're after and that they're following him and that they want him to know that they're following him, Cynthia Thompson's sitting at an outside table at the Starbucks across the drive.

Her legs are crossed—showing leg—and she's sitting there going through what looks like a stack of bills. She looks up occasionally, and then looks back down again. At one point it looks as if she sees me, although—with a row of Mercedes, Lexus, and BMWs parked out front—it's highly unlikely.

Lemon breaks into a litany about needing his disability check to arrive. Everything's falling apart. He's not the only one in trouble. His mother's in debt up to her eyeballs. The lease on Conspiracy Books is about to expire and the owner of the building's going to kick her out. He's going to sell-out to a group of investors hoping to put a high-end hotel slash high-end lofts in its place. If he doesn't find some way to help her out, all that she has worked so hard for's going to go up in smoke. I'm nodding my head—trying my best to listen—but I can't get past the sight of Cynthia Thompson sitting at the outside table at the Starbucks across the drive, showing leg.

———◆———

I'm well over my five minutes—closing in on the amount of time it takes Debra to blow her stack—when I tell Lemon that I have to be going. I walk across the drive to Starbucks to pick me up a Grande Black Eye and to further my chances of chatting with Cynthia Thompson. Not that we're going to chat or anything, but suddenly I have this urge to be near her. I don't know if it has anything to do with the jealousy I sensed in Maggie's *Grrr Grrr* comment, or that I'm drawn to long legs and short skirts. Maybe I have a connection with Cynthia Thompson because I masturbate to a series of photographs that happen to include her husband and his mistress. Regardless, here I am, walking across to the Starbucks not certain what I expect to find there.

By now, Cynthia Thompson's talking on her cell phone. I look down at her as I pass and sneak a look at her long legs and her short skirt. I notice a manila envelope sitting to the left of her stack of bills. It's ragged where it has been opened and the tip of a photograph can be seen sticking out of the top.

I forget why I'm walking over to Starbucks. I have the urge to get back to work in order to get all of this—quickly and suddenly—out of my head.

———◆———

When I arrive home, I immediately know something's wrong. That feeling that you get in the pit of your stomach telling you to get the hell out of there. Something isn't right.

The door's unlocked.

Which isn't normal.

I don't leave the door unlocked.

It's slightly open.

I check around the door jamb. I look carefully around the door knob. It wasn't forced open.

Although my gut tells me to run, I almost never go with my gut. I ignore it. I stuff it down. I've had a long day. I need to drink less coffee. I'm being ridiculous. I'll laugh about this later when I find out that everything is how I left it. There wasn't anything to be afraid of at all.

Charlie's skittish. He's waiting for me by the door—as usual—but something's wrong. He's in that low-crouched position. It's like he's been kicked. He's afraid of something.

But Charlie's afraid of everything. He's the kind of dog that gets spooked when there's a storm coming, crawls under the bed when there's the slightest sign of rain.

I don't have to fear the worst.

I walk through my apartment and nothing's out of place. No lights are turned on that I left off. No lights are turned off that I left on. No sign of forced entry. My computer hasn't been touched. Everything's where I left it.

I need a nice long shower. All of this will go away. I'll take a nice long shower, I'll take Charlie for a long walk, and all of this will go away. I'll laugh about feeling anxious when there wasn't anything to be afraid of at all.

I walk down the hallway—stopping to grab a towel, Charlie following closely behind me—and walk into the bathroom.

It's funny, getting myself worked up this way. It's old behavior, this paranoia. I need to have faith. I need to accept the fact that I'm safe. I need to let go of my fear.

My bathroom's small.

It's a tight, small square with the bathtub squeezed into the corner. It's a tight, small square with a tiny sink with a tiny mirror hanging above it, a tiny sink with little or no space for clutter. A razor. A toothbrush. Some toothpaste. A can of shaving cream.

The mirror's the first thing I see when I walk into the bathroom and turn on the light. Which can be disturbing in the morning. When the first thing that greets me is a vision of myself unkempt and tired. A vision of myself who's only half awake after a long night of restless sleep.

But I'm not groggy. I'm not half awake. Outside of the slight hangover from my brief bout with fear and paranoia, I'm relatively clear-minded and self-aware.

Which changes when I turn on the bathroom light and the word *Patsy* is scrawled in blood across the tiny mirror hanging above the tiny sink with little or no space for clutter.

Fear's not a sufficient explanation for what I'm feeling. I won't slip into cliché by telling you I cringe in horror or shrink back in terror or that goosebumps creep up my spine. I won't slip into cliché by telling you that I'm frightened speechless, that I can't find the breath to scream, that a sudden coldness creeps over my body like I have taken a plunge into icy waters.

Although, all of this is true.

I feel no safer when I swipe at the bloody word with my bare palms, watching the water in the sink turn crimson as I wash my hands in manic desperation. I feel no safer when the blood's gone.

I check the shower. I check under my bed. I open every closet. I check the balcony. I lock all the windows.

I make absolutely certain that I'm alone.

I walk Charlie and I feel no safer outside.

The heavy air—weighing me down with its humid fingers—causes me to forget to breathe. I should put Charlie in the car and drive away. I'll drive and drive and drive and drive. I won't look back. I'll start my life over. I'll move to a small town. I won't call my parents. I won't call Debra at Lone Star. I won't call Maggie. I won't look back. I won't have regrets.

7

Bob's funeral's like any other funeral.

———◆———

His plot's in an area called the Garden of Grace.
  We stand under a green pavilion.
  The preacher reads from the Bible.
  We're all somber and sad.

———◆———

"It was a nice service," Martha says.
  "Yes."
  "I thought everything turned out rather nicely."
  "Yes."
  "It's a shame. I never dreamed that it would end this way." She shakes her head. She looks at the television. She looks away from the television. She stares off into space. She watches something that's not there.

"I'm sorry."

"Bob's father drank for many years. But not since I've been with him. He's been sober the whole time. Harold would give the shirt off his back for you. He was that kind of man."

"Right," I say.

"He loved Bob. He wanted to take back all of those years when he wasn't there. He wanted to make everything right."

"I'm sure."

"Bob came over shortly before Harold passed. Sat right where you're sitting. He bawled like a baby. They hugged for the longest time. It made me so happy."

"I imagine," I say.

"That's all I have to hold on to. They made their peace with each other."

"That's good."

"I miss them both," she says.

"I know you do."

"I'm glad you stopped by," she says. "There's something I need to know."

"Ok."

"He'd been drinking. Right?"

"Yes."

"You're a good friend," Martha says. "You're a good friend."

———◆———

The two detectives are sitting on the steps at the bottom of my stairs, smoking cigarettes. I'm not surprised to see them. I had a feeling they'd be back.

"Mind if we ask a few questions?" Jacobs says. He pushes his shades up on the top of his head, takes another drag of his cigarette.

Up until now, I didn't think he could talk. And his voice doesn't match his body. He sounds like an accountant. But it's not the voice that concerns me. He's bigger than I remember. Thick. His arms are as big as my legs.

I imagine he has them filled with tattoos. Skulls and Crossbones. Military bullshit. Daggers through bloody red hearts imbedded deep in his skin by dirty needles late in the evening in some war-torn barracks between killing sprees during the Gulf War. Slings blood deep in the trenches. Slings drinks at a dingy bar on the way back from slinging blood. When he gets back to his barracks after closing time, another jarhead slings ink into his flesh—a half naked lady with his girlfriend's name in wavy letters underneath—which he covers later with a dagger through a bloody red heart, which was symbolic of what she had done to him.

But the killing wasn't over. He came back victorious, but once you start killing, you don't ever stop. Just because some treaty gets signed or some bill gets passed—and you're airlifted away from battle—the battle stays in your head.

Pushing pencils in some nine-to-five won't satiate his need for blood. He'll wave his military record around in front of some hungry recruiter, find himself wearing a badge and carrying a gun. He's lucky he passed his PHQ because he's crazy as a loon. Maybe that's why they want him. He's got a taste for blood and a pair of arms to back it up. He's here for his bulk. For his brutality. For his inability to feel. For his total lack of fear. He's a machine. A killing machine.

I won't walk up the stairs to my apartment until Jacobs decides that he wants me to walk up the stairs to my apartment. He could crush me like a bug, this guy. He could take me out in his sleep.

"I'm talking to you," he says, his eyes bearing into me like he's having a flashback. "Mind if we ask a few questions?"

"Do I need an attorney present?"

"Are you guilty of something?" Cohen says.

"We're all guilty of something," I say.

"You've got that shit right," Cohen says.

Cohen's the brains behind this operation. He's here to keep Jacobs from killing first and asking questions later—but he's not beyond turning me black and blue. He's done his share of beating the shit out of guys who never saw it coming.

When you first see Cohen, he doesn't look like the kind of guy who could tear you apart, but if you look into his eyes long enough, you can see enough rage to fuel a million fires. Cohen doesn't have a soul. He doesn't have a conscience. While he may be small in comparison to Jacobs, he doesn't have anything to lose. When you don't know right from wrong, you're capable of anything.

More than likely, Cohen got the shit beat out of him by his old man when he was growing up. He learned to walk quietly when the old man had been drinking—doing his best yessir, nosir—and when the old man got violent, took it without making a sound. He stored all of that anger real deep. You wouldn't have a clue that he was at a boiling point—that he was at the point of losing it—until you pushed him into a corner.

You would regret it.

Cohen would reach into the back of his psyche—would open that little trap door that stored all of that anger—and he would let it loose. You would never see it coming. Every time he beat you, he would be beating his old man. That kind of guy.

And I'm about to invite these gentlemen in for a cup of coffee.

———◆———

I walk around my kitchen. I make coffee. I open the refrigerator. I take out the milk. I add milk and sugar. I walk around my apartment like two detectives sitting in my living room's nothing out of the ordinary. I have absolutely no fear of them finding out anything. There's nothing to find out. I'm blameless. I have no past. I have nothing to run from. They're here for a friendly visit. I have no feelings of anguish or dread. No feelings of guilt. No feelings at all, really. I'm not the man they're looking for.

"You going somewhere?" Cohen says. He takes a sip of his coffee.

"What do you mean?"

"Your apartment. Not much stuff in it. You're either coming or you're going."

"I'm not going anywhere. I'm just not the kind of guy who needs a lot of stuff."

"So what kind of guy are you?" Cohen says. He lights a cigarette, stretches his legs out in front of him like he's expecting me to tell him a long story.

I'm not going to open myself up to this guy. I'm not about to go into my history, not about to go into some kind of rant about myself like he's my goddamn therapist or something.

"The kind of guy who doesn't need a lot of stuff."

"Fair enough," he says. "So what kind of guy was Bob?"

"What do you want to know?"

"You mentioned him being caught up in some kind of scam. The Canadian Lottery thing."

"He didn't tell me much. Just that he got scammed."

"Was he in trouble financially?"

"I was his friend. Not his banker."

"I'll tell you this much, Hal," Cohen says. "It just doesn't add up. A guy his age isn't typically ripped off by lottery scams. Eighty-year-old grandmothers, yes. Not many men in their forties fall prey to that kind of thing."

"So, he was a sucker," I say.

"Evidently," Cohen says. "So, we don't have much, but we know your buddy was in trouble financially. We know he was looking for a quick buck. Fast money. Sounds like a desperate fellow. That a fair assessment, Hal?"

"I suppose."

"You ever hear of birds of a feather?"

"I'm not desperate."

"You seem desperate."

"Why all the questions about Bob? I thought you were looking into the death of Billy Joe Harris?"

"Oh, we are. But we're not ruling out a connection."

"We're not ruling out anything," Jacobs says. "No, sirree. Have to check all the leads. We don't want to overlook something. You never know what's staring you right in the face. You never know when the culprit's sitting right in front of you."

And he says this like we're going over my tax returns and he's found a way to save me some money. He sounds cheerful. But he's looking at me like he's about to rip my head from my neck and toss it around my apartment.

"Sounds like you think I had something to do with it," I say.

"Oh, I wouldn't go that far, Hal," Cohen says. "But I think you know more than you're telling us. Why don't you tell us about the night you found Bob."

"I didn't find Bob. My friend Gerald found Bob. He called me."

"Oh right," Cohen says. "My bad. So tell me about the night Gerald found Bob. Surely you talked to him about it."

"I can't say that I did," I say.

"Why don't you call him up?" Cohen says.

"Now?" I say.

"Just as good a time as any," Cohen says. "We wouldn't mind talking to your friend, Gerald. Maybe he has something that he can tell us."

"What kind of stuff do you want to know?"

"I'm thinking Bob had something somebody wanted. Maybe that something got him killed."

"Bob killed himself. Shot himself in the mouth."

"Hmmm," Cohen says. "What else do you know about Bob's death?"

"That's all I know."

"Bob have a girlfriend?"

"Look," I say. "If you guys want to interrogate me, take me downtown. In the meantime, I'll get an attorney—"

"He either had a girlfriend or he didn't."

"He was seeing someone."

"Does that someone have a name?"

"Rachel," I say.

"Tell me about Rachel," Cohen says.

"Seems like a good enough girl," I say.

"Did they fight?"

"Not anymore than anybody else—"

"So they did."

"They had their ups and downs."

"Was Rachel the jealous type?"

"I don't know about that."

"Let's say that Rachel caught Bob cheating. Was she the kind of girl that would lose her mind? Maybe shoot him in the face?"

"Rachel didn't kill Bob."

"How about Bob? Was he the jealous type?"

"Don't know that either."

"It works both ways, you know. Women cheat on their boyfriends all of the time."

"They loved each other," I say.

"You ever been in love?" Cohen says.

"I'm tired of these games," I say.

"Tired enough that we're pissing you off?" Cohen says. "You're probably thinking about whipping up on us or something. Better think that through, cuz Jacobs here, he's the kind of guy who just sort of snaps. You ever just snap, Hal?"

"What are you trying to do here?" I say. "All this is making me a little uncomfortable."

"Sort of makes you want to have a drink, Hal? Because if you need a drink, we'll wait while you make yourself one. Hell, if you need a drink, I'll make one for you. If you'll just steer me toward the booze," Cohen says.

"I don't have any booze," I say.

"Teetotaler, huh? You on the wagon, Hal?"

"One day at a time," I say.

"How about your friend, Bob? He a teetotaler—"

"That's not my business."

"—cuz toxicology came back different. A body full of booze. Pretty much pickled."

"Ok, gentlemen, I'm going to ask you to leave."

"You know the drill," Cohen says. "If you remember something that you think we want to know, give us a call."

"I'll do that," I say.

"One more thing," Cohen says. "You ever talk to Bob about his sex life with Rachel?"

"I'm finished," I say.

"Some people are curious about that kind of thing. They like to know other people's business. You know, voyeurs. They like to watch. You wouldn't fit into that category, now would you, Hal?"

"No more than you," I say. "You're the ones getting into everybody's business. And you're getting off on it."

"How about Billy Joe Harris?" Cohen says. "Now that's a good example. He certainly cared about other people's sex lives. Made a pretty good living at it. Any reason he would want to know about Bob's sex life? Or yours?"

"You tell me," I say.

"Doesn't work that way, Hal," Cohen says. "Thought you would have learned that by now."

"I'm a slow learner."

"That's where you're not giving yourself credit, Hal. You know a lot. You might want us to think you don't know anything, but you know a hell of a lot more than you're telling us. Billy Joe Harris knew a lot too. And someone killed him for it."

———◆———

I didn't kill Billy Joe Harris.

I didn't kill Billy Joe Harris.

I didn't kill Billy Joe Harris.

It wasn't me. I had absolutely no reason to kill Billy Joe Harris. There was no connection. So, I paid him a visit. So, I beat the shit out of him in a sudden blind rage. But kicking the shit out of someone and killing them are two different things. Kicking the shit out of someone doesn't give me a motive for murder.

The twins can question me all they want.

I had no motive.

The twins don't really think I did it. They don't have anything other than I paid him a visit. The only thing they have is the testimony of a woman who was looking for a lost dog. A woman who got the license plate on my car.

That's all.

It's not enough.

They know it. They're talking to me for other reasons. They're suspicious that they have stumbled onto some kind of conspiracy—something bigger than all of us—and they're going to harass me until I tell them what they want to hear.

But that isn't going to happen. I've got an alibi. My alibi is this: I'm not a killer. I didn't kill Billy Joe Harris.

But there are plenty of people who would want him dead. There are scores of cheating husbands wiped out in their divorce proceedings due to Billy Joe Harris catching them in compromising positions. He followed them as they were taking their eighteen-year-old babysitters home on a Friday night after they took their wives out to dinner and a movie. All they had to do was run Stacie home, and then they would be back in a jiffy. But their wives know better than this. They know better than this because they have seen the signs. That's why they hired Billy Joe Harris in the first place. Billy Joe Harris follows their husbands as they take Stacie, or Kendra, or Jasmine home. He photographs them as they kiss

Stacie. Photographs them as they fondle Kendra. Photographs them as Jasmine disappears from view. Photographs them as their back stiffens and they moan with pleasure. Billy Joe Harris photographs those faces of pleasure, which become faces of rage when their wives show them the photographs that Billy Joe Harris snapped of them, those pictures of their late-night indiscretions. This rage carries over. They want to kill Billy Joe Harris. They have every reason in the world to slip into his house and cut his throat. Or shoot him. Or strangle him. Or stab him in the chest.

Photographs of men who have been selling company secrets to the highest bidder. Men who have been involved in corporate espionage. Men who have become so dissatisfied with their lives—who have lost their ability to wait until they achieve success the good old-fashioned way—that they're willing to lose it all.

Billy Joe Harris compiles the evidence until it's beyond a reasonable doubt. The evidence will be turned over to the prosecution. Our man will go to prison to do some really hard time. He'll meet someone in the pen who knows someone who knows someone who knows someone who will kill Billy Joe Harris for less than a thousand dollars. When Billy Joe Harris is least expecting it—when he has tucked his daughter into bed and is brushing his teeth—the bullet goes through his back and rips his chest open. He has long forgotten the man who he had put behind bars, the man who nursed his anger in prison until he couldn't take it any longer.

Billy Joe Harris tracks small-time drug dealers. He tracks Kingpins. He spends his life uncovering the secrets of others. For a small fee. He spends his life uncovering the secrets of others so he can pay his bills. But he fails to realize that uncovering secrets isn't the safest job in the world. This profession has repercussions.

Or maybe he knew. Maybe he was willing to make the ultimate gamble, the ultimate sacrifice. Maybe he was willing to give it all up for the satisfaction he obtained from slipping behind the exacting lens of a camera, where eighteen-year-old babysitters give blowjobs to men twice their age. Getting this all on film and getting paid for it. Maybe he was willing to give it all up for the satisfaction he obtained from rummaging through the lives of others, regardless if it would break up a family, lose an election, or get him killed.

The only reason I came up as a suspect at all is because they got my license plate when I paid him a visit. They don't have any real leads.

So they pick me.

They're going on a wild goose chase.

I promise you this. I've got an alibi. I had no reason to kill Billy Joe Harris.

I'm not cheating on my wife. I'm not getting blowjobs from my children's eighteen-year-old babysitter. I'm not selling company secrets to our competitors. I'm not running for governor of the State of Texas while fucking my assistant in the bedroom of her tiny apartment.

I'm innocent.

I didn't kill Billy Joe Harris.

———◆———

I walk through the double doors at Minyard's—about to do some grocery shopping—when I see Celia. Or I should say a picture of Celia, stuck on one of those missing posters. Slapped in the center of the cork bulletin board surrounded by fliers with washers to sell. Juaquin will mow your yard. Bishop Lynch High School Drama Department is presenting *Noises Off* the first and second weekend in October.

Surrounded by fliers advertising this and that, a picture of Celia in a white sweatshirt and a beautiful smile. Right under large block letters that tell you that she's missing. Below the picture's a blurb telling you that their beloved daughter has been missing since the last week in August. If you have any information, you should call such and such number. There's a reward for information leading to her safe return. When I read it—when I look at the picture—it's like I'm reading about the disappearance of a long-lost friend.

I stand there for a nice long while.

I'm half expecting her to talk to me. If I stand here long enough, she'll ask me why I pulled her into this mess. She'll tell me that I know good and well that it's not her in the pictures I jerk off to every day. But she doesn't say anything. She only smiles. There is no hint that she's a dead corpse lying in a field somewhere—an unclaimed body in a morgue awaiting identification—no hint that she's lost and lonely and nowhere to be found.

Nothing.

I walk around the store in a daze—pushing my cart—my mind in another world, when I see Rachel.

She's a disaster. She's pale. She's paranoid. She darts her head from side to side knowing that something's about to happen to her. She keeps her mobile phone off. She doesn't take phone calls. She has no family. Very few friends. She's done with loss. Her grandfather died. Her father has cancer. And now, Bob. It doesn't get any worse than that.

What do you say? I've got seconds to figure it out. She pushes her cart down the aisle, lost.

"Hello," I say.

She barely recognizes me.

"Hello."

"I'm so sorry," I say.

"Thanks."

She pushes her cart past me.

I want to run after her. I want to say something that will make it all better. There's nothing I can say. Nothing at all.

I get a box of cereal, a half-gallon of milk, a twelve pack of Dr. Pepper, a Snickers bar, three packs of gum, a tube of toothpaste, some shaving lotion, and I pay with a credit card. I say paper when they ask paper or plastic. I push my cart through the double doors without looking at the picture of Celia because I'm afraid she'll haunt me in my dreams. I'm on my way to my car—thankful that I didn't have to deal with Rachel—and she's waiting by my blue Saturn, smoking a cigarette.

"Hello . . ."

"I miss him," she says.

We'll have sex. I know we shouldn't. It's like sleeping with family. We have no right to be clinging to each other. But, at the same time, there's nobody else. We're alone here. Wrong or not, we don't have a choice.

"I know. I miss him too."

"I don't understand."

"I know."

"I really don't understand."

"Yeah."

"I just buried my grandfather. My father has cancer. And Bob has to shoot himself in the mouth? It makes no goddamn sense."

"I know what you mean."

"They say God never gives us more than we can bear. That's a crock of shit. God's heaping it on whether I can bear it or not. I wish he'd ask for my goddamn opinion every once in a while."

"If he does, let me know," I say.

"Do you want me?" Rachel says.

What do you say?

"I'm not going to ask you again."

"Well, then," I say. "Then I should say yes."

We get in our cars as though it's the end of the world. We get in our cars and drive toward my apartment as though there's been some kind of announcement that the red button has been pressed and we have fifteen minutes to say goodbye to our loved ones.

This sense of urgency zaps our memory. We can't recall how we know each other. We didn't just bury my best friend and her lover. We met each other in a grocery store and the world's ending and we don't have the time to get to know each other. We have a mission without thought of repercussions. It'll be empty. It'll be meaningless. But it will be. And that's enough.

Five minutes later we're at my apartment—at the bottom of my stairs—ripping off each other's clothes. I feel guilty, but that doesn't keep me from kissing Rachel and pretty soon we're on the second or third step from the bottom and we fuck all the way up the stairs until we make it to my bed.

We collapse in a heap—breathless, empty—with Charlie looking at us from the foot of the bed, like we've lost our minds.

I've lost my mind. I've betrayed my best friend without thinking it through. I feel nauseated. Rachel will take this personally. What's wrong? Is it something I said? Don't you enjoy making love to me?

I stumble from my bed and into my bathroom—my head spinning, my world instantly dizzy—and I bend over my toilet, vomiting. I puke my guts out.

I wash my face in the sink. I rinse my mouth out. I gargle. I let the water roll down my throat. I've taken a bite out of an apple and I have this premonition. I'm all knowing. I want to die.

8

IF ALL YOU HAVE ARE THE PICTURES—and you know that they
were found in Bob's apartment the night of his death, and you buy
into the fact that they are pictures of Celia and not someone else—
there are certain assumptions you have to make.

Bob has been stalking Celia. There's no other way to put it. He's
watching her. He's hoping to connect but this connection isn't
possible. He's been watching her—has been masturbating outside
her window—and realizes that all those times that they go to lunch
during their lunch breaks, all those times that he thought they'd
achieved some kind of intimacy, wasn't really intimacy at all. When
they went to lunch during their lunch breaks and Celia supposedly
spilled her soul, she was doing nothing more than telling him what
he wanted to hear.

Bob's desperately seeking salvation. Answers. The meaning
behind the slow drudge. But nothing's adding up here. He's sitting
behind his computer—masturbating to a scenario created by
someone on the other side of the world—and it's just like having
lunch with Celia. There's no difference. There are moments during
this computer conversation where they reach the same emotional

levels that he and Celia had reached, and he suddenly realizes that relationships are nothing but frauds. He no longer has a reason to be here.

He calls Celia and listens to her answering machine. He doesn't leave a message. Even if she wasn't missing—if she would've answered—he would've hung up. He wouldn't know what to say to her.

He thinks of the last five years of his sobriety. He thinks about the highs and the lows—the joy and the pain—peruses this new life for any shred of hope. But ends up empty. He loses sight of the happiness. He loses sight of the joy.

He combs through his bills. He rifles through the letters from collection agencies. He tells himself if he cuts back here and there, everything'll work itself out. At the same time, he's paying almost 200 dollars a month on at least two credit cards. These are minimum payments, mind you. It's like he didn't pay them at all. It's a circle without end.

He opens his wallet, and all he has is thirteen bucks. He doesn't get paid for another week. Christ, how'll he even pay his electric bill? Gas for his car? How'll he pay to get the inspection for Christ's sake? Over and over, this continual circle of despair.

He puts on his pants, grabs his wallet, lights a cigarette, and walks down the stairs—past the pile of leaves—and into the street.

He crosses over at Ross and walks to the Centennial at the corner of Skillman and Live Oak. The Dallas skyline's a dream. Its buildings are empty, wishing its workers would work around the clock, wishing that its insides were vibrating with the travel of leather and high heels. Its elevators should be pulsing with the silent breath of passengers avoiding eye contact, looking at their watches, staring at their shoes, watching their mobile phones. These buildings wish they could be utilized around the clock, wish they could be utilized for more than this nine-to-five monotony.

The streets are empty. A car here. A car there. But otherwise, most folks are safe and secure in their homes. There's darkness all around him outside of the dim blink of the streetlights.

The Centennial Liquor Store's lit up like a church. Salvation can be found here. *You who are weary, come unto me. And I will give you rest.*

He doesn't feel guilty. He remembers where to find the Jack Daniels. At the end of the middle aisle. He grabs a fifth of Jack Daniels, stops by the cooler and grabs a Coke and walks to the front of the store to check out.

There's a young girl in front of him talking on her mobile phone. She's wearing a pair of denim overalls and a tank top. He doesn't take his eyes off of her. She isn't twenty-one. She licks her lips when she reaches the cashier in hopes that the urges of his dick will be stronger than his common sense.

"Next."

Bob asks for a pack of Camels and sits his Jack Daniels and his soda on the counter.

He says *fine* when the clerk asks him how he's doing.

He says *thank you* when the clerk tells him to *be safe* and to *have a nice evening.*

He doesn't tell the clerk that no one's safe anymore. Safety's a construct. Women are raped in the parking lots of liquor stores. Presidents are assassinated in the angry streets of Dallas. Coworkers disappear all the time. Future governors fuck women other than their wives. He doesn't tell the clerk that he's going to drink a fifth of Jack Daniels and wash it down with a bullet.

The young girl's having trouble starting her car.

It sounds like the battery.

Bob walks away from her. There's nothing he can do.

When he walks upstairs and into his apartment, he's walking into the home of a stranger. He's never been here. He pulls books from the shelf—glances at their covers—and wonders if they're any good. He looks at the picture of him and Rachel at Disney World and has no recollection of having ever been there.

He walks over to his cabinet, takes down a glass and fills it with ice. He fills it to the brim with Jack Daniels. There's no room for Coke.

He sits in his chair and starts watching television.

He doesn't care what's on.

He's not really watching television.

He's listening to his father. They're fishing. They're in his father's boat—a small number—a little, gray boat without a motor. They row out near a little island swamped with trees. It's early morning.

His father tells him how to bait the hook. He watches as his father takes a worm—hooks it, doubles it up—and casts it into the water. His thumbs are calloused, his fingernails uneven. He has big hands. Big hands that are comfortable with baiting a hook. Big hands that swivel when he sends the line spinning into the water.

His father tells him they should whisper. "We don't want to disturb the fish." His father reaches down into the cooler and pops a Budweiser.

Bob takes a long drink of his Jack Daniels.

His father takes a long pull from his Budweiser.

It's beautiful. Watching the water lap up against the shore. It's beautiful. The quiet bob of the boat. It's beautiful. The stillness of the morning.

When he gets old enough, Bob will drink Budweiser.

The first time he has one, he thinks of the water lapping up against the shore, the quiet bob of the boat, the stillness of the morning. He remembers his father's thumbs.

Bob walks into the kitchen and pours himself another drink. He opens the middle drawer. Removes the manila envelope. Takes it into the living room. He changes the channel. He turns on his CD player. He plays *Purple Haze*. He sits down and places the manila envelope on his lap.

He's not thinking about the fact that he's drinking.

He's not thinking about anything but Celia.

When he went to work that morning, he had absolutely no idea that when he went down to the mailbox it would change his life.

There wasn't that much mail. Before he took it upstairs, he stopped outside and had a smoke. He said hello to Gretchen, a young woman who always wore tight shirts. And jeans. He always jokes with her about not being able to wear jeans to work. He has to wear dress slacks and a tie. He talks about not being able to wear jeans so he can justify looking down at her crotch. At her ass, when she turns away to blow her smoke in the opposite direction. She doesn't want to get it in his face. Despite the fact that he's smoking.

It saddens him—as he walks back to his office—that he doesn't know her. He smokes a cigarette with her several times a day and he barely knows her name. It saddens him that he doesn't care who she is. He's content at staring at her crotch and watching her gradually disappear.

He sorts the mail—throwing out the junk—and starts slicing open the envelopes. It's his job to check the mail for checks. He walks the checks to Claudia's office. She puts them up on the system, gives them back to him. He fills out a deposit slip that afternoon and walks them down to Lone Star Bank, where he says *hi* to me, asks me if I'm having a good day.

But before that—as he's opening the mail—he comes across a large Tyvek envelope with a label addressed to Mr. Gavin Thompson on it, written in blue ink. It's printed in small block letters. It doesn't catch his attention. There's no moment—before opening the envelope— that Bob thinks that there's something unusual about this envelope. There's no moment where Bob gets the feeling that something isn't right. He has no premonition.

There's a small manila envelope inside the larger Tyvek envelope. He opens the manila envelope and discovers the pictures of Celia fucking Gavin in the middle of a rather large bed.

His first instinct is to hide them somewhere.

But first, he takes them to the men's bathroom and jacks off.

It's clear that the pictures are of Gavin and Celia. There's no denying this. There are pictures of her sucking his dick. There are pictures of him eating her out. A picture of her sitting on top of him. One of them kissing. One of her lying on the bed with her legs spread open, waiting. You can see Gavin's silhouette at the foot of the bed.

He does all this before he thinks of the ramifications. He does all this before he even wonders who might have sent those pictures.

But now—as he slides the manila envelope in a hanging folder in the bottom of his desk drawer—his head's full of ideas.

Someone's blackmailing Gavin.

The note will come later.

It's probably Cynthia Thompson.

She's gotten the kids off to school. She walks upstairs to their bedroom and removes her panty drawer and reaches into the back of their dresser with her well-manicured fingers and fishes the manila envelope out from the back wall of the dresser. She carries the envelope over to their bed like she's carrying her grandmother's china. She opens the envelope and looks at the pictures one more time.

That bitch.

That limp dick bastard.

She slides the manila envelope into the larger Tyvek envelope and she writes her limp dick bastard-of-a- husband's name in small-blocked, blue letters. She licks the stamp thinking of revenge. She almost smiles as she drops it off at the Highland Park Post Office on her way to play Bridge at Suzanne Parker's house.

Bob's angry. And he's angry because he's had to listen to this sack-of-shit preach moral values—going on and on about the importance of his family, parading them around at the office party every Christmas, giving a toast to his wife, telling them how important his family is to him and that they should all love and cherish their families because they're the only thing that a man can really value at the end of the day—and all the while he has been fucking girls young enough to be his daughter. And this asshole's about to become governor of the State of Texas. This asshole.

He should walk around the office showing them to his coworkers. He should walk around to every poor soul who has had to listen to Gavin's incessant sermons about the importance of his family— and as soon as everyone has had their fill—he'd walk down the street and hand them over to the front desk at the *Dallas Morning News*. These pictures deserve to be on the front-page of the next morning's early edition.

But then he has to consider Celia. What's this going to do to her reputation? After all, she's not the only one in these pictures. It's not her fault, really. She's young. She's impressionable. She didn't do anything to deserve this.

So, Bob won't show them to anyone.

He'll burn them.

But every time that he starts to set them ablaze, he slides them back in the manila envelope and puts them in his kitchen drawer.

Bob makes himself one more drink.

He's close to the end.

He gets his gun from the top of his bedroom closet and walks back into the living room. He sits in his chair and thumbs through the pictures. He takes off his pants and masturbates. He curses his life.

He curses everyone he ever called a friend. He doesn't think about writing a note. That would be too generous. They deserve to suffer.

The last thing that crosses his mind as he pulls the trigger of his gun—its barrel in his mouth—is that his father never took him fishing. He didn't even own a boat.

9

LEMON. LEE MONTGOMERY PICKENS. I should fill you in.

If you remember, he made the cover of the *Dallas Observer* in the early nineties. That local rag where they're always lampooning local politicians, doing in-depth interviews with local bands, running an occasional spread about a local socialite, but usually only if they've done a stint in jail or rehab. But anyway, Lemon's on the front cover in the early nineties, and there's this large picture of his face, but mostly shadow. He doesn't look sober. He looks out of his mind. Underneath, in bold letters, *Confessions of a Patsy's Bastard Son*, and then in smaller letters, something about delving into the dark world of the self-proclaimed bastard son of Lee Harvey Oswald.

It's sad, really. The story's one of those wannabe lurid tales reeking of conspiracy. By the time you plow through it, you understand that they think Lemon's batshit crazy. The story's written as sort of a *wink wink nudge nudge* exercise, reminiscent of the high school bully kicking the shit out of the president of the chess club.

The article spends a lot of time on Lemon's extracurricular begging activities. It paints him as a huckster. A couple of days a week, Lemon throws on an old pair of pants and a beat-up shirt and wheels himself to the corner of one of the access roads, right next to one of the overpasses, and turns into his alter ego to beg for change.

You wouldn't know that he's a fraud. If you've ever seen him—at least until the article came out—you would swear he's a young man with cerebral palsy trying to make a dime to make ends meet. It's almost spooky how well he has it down.

I tell him he needs to stop. It's dishonest. How the hell can he expect people to believe the other stuff he tells them—like that he's the bastard son of Lee Harvey Oswald—when he spends a good portion of his free time trying to con people out of their money?

I'm not certain that *I* don't think he's just another nutjob. That is, until Lemon discovers the equivalent of the Holy Grail of conspiracy theories when we're helping his mother move boxes down from her attic.

It changes everything.

But, for now, Lemon wants me to go with him to an exorcism.

Lemon and his cousin Ben are going to an exorcism. He wants me to come along.

"A what—"

"You heard me," he says. "An exorcism. Devil shit."

"They really do those?"

"We're about to find out."

"Are you possessed?"

"Not that I'm aware of," he says. "But Ben is."

"I don't know if I'm up for that."

"Where is this place?" I ask.

We're driving down Ross. Of course, we're driving my car.

Ben's in the back seat, looking dizzy.

Lemon's up front, smoking a cigarette.

The City's friendly again. Its citizens are no longer threatening. The skyline's suddenly bright and colorful. The night's breezy and cool. No humidity. No heavy air. No heavy breathing. Suddenly, I feel ok.

Unlike Ben, who doesn't look good.

"Are you going to be ok?" I say to Ben.

"Once this is over," Ben says.

"Have you been drinking?"

"It's the only way he could go through with it," Lemon says.

"You're drunk?"

Ben nods.

"You're going to your own exorcism drunk?"

He nods again.

"Don't puke in my car."

———◆———

There's an apartment building on the corner of Ross and Haskell. Lemon's dealer lives there. I guess I should say his ex-dealer.

"How big of a coincidence is that?" I say.

"What?" Lemon says.

"That we're about to go for an exorcism in the same apartment building where you buy your crank."

"Bought. That I bought my crank," Lemon says.

"I don't know if I like that," Ben says.

"Is that the Devil talking or is that you, Ben?"

"Fuck you," Ben says to Lemon.

"Must be the Devil. You let go of my cousin, you old Beelzebub son of a bitch."

"We should probably stop mocking exorcisms before we get inside," I say. "That's bad Karma."

"Maybe," says Lemon. "What do you think, Satan?" Lemon says, turning to Ben.

"Knock it off," Satan says.

———◆———

This place's a dump. Really. The bricks lining the walkways are falling apart or missing. The flowerbeds are empty, flowers non-existent, a few dead hedges. Dry, lifeless bushes sit awkwardly under the windows of the downstairs units, and the stairs leading up to the second floor are anything but reliable. Every other lamp's missing a bulb, their coverings dry and cracked or totally missing. The windows are covered with screens pulled away from the frames. Men sit on their porches—surrounded by cracked and decaying bricks—smoking their cigarettes and drinking their beer, wishing they had enough money to score some crank. They're wondering where their girlfriends are, who they're fucking to get another fix. A few kids here or there—searching for their mothers, never knew their fathers, locked up somewhere in a federal penitentiary—wondering if they'll ever get out of this place alive.

We make it down the hallway without getting shot. A woman standing in the doorway tells us that she won't cost us much at all. She's the best fuck in Dallas. For a second, it looks as though Lemon's considering her proposition, tells me—as we pass her apartment and continue on down the hallway—that he thinks she likes him. When we reach 216, I consider telling Lemon and Ben that I'll meet them in the car. This is a bad idea.

But Ben has bigger problems. He's got a devil inside of him. He needs to rid himself of evil so he can have a family, marry his high school sweetheart, have a couple of children, and spend the rest of his life going to little league softball games and PTA meetings, devoting his life to the betterment of his family.

First things first. Deal with that pesky little devil.

———◆———

The Conductor's a really short man with bad hygiene. This guy hasn't brushed his hair in weeks. He hasn't brushed his teeth. He's wearing a Nirvana T-shirt and a pair of purple sweats. He hasn't eaten for days. He's been on a caffeine binge, cups of coffee strewn around his place, ashtrays overflowing. He looks like a drug dealer. He tells us to call him the Conductor. It feels awkward referring to him as the Conductor—seems like a really bad joke—so we don't refer to him at all.

"You do this in your apartment?"

"Did you think I would have an office?"

"I hadn't really thought about it."

"It's not like I'm getting rich off of this. I'm a servant. I'm serving. I'm serving where I live."

His apartment reminds me of Lemon's apartment with all his shit strewn everywhere. I half expect him to turn on NASCAR.

"How long have you been possessed?" he says, looking at me.

"Wrong guy," I say.

"Are you sure?" he says.

"Yes," I say. "Ben's the one with a devil."

"If that's what you say," he says. "Take off your clothes," he says to Ben.

"Really?" Ben says. He looks at us like we're going to save him.

"I won't beg. You either want it or you don't. If you want it, you'll do as I say. If you don't, there's the door."

He takes a long drag from his cigarette and he disappears in a cloud of smoke.

"Gotcha," Ben says, taking off his shirt. His pants. His shoes. His underwear.

The Conductor points at me and Lemon.

"You too, gentlemen."

"You're kidding me," Lemon says.

That's exactly what I'm thinking.

"We're in this together," he says, taking off his shirt.

"Jesus."

"Come on," Ben says. "Do this for me."

"I'm not doing this for you, Ben," Lemon says, taking off his underwear. "I'm doing this for the benefit of all mankind."

———◆———

The Conductor convinces us to all get naked in the middle of his living room, lights a shitload of incense, and tells us to free our minds of any of the wicked deeds that we have ever done against humanity. Splashing holy water on us from an Ozarka bottle, the Conductor tells us that if there's anyone among us who harbors the darkness of secrets, he should cleanse himself of that and announce in a public forum—in front of his brethren—his sins and short-comings, or the Devil will remain in Ben for all eternity. He tells us that if we keep these secrets harbored in the secret place that is our hearts—without true confession before our brethrenpoor Ben will be consumed by evil incarnate for all eternity.

Ben doesn't want any of that. Ben lets us know right away that we'd better confess our asses off so that he doesn't become forever imprisoned by the bondage of the Devil.

We're looking at each other to find out who will confess his sins first, so we can get it over with and get the hell out of this freaky apartment. Lemon looks at me. I look at Lemon. Lemon looks at me, like I'd better go first. I look at Lemon. *It's your cousin. You got me into this mess, you get us out.*

———◆———

The Conductor looks at us with this weird-ass look on his face, which tells us that—if we don't want Ben's soul to be in the eternal hands of Satan—we'd better start talking.

Lemon's convinced that I'm not going first, so he raises his hand like we're in the third grade. The Conductor calls on him like he's the teacher, and Lemon starts spewing out details of his sordid past.

When he was in high school and his mother was at work, Lemon would put on his mother's high heels, put on one of her old burlesque getups, and traipse around the house half naked.

Lemon spews out details of masturbating in the church bathroom when he went to Vacation Bible School with his little neighbor friend, says he felt guilty about getting his rocks off in God's house. He had placed a stain on something holy. He got on his hands and knees in an effort to rid the church bathroom of that stain. He talks about how he got himself all over the walls. On the back of the commode. On the sink. Once he got back to the Vacation Bible School class and the teacher was teaching about Adam and Eve in the Garden of Eden—how they didn't have clothes on, how they were naked in the Garden—he had the urge to masturbate again. Knowing that he would burn in a lake of fire and everlasting brimstone, Lemon found himself back in that same bathroom, getting his rocks off to images of Adam and Eve fucking themselves silly all over the Garden of Eden. Lemon says that he's sorry from the bottom of his heart. He hopes that his sins will be forgiven so that his drug-riddled cousin Ben can be saved from the great and mighty Dragon that is the Devil.

The Conductor asks Lemon if he's finished—does he feel free from the bondage of self—and is about to move on to me when Lemon starts babbling on about visiting one of those bathhouses off of I-35 and Harry Hines. He got shitfaced drunk and shot something into his veins and jumped the DART Bus over to one of those bathhouses so he could get laid for the first time. A Vietnamese woman greeted him at the front—supposedly came through a beaded entryway—and told Lemon that his wish was her command. Lemon knew that he shouldn't be at this bathhouse. He shouldn't follow this Vietnamese woman to her lair—a little room with a bluish hue, tile floors and drains, smelling like sex—but he stayed anyway.

The woman teased him by lifting up her robe, but it was too dark for Lemon to really see anything. The woman basically straddled him on the table. Before it actually happened, as this Vietnamese woman placed herself on him, he suddenly realized that it was a man. Lemon babbles on about knowing that he should tell her/him to stop. He knew it was a mortal sin—or whatever the hell you call those things that God will never forgive—but he did it anyway.

Lemon was almost crying, running his fingers through his hair, begging God, Ben, me, and the Conductor to forgive him for his gay ways. And, in an effort to save Lemon from himself, I admitted—in front of them all—that I killed Sam.

———◆———

I'm stumbling around my apartment like I'm losing my mind. I've got all of this guilt rushing through me. The exorcism stirred something up. It's bubbling to the surface and I don't have any choice but to deal with it. I'll let all of this shit bubble around in my memory in hopes that if I entertain it, it'll disappear.

———◆———

Sam invites her sister over for dinner.

That's what she does when we're having marital problems.

We have company.

I don't mind, really. At the same time, I've got things to do. I've got other things on my mind. But I don't mind Cheryl. I like her. She's nice enough.

"It's hotter than holy hell," she says.

She steps into the foyer—hands me a bottle of wine—and kisses me on the cheek. She has a pair of sunglasses propped up in her short bob, an almost platinum blonde with dark roots. She's wearing a green sundress.

"So what did you do to piss Sam off?" Cheryl says.

"You tell me."

"You had to do something," Cheryl says.

———•———

I shouldn't be thinking about Sam's sister. I shouldn't be thinking about taking off her green sundress and cradling her breasts in my hands while running my tongue up the side of her neck.

I walk into the living room and start watching television. I flip through the channels. I settle on some nature show on the mating habits of whales.

Sam and Cheryl are sitting at the kitchen table smoking a joint.

No pot for me. It makes me paranoid.

Cheryl's talking about a guy she's dating. They met in a philosophy class. He's a poet. Theo. A trust-fund baby. A trust-fund baby with a big dick.

She winks at me as she drops ice into each glass.

It turns me on. It makes me uncomfortable.

———•———

Sam lights a candle in the center of the table, and we find our seats and ooh and ahh over how good everything looks. "Doesn't every-thing look so good, Hal? It must be nice to have a wife who cooks. Maybe I should switch sides so I can have a wife who cooks. Theo can't cook. But did I mention he has a big dick? And good cock is hard to find."

"Cheryl," Sam says. "Not at the table."

"Hal has a big dick. Now don't you, Hal? Don't you have a big cock?"

"Have some more wine, Cheryl," I say.

"That's a good idea," says Cheryl. She pours me a glass of wine, pours Sam a glass of wine, raises her glass to toast us.

"To big cocks," she says.

———◆———

"You can't drive home like this."

"I'll be fine."

"No really. Hal, tell her. Hal, tell her that she can't drive home like this."

"You can't drive home like this."

"Thank you."

"Where will I sleep?"

Sam doesn't say anything.

Cheryl needs to pee. She needs to pee badly. She gets up from the table and runs her fingers through my hair on her way out.

"Are you ok?" Sam says.

"Yes," I say. "A little drunk."

"A little?"

"Ok. A lot drunk."

"I'm sorry," she says.

"For what?" I say.

"I'm just sorry."

"Me too," I say.

———◆———

"Let's do more shots," says Cheryl. She's wearing a T-shirt and a pair of white panties. The shirt barely covers her belly button. Her nipples are poking through her shirt. Through the haze, her face is lit up in a perpetual glow. She's wearing a halo. She's magical. She's sacred.

"I'm yours," Cheryl says.

"And Sam—"

"Sam who?"

She points to Sam's empty chair. Sam has vanished. Sam's no longer with us.

I forget who Sam is. I have no recollection of her. I don't remember when we first met. I don't remember going to Deep Ellum, the skies, threatening. I don't remember the concert at Club Dada, a slight mist coming down, the world smelling like rain. I don't remember holding hands. I don't remember being surrounded by young punks in full sleeve tattoos with girlfriends in low-cut shirts and short shorts, pierced lips, earrings, and nose rings.

I don't remember the blue light filtering through the tables, smoke rising from cigarettes and their red glow. I don't remember getting a drink at the bar. I don't remember Edie Brickell and New Bohemians playing their first song. Edie, looking angelic. Sam singing along silently with the music, her lips moving with each lyric. I don't remember running toward the car, Sam sliding out of her sandals, jumping on my back, carrying her through the rain. I don't remember any of this.

———◆———

We're all lying in bed in our own blackness.

Each of us has our own room spinning in our heads.

Cheryl takes off her T-shirt.

She knows I'm watching her.

Sam's drunk. But not asleep. She's rubbing my leg.

"Pretend I'm not here," Cheryl says.

Pretend I'm not here.

I'm turned on. Sam rubs my leg. Cheryl—in her panties—touches her nipples, licks her lips. I roll over onto Sam.

Cheryl watches us. She masturbates. I'm about to come and Cheryl slides over and sticks her finger in Sam's mouth. Sam sucks on Cheryl's finger. I pull out and pull Cheryl closer to the foot of the bed. I start kissing her. I start fucking her. Cheryl and Sam kiss. When I come, it's the end of the world.

———◆———

This memory's as vivid as the day it happened. Or the day it didn't happen. Memories are unreliable. With the passage of time, it becomes difficult to distinguish the truth from pure fantasy, what you wish would have happened.

These memories are a direct result of visiting the Exorcist.

He creeped me out.

What creeped me out the most was that he seemed afraid of me. This wide-eyed lunatic wanted nothing to do with me. He avoided me at all cost. Once the hocus pocus was over and done with, he had been all too anxious to get us out of his apartment.

10

MAGGIE LIKES BUTTERFLIES, almost lights up when she sees one soaring on the wind, soaring over a plant, easing between the leaves on the bush outside of my apartment. She'll peer down from the balcony—transfixed—like she's flying along side of it, that somehow she has taken flight, has transformed herself into a butterfly.

She prefers warm to cold. Complains incessantly about *bad weather*, always holding out for the spring, when she can throw Tyler into his jogging stroller and jog with him down endless sidewalks— the sun pouring down on her shoulders—filling her up with an unending joy. Maggie enjoys the satisfaction of having the sun on her back and a cool breeze in her face, the kind of weather where she can take off all her clothes—throw on a bikini—and hang out by the pool smoking cigarettes. She'll look at me through her dark shades—her skin already becoming a golden bronze—telling me she wishes she was lying on a beach somewhere—an endless white beach right next to the cool lap of ocean water—sipping drinks out of tall, hollow glasses with little umbrellas sticking out of the top.

Room service. She loves room service. Throw on a white fluffy robe, a towel on her head—after showering, after laying out by the water—and ordering room service while watching cable television, looking out at the water through the half-open blinds. Oohing and Ahhing over the bowl of fresh fruit. Over the crepes filled with berries, topped with whipped cream. Taking in each and every taste, forgetting that hunger that has been plaguing her for a lifetime.

I'll see this hunger, even when she's overtaken by the food brought in on fine china and covered in shiny metallic food covers. I'll spot her ribs winking under her taut skin, watch them shift as she saunters around the room in her panties, her breasts small and firm, small mounds of skin connected to a rib cage. I'll do my best to ignore her disappearance. I'll enjoy her until she's faded away.

I wonder if it's possible for her to fade away here—precisely because it's all a dream—this facade of room service and lying on the beach at exotic locations. This dream will come to fruition perhaps in the future, but for now, it's simply the thing of conversations, the kind of thing that's on the tip of her tongue while she fantasizes about the future in order to forget about the past. Fantasizes about the future in order to push back the reality of things.

Things like a fussy baby who never gets enough to eat. A fussy baby who cries when he isn't sleeping—and even then—makes these cries of discontent that jut through her fantasies like barbed wire strung through her living-room. As much as she wants to ignore it—stay in her apartment long enough—she's liable to get cut.

She likes romance novels and bad TV. The color purple. The sound of the air conditioner humming on the hottest of summer days. The tick of a ceiling fan—that tick between whirls—the constant churning. Wearing all white—no matter the season—and preferably white shorts and a white tanktop that shows off her tan. Sandals as opposed to tennis shoes. Little trinkets that she picks up at busy airports. The *do not disturb* signs in cheap hotels. Seashells. Smooth stones. Turquoise jewelry. Anything made of pearls.

Receiving greeting cards when there's nothing to celebrate. Flowers as opposed to roses. Preferably something in a pot as opposed to a vase. The paper menus at the International House of Pancakes with the children's menu on the back, one of those that you hand to your child and tell him to color until the food arrives. Endless cups of coffee at Cafe Brazil—preferably on the patio in the middle of a warm afternoon, preferably Sunday—when she has nothing else going on, no place to be, no errands to run. The endless pursuit of nothing.

Sunsets. Sunrises. Walks on the beach. Lunch on the patio of a beachside cafe. Quad Venti Breve Cinnamon Dulce Lattes. Dinner on that same patio of that same beachside cafe. Forgetting what day it is. Forgetting what time it is. Losing time altogether. Forgetting her name.

Fucking absolute strangers. Picking them up in some hick-town bar, calling herself Sarah or Susan. Creating something out of nothing. Creating this persona that looks nothing like her.

Watching men beat up other men because they looked at her the wrong way. Watching clean-cut, fresh-shaven faces turn purple in the blue bruised knuckle of an instant. Watching wounds open and close, turning into scars right in front of her.

Faces that carry the scars of drink. Of thirst. Hunger. That moment before she gets what she needs. That moment before she takes the food into her mouth. Not the food itself, but the longing. The need, right before it's met.

She longs for that brief moment when she realizes how good it will taste. The moment between need and plenty that's lost in an instant but will last for eternity. She loves this more than life itself.

She's a vampire.

She's a vulture.

She's the captor and the prey.

All rolled up into one.

"Good morning," she says. Maggie's standing over me with a video camera.

I don't have the chance to wake up and note my surroundings, wonder if it was all a dream. I don't have the chance to wake up and enjoy the rhythm of her breathing as I relive the night in my head.

The video camera steals all of this from me. It doesn't give me the chance to do anything at all.

"Good morning," she says.

"Yes . . ."

I don't know what else to say. I'm in shock. I'm not accustomed to waking up this way.

"What are you thinking?"

"What are you doing?"

"I'm asking the questions."

"What are you doing?"

"What are you thinking?"

"That it's weird to wake up with a video camera in your face."

"You're breaking the illusion. I'm not here."

She smiles.

But it's not the kind of smile that arises out of unfamiliarity. She has done this before.

"So who's asking me questions?"

"Fine. Talk. I won't ask questions."

"I'm not comfortable with this."

"Relax," she says. "Get comfortable."

She's naked. I wonder how it's possible for her to feel so comfortable naked—exposed—holding a video camera.

"Can I at least put my clothes on?"

"If you insist."

She shrinks back for a moment. She's taken aback by my discomfort. She thought I would be different. She thought I would be comfortable under the scrutiny of her camera.

I'm sorry to disappoint her. But not enough to go along for the ride. I hold the blanket up to me as I lean over the side of the bed and search for my jeans. I find them. I put them on under the blanket.

"That's cute," she says.

"What?"

"Your shyness."

"Oh," I say.

"You weren't shy last night."

"You weren't holding a camera in my face—"

"You got lucky."

"What does that mean?"

"You were the first."

"The first for what?"

"Sex before confession."

"Whatever that means."

"Nothing's free, Hal. There's a price to pay."

"Ah," I say. "This is the price I pay."

"So was it worth it?" she says.

"It depends," I say.

"On what?"

"On what you want to know."

"I want to know everything," she says. She's an absolute lunatic—standing over me naked—with a camera.

"Oh—"

"But I don't have to know it all today. There'll be plenty of time for that."

"That's good to know."

"Yeah," she says. "At least you know you'll get fucked again."

"Is that what this means?"

"Yes," she says.

"Ok."

"Let's eat," she says.

———◆———

"Are you going to eat?"

"It's hard for me to eat with you sticking a camera in my face."

"Pretend I'm not here."

"But you are here. You're sticking a camera in my face."

"Pretend."

"Ok, you're not here."

———◆———

"Tell me about yourself."

"What do you want to know?"

"What's your favorite color?"

"I don't have a favorite color."

"If you had a favorite color, what would it be?"

"Beige," I say.

"How do you like your coffee?"

"Black and bitter."

"How old were you when you lost your virginity?"

"Ten," I say.

"Be serious."

"Sixteen."

"Where?"

"Where what?"

"Where did you lose it?"

"In the track and field storage shed at my high school."

"The track and field storage shed?"

"Yeah. It was late. We were drunk."

"So you lost your virginity and betrayed your best friend all in the same evening? Sex and betrayal."

"How does this have anything to do with my best friend?"

"I know things."

"What was her name?"

"Katie—"

"Katie what?"

"I don't remember."

"Try."

"Next question."

"I like this one."

"Next question."

But I know her name. Katie Jackson. I know it well. I whispered it under my breath. That night—a Saturday—we had been drinking Boone's Farm during a practice of some God-awful play produced by the Drama Department. I was some third-rate character without any lines. She was the star. We snuck to the back of the auditorium and slipped out the back exit.

Drinking the Boone's Farm that Katie smuggled from her car and smoking cigarettes, I never considered that Katie was my best friend's girlfriend. I never considered the consequences.

Katie and I walk out to the empty track—this huge, never-ending circle—and the sky's lit with stars.

The side door to the track and field storage shed is open. I feel around for a light switch and find nothing. We push through what seems to be the wooden horses that they use for track events on Saturday mornings and we ease over to the large blue high jump mat. We lay there in our drunken state—our heads spinning with the sweet nastiness that is Boone's Farm—and I have no doubt that I'll fuck Katie.

As she's leaving, she says what has happened will be our little secret.

I drive home in my dad's truck—drunk out of my mind—tasting the aftertaste of the sweetness of her tongue in my mouth. My parents are asleep. I masturbate in my bedroom for what seems like hours because I don't want that little secret to slip out of my mind. I recreate that moment until it's forged in my memory. I carry that little secret around in my head for the rest of my days. As though it were a dream.

"Next question."

"Dogs or cats?"

"Dogs."

"You have egg on your face," she says.

11

GENERAL EDWIN WALKER was a right-wing conservative nut who worked his way up the ranks of the United States Army. In his free time, he attended covert meetings of the John Birch Society, a group of tightly lipped men who were in love with their rituals, sworn to secrecy, and convinced that the government was out to get them.

He quickly decided that his salvation depended on the recruitment of other souls into the folds of the John Birch Society. Against the rules of the military, Walker set out to convert the troops in his battalion. Which included handing out pamphlets critical of the United States Government while praising the virtues of the John Birch Society. Which included a set of precepts demanding allegiance to the JBS over anything else. Which included the United States Army.

Word leaked out that General Edwin Walker was handing out tracts promoting the John Birch Society, and the Kennedy Administration relieved him of his duty to the United States military.

General Edwin Walker wasn't pleased. It further illustrated that the government wasn't content until it meddled in your affairs and stole your freedom.

There are those out there who would argue that General Edwin Walker was behind the assassination of President John F. Kennedy. General Edwin Walker was not only a plausible candidate, he was entirely capable.

When the United States Secret Service Agents stormed Lee Harvey Oswald's boarding room—and later his rental house in Irving—they supposedly uncovered a letter written by Oswald to Marina, outlining his plans to assassinate the general. Along with detailed blueprints of General Walker's house and the surrounding landscape.

But, what the Warren Commission doesn't tell you is that Lee Harvey Oswald was not the man who attempted to assassinate General Edwin Walker.

That was a man by the name of Colonel ███████.

The attempted assassination—a bullet that shattered the window and lodged itself into a bookcase, landing in a leather-bound copy of the Holy Bible—had less to do with The Colonel thinking that General Edwin Walker was a stark-raving-mad lunatic who needed to be stopped, than it had to do with General Edwin Walker getting blowjobs from a woman named Becky Lynn Bardow. Becky Lynn strutted her stuff in the equivalent of a devil's costume—complete with horns and a tail—at a little burlesque joint by the name of the Carousel, owned by a rather shady character by the name of Jack Ruby. She did things with a pitchfork that were unforgettable. If she got drunk enough—and Jack was passed out in his office— Becky Lynn would use the pitchfork as a dildo while strangers threw her wads of cash. Becky Lynn Bardow just happened to be engaged to a man by the name of Colonel ███████. If you can't pull a conspiracy out of that, you can't pull a conspiracy out of anything.

But in Lemon's mind, the Colonel's one of the last living human beings who can prove that Lee Harvey Oswald had nothing to do with the near assassination of General Edwin Walker. If he was framed in the near assassination of General Edwin Walker, then why in the hell couldn't he have been framed for the more infamous assassination of the President of the United States?

Now that Lemon's got his hands on something that he feels will set the record straight on the misinformation that his father was the lone shooter of the President of the United States, finding the

Colonel has become an absolute necessity.

———◆———

We're sitting in the IHOP off of Mockingbird and Abrams, and Lemon's going on about the Colonel. And frankly, it's a nice distraction. Anything to get me out of my head.

Cohen and Jacobs nosing around. Bob blowing his brains out in a drunken haze. Dreams of Sam doing little mundane things that have absolutely no attachment with reality—things that Sam would never do—like scrubbing the kitchen floor until her hands bleed. Dreams of Sam cleaning out the fridge absolutely bare-ass naked. Dreams of Sam crocheting in the middle of the living-room floor while watching the Home Shopping Network. Random occurrences filtering through my sleep like bizarre messages from the dead.

Or the constant urge to call Rachel up for one more indiscriminate meeting in the supermarket that will end up with us losing our minds all over my apartment. Or an absolutely spontaneous thought like driving over to Maggie's apartment and telling her to get in the car, that we're driving to Vegas to get married. All of these random things bouncing around in my head. Thoughts of going to the Lakewood Landing to have myself a drink—drink myself into oblivion—and drive my car head-on into oncoming traffic. Thoughts of throwing myself off of the Triple Underpass. Thoughts of slicing my wrists in a warm bath and dozing off into the Great Beyond listening to Edie Brickell and New Bohemians.

Anything—even Lemon's incessant ramblings about some nutjob Colonel—is better than this.

"Are you paying attention?" Lemon says.

"No, not really," I say.

"What's wrong with you?"

I'm trying my best to pay attention, but I have this strange feeling that I'm being watched.

You know what I'm talking about. You get that feeling. You're walking down the street and it feels like a pair of eyes are boring a hole into your back.

You turn around and look and nobody's there.

But that doesn't mean they're not there. You just don't see them. I sound like Lemon. He's rubbing off on me. If I'm not careful, I'll be locking myself up in my house afraid to look out of the blinds or answer the phone, be locked up in my house thinking that the mailman works for the CIA and my junk mail contains hidden messages containing the times and locations of JBS meetings. But with that said, this isn't some psychotic paranoia set on by latent schizophrenia, I'm being watched. I'm being watched. Period.

"So how do I go about finding the Colonel?"

"Call him," I say.

"It's not as easy as that."

"So, do you have his number?"

"No. Maybe I had it before. But not anymore."

"Wouldn't your mother have it? Isn't she connected at the hip with all of these conspiracy people?"

"Watch your mouth. But no. She doesn't like the Colonel. I've told you that. She doesn't want me hanging around him. Says he's dangerous."

"Well, Lemon, that's exactly what we need. Let's go look up Mr. Dangerous. That's exactly who we need to be hanging around. Dangerous people. It's not like we're in enough danger already."

"He's not dangerous."

"Why exactly do you need to hook up with the Colonel anyway?"

"I need to know what to do with this." He pulls a manila envelope out of his backpack and waves it at me.

"What is that?"

"It's what's going to get me out of debt. It's going to save Conspiracy Books. It's going to keep some rich-ass corporation from turning it into a high-rise. That's exactly what it is."

"You think you can save Conspiracy Books with that?"

"Yes. As a matter of fact, I do."

"So, I guess it's important."

"Yes it is."

"I guess you think somebody else wants it."

"Yes I do."

"You think someone's willing to pay you a lot of money for it."

"Yes I do."

"Well, then, let's find the Colonel."

———◆———

Crazy Larry hangs out at the exit of the Sixth Floor Museum every day of the week. After these fine folks from out of town have spent their twelve dollars to get their whitewashed tour of the day President Kennedy got shot in Dallas—the government version, the one where Lee Harvey Oswald, crazed lunatic that he was, sticks his head out of the sixth floor of the Texas School Book Depository building and does some magic with a mail-order rifle and three magic bullets and then slips on down to Oak Cliff where he'll shoot Officer J.D. Tippit and then get the sudden urge to go see a movie, get arrested without so much as a fight, be escorted to the court-house where he'll undergo a debriefing of sorts, on his way to being transferred to the jail, he'll be shot by wannabe mafia/strip joint owner/small-town gangster, Jack Ruby, and after a *thorough investi-gation* by the Warren Commission, will be ruled the Lone Assassin of the President of the United States—they'll be on their way out the door, thanking God for justice, and waving their little flag and humming "God Bless America" under their breath. And Crazy Larry will catch them by surprise.

"You buy that horseshit?" Larry screams from his wheelchair. "You buy their Godless version of the truth? Then you go sit your ass in your gas-eating SUV and drive on home to your comfortable house and forget you ever wanted to know some semblance of the goddamn truth. But, if you had a little doubt on their goddamn worthless whitewashed tour, then march yourselves over here for a quick unveiling of the God's honest truth about the cover-up of the millennium."

They'll get in their cars and drive home.

They'll talk about Crazy Larry. They'll say that people like Crazy Larry need to be locked up. They'll whisper to themselves that he's on drugs. He's probably into child pornography. They'll tell all their friends about him and when they go home at night they'll thank the dear Lord in Heaven that they're not like Crazy Larry.

Larry curses every last one of them—in their gas- guzzling SUVs—curses their goddamn nine-to-five white-collar jobs, their support for rounding up all the illegals, except for the ones that watch their kids, and shipping them back to where they came from, curses their

Ivy League educations, their trust funds, their family foundations, their CRUTS, their CLATS, their 529 Plans, their 401(k)s. They don't know a goddamn about what it's like to fight for your country. They don't know what it's like to get both of your legs blown off in Vietnam and then have to give goddamn Conspiracy Bookstore fliers out at the goddamn Sixth Floor Museum so they can have enough money to wheel their goddamn legless selves down to the VFW and have a watered-down goddamn drink. They don't know what it feels like to waste the last goddamn money you have in the world on a hooker that doesn't have any teeth—thank God for small favors—and then wheel your legless self down to the local homeless shelter and hope they'll let you have a bed for the night even though you haven't followed their sobriety requirements and are drunk out of your goddamn mind.

Every evening, that's the scenario. Crazy Larry's day in a nutshell.

If Crazy Larry doesn't rustle up enough money at the Sixth Floor Museum, he'll wheel himself over to Conspiracy Books—where Claire will usually give him a sandwich and some spare change—and he'll wheel himself down the street to the VFW to get his drink on.

By the time we get to the Sixth Floor Museum, Larry has already made it over to the bookstore and by now is three sheets to the wind at the VFW while "Friends in Low Places" grinds itself out on the jukebox.

We know that he's three sheets to the wind because Claire gave him ten dollars. That's what she tells us when we walk in the door of Conspiracy Books and she's counting change to a little old woman in a kerchief and socks that come up to her knees and an armful of Jim Thompson crime novels. Once the little old woman has staggered out of the bookstore—the bells ringing in the door to prove that she's gone—Claire tells us that it's been well over an hour since she saw Crazy Larry.

She's right. By the time we reach Larry, he's drunk to the gills. He has his chair parked in a dark corner and he's slamming down Vodka Sprites like he's drinking his final meal.

He smiles when he sees Lemon. Tells him—as best as he can—that it's good to see a kindred spirit. In a complete reversal, Crazy Larry screams at him for stealing his business over at the access road on Interstate 30. Says it's goddamn disrespectful. Worse than that, it's goddamn stealing. You have two legs that work and you could go out and get a goddamn job, but you'd rather play cripple and steal all of Crazy Larry's business, begging for change. If he had the strength, he would climb out of his chair and ring Lemon's neck. That would teach Lemon not to disrespect the Country's Veterans. He slaps his hand over his heart and starts singing "God Bless America."

In another complete reversal, Crazy Larry goes into a tirade about needing to clean up his act. Lemon's mother had a right to get mad at him when he came into the bookstore begging for change, but a man has to do what a man has to do. After all, he's got a family to feed. By family, Crazy Larry's talking about his dog—Zoot—and a couple of pigeons that have taken to him when he sleeps under the bridge off of Haskell. Your mother—God bless her heart—is an angel.

He'll go on and on about Mary. She's the sweetest woman that he has ever laid his eyes on. He doesn't mean any disrespect when he says that the worst mistake he ever made in his life was when he turned down her marriage proposal. We don't know if this is true or not—don't have a clue if Crazy Larry's lying his ass off about everything he says or not—but we're forced to listen to him go on and on until he finally wears himself out—shuts his mouth long enough for Lemon to ask him a few questions—and then he's off to his drinking again.

———◆———

Watching Crazy Larry drink Vodka Sprites gets old fast. This is a dead end. After all, what do we expect to gain from standing over a drunk for half an hour while the guy literally slobbers all over himself. At one point, he falls out of his wheelchair and onto the floor. Crazy Larry's so drunk out of his mind that he won't let anybody help him up. Whenever we bend down to help him, he accuses us of aiding and abetting the conservative right. He accuses us of aiding and abetting the status quo. I'm not sure what he's talking about. Nobody's sure what he's talking about.

But I'm sure of one thing: we're not getting anything from Crazy Larry. At least, not tonight.

But of course, I'm wrong.

———◆———

I'm down to two bucks in my pocket when Crazy Larry gives us the first lead of the night. Before Larry passes out for the final time—and the bartender and a few of his friends carry Larry out to a fenced-in area behind the bar, where the bartender keeps a few of his junk cars, so Larry can sleep his drink off for a while, crunched up in a fetal position in his wheelchair, cradling the stumps of his legs like he's cradling a set of twins—he points across the bar and tells us that Mo knows how to contact the Colonel. Larry says that Mo screws the Colonel from time to time. He goes into a spiel about how the Government encourages a proverbial free market, and yet they don't let women charge money for sex. With that, Larry curls up in his fetal position, passed out and ready for the bartender to cart him out the door.

———◆———

Mo's sitting at the bar drinking a scotch and soda and smoking a Kool cigarette. This woman has hair so black it almost looks purple, a face the color of a hospital sheet, a pair of red lips—the lipstick smeared around her lips like she did her makeup while riding bareback at the Mesquite Rodeo—and she's wearing a black sequined dress that's missing most of the sequins.

She's been drinking since ten o'clock this morning. Her eyes are bloodshot. Half spheres of glass that you could use to comb your hair while you're talking to her.

When you're talking to Mo, you're going to be doing most of the talking. She's not the kind of woman who's going to spend much of her time telling you anything. She's old. She's tired. She's washed up. Unless she thinks you're interested in a blowjob or a screw at the Daisy Chain Motel down the street—where she rents a room by the hour from a guy named Plug—she's got nothing to say to you. But she's not going to cut you off because everyone that approaches her is a chance at a few extra dollars to get her next drink. That's what she lives for.

That's the impression I get when we walk over—sit next to her at the bar—and Lemon starts asking her questions.

I take one look at Mo, and I'm convinced that this is another goddamn dead end.

Yet again, I'm wrong.

———◆———

Lemon's the first one to say anything. He pulls a stool up next to the bar—orders a Tab, lights up a cigarette—turns to Mo and tells her that Crazy Larry said she had the scoop on Colonel ████.

She takes a pull from her Scotch and soda, takes a pull from her Kool cigarette—rests it on the corner of her ashtray—and blows a cloud of smoke in Lemon's face.

"Crazy Larry's full of shit," she says.

"I'm with you," Lemon says. "But I think you know how I can find the Colonel. Just tell me and you can get back to drinking your Scotch and soda and smoking your Kool cigarettes."

"Who's asking?" she says.

"Lemon Pickens."

"Ain't that the shit," she says. "Goddamn, it is you. Last time I saw your ass was on the cover of that shit-rag *Dallas Observer*. I thought you dropped off of the face of the earth."

"No," Lemon says, "I'm still here."

"Jesus Christ," she says. "So Mary still doing that bookstore thing?"

"Still doing it," Lemon says. "Although it looks like they're going to shut her down if they have their way. Putting up a shitload of condominiums."

"You bet your ass they are," she says. "I read something about that. Well Goddamn, Mary Pickens's son."

———◆———

The way Mo goes on and on about Mary, you would assume that they'd danced together at the Carousel. The way Mo goes on and on about Mary, you would assume they'd done time at conspiracy convention after conspiracy convention, but that wouldn't be accurate at all.

When Mary was pregnant with Lemon—and John F. Kennedy was getting the back of his head blown off—Mo was getting her doctorate in Fort Lauderdale, Florida. When Jack Ruby was busy shooting up Lee Harvey Oswald in the basement of the downtown courthouse, Mo was juggling raising a daughter and being married to a divorce attorney with a really bad drinking problem and an even worse temper.

All Mo knows about Mary is what the Colonel has told her. And that would be plenty. When Mo's off giving the Colonel a blowjob in Room 69 at the Daisy Chain Motel—with old Plug threatening to throw her out at any moment—and things settle down and she's watching some bad television with the Colonel in the bed next to her getting his drink on, the Colonel will settle in with story after story of his days at the Carousel. The drinking. The carousing. The women. And mostly, the women.

And by God, this isn't the first time some half-drunk Colonel lay next to her in bed telling her stories of the women who broke his heart. Well, maybe the first time from a colonel, but if you've been with as many men as Mo has, they all start sounding the same. All of them.

But the Colonel's story is different.

———◆———

There's no greater love than a man who will lay down his life for a friend. Outside of a man who's willing to spend his life in prison by killing the man who's sleeping with his girlfriend.

And that man's the Colonel. Mo will tell that story with such detail that her eyes light up and you would swear that she had been the object of the Colonel's affections.

That isn't the case. The woman who the Colonel was willing to go to prison for was the dancer—by the name of Becky Lynn Bardow—who danced night after night on the same stage as Mary Pickens. Mary had her angel outfit. Becky Lynn, the devil. The Colonel should have known better than to get involved. Should have known better than to dance with the devil.

According to Mo, everybody who was anybody had wanted to sleep with Becky Lynn Bardow. And those who didn't want to sleep with Becky Lynn Bardow, wanted to sleep with Mary Pickens. They both had that special something—that ability to turn it on like a light switch—and they all came running.

To give Mo credit—in her day—she had been that woman as well. But it had chewed her up and spit her out. It wasn't all that it was cracked up to be.

As soon as she left her husband—when she had been beaten to an inch of her life one too many times—she didn't have a shortage of pursuers. Fellow doctoral students. Professors. Neighbors. Customers at the Sunset Bar and Grill, where she slung drinks at night to make ends meet. All of them wanted a piece of her.

Perhaps they knew she was broken. And defenseless. And then she ran out of money to pay the bills—started drinking—and pretty much gave her daughter away to her sister so she could do whatever it was she had to do to forget what she had done with herself.

She meets a guy—a trucker or something like that—follows him to Dallas, and he leaves her for a woman half her age. She wakes up one day giving blowjobs to total strangers for ten bucks to settle a score—or to pay off her tab—and suddenly she wonders where her life went.

But listening to the Colonel tell his stories filled her up. Brought back memories. Gave her a reason to believe in a thing called love.

12

THE COLONEL'S NOT an easy man to find. Never has been. He's one of those guys who disappears at a moment's notice. That much is clear. Mo said it is out of necessity. But not the kind of necessity that you might think. Not that he's *not* being followed by the government. There are plenty of men with badges who want to keep an eye on him. But he has been running his whole life. It's pretty much what sent him to the military. An abusive father. A not-so-stable home life. But even after he joined the service—learned the code of honor and all of that horseshit, love of brother, love of country, learned a shitload of discipline—his ability to settle down and start a family never came together.

He would tell you that's what he wanted.

He would tell you that's what he was searching for.

But if you look at his actions, you would guess that what he really wanted was to wander around aimlessly wishing he were somewhere else.

He always went for the girl who was unavailable, always wanted the job when they weren't hiring, always showed up at the parties that required invitations. The Colonel had become so accustomed to being an outsider—even if he made it into an inner circle of sorts—he was always wanting out.

Which makes the government extremely nervous. They aren't worried about the guy with a family, aren't worried about the guy with a stable job and home life. They've got those things to occupy their time. But those individuals with wanderlust, those individuals who are always searching for something else—anything—now those are the kind of guys you have to worry about.

These guys won't take no for an answer. They're willing to give all of that up in order to uncover the kinds of things that the government has become an expert at hiding.

Guys like the Colonel are destined to fall right in the middle of the kinds of conspiracies that the government doesn't want you to know about.

And Mo added, similar to Lee Harvey Oswald.

Mo told us she didn't know Oswald. But if she did, she wouldn't cop to it. You start telling people that you knew Lee, and suddenly they find your body in a ditch somewhere. Instead, you keep to the company line. Whether you knew Lee or not, you say Oswald didn't have any friends or acquaintances. You tell them he was the kind of guy who hung out by himself. And, in a lot of ways, you wouldn't be lying. Plenty of people knew Oswald—hung out with him— had a few drinks with him from time to time. But as far as really knowing the man—and what made him tick—that was impossible. It was true that Oswald probably wouldn't open up to many people.

But then again, there are plenty of people who knew what he was up to, but they knew better than to go around handing out all of their info to the general public. You start doing interviews, and guys in suits show up on your doorstep and suggest that you keep your mouth shut. If the old scare tactic doesn't work, you find yourself overdosing on a shitload of pills and you wake up and read your obituary in the paper.

That's why the Colonel's hard to find. He doesn't talk. And you don't talk. You learn to keep your mouth shut. Despite not being too keen on how everything went down concerning his life, he wasn't too keen on the alternative.

You've got to know that there was a whole lot going on at the Carousel around the time of Kennedy's assassination. There were a lot of players involved. And most of them had either had a drink at the place, taken a punch from Jack Ruby, or had taken off their clothes to the sound of a cheesy Broadway number.

And most of them were dead.

The Colonel wanted to get away from all of that.

Dying, that is.

———◆———

Mo said the Colonel was a man of few regrets.

If there's one regret that he had in life, it's that he wishes he had been a better shot.

Mo retold the story the Colonel told to her. She had heard it a thousand times. The Colonel had been drinking cheap champagne over at the Carousel in the wee hours of the morning. He had already pissed Jack off by groping Becky Lynn, and an argument started. After taking a cheap shot in the nose, Jack punched the Colonel in the mouth—took a few of his teeth—and then—in an effort to pay him back for the cheap shot—told the Colonel that if he thought Becky Lynn was his girl, he had another thing coming.

Why don't you ask her, you son of a bitch, the Colonel said.

And Jack said, I've got something better, why don't you ask the General.

The Colonel knew right away. He couldn't—even long after they had gone their separate ways—get the image of Becky Lynn sucking the General's dick—in the backseat of his black coupe—out of his head. He couldn't get over the image of Becky Lynn taking it in the ass in the middle of the General's bed.

According to Mo, the Colonel shot down a couple more bottles of Jack's champagne, drove home to his upstairs apartment and loaded up his rifle and a box of shells and drove his ass over to the General's place.

The Colonel was a good shot. Anybody would tell you that. But he was drunk off of his ass, and the General was extremely lucky that night. As soon as the Colonel had pulled the trigger, the General moved half an inch. The bullet almost took off the tip of his nose.

The Colonel missed.

But at the same time, he was so drunk he probably didn't notice. The loud crack of his rifle stirred his senses, so he drove out of there thinking he had killed the General. Only to find out the next day—after beating the shit out of Becky Lynn at the apartment supplied to her by Jack Ruby, throwing her around like a rag doll, doing everything but mess up her face, because even drunk he knew that if he messed up her face, Ruby would kill him—that the General was alive and well.

By then—waking up with a hangover but sober all the same—he had regained a little of his common sense. He figured killing the General might not be the thing to do. If he wanted to marry Becky Lynn. It's hard to enjoy marriage when you're doing hard time in prison.

But regardless, every once in a while—more often than not probably—the Colonel fantasized about blowing the General's head off of his shoulders.

This feeling wouldn't go away.

But it softened.

Through the years, it would pop its head up, and the Colonel would feel like tracking him down and killing him. Time moved on. The Colonel got old. The General got old. And one day the Colonel woke up and read the obituary section and the General had died of old age, in relative obscurity.

And the feeling was gone.

He realized that he didn't have any reason to continue to harbor his anger. So he let it go. He didn't want to die with thoughts of the General on his mind. He let it go. He didn't want to think about the General. He didn't want to talk about the General. He didn't want to relive any of those old times. He would live in the now.

But if Lemon could find him, that would change. Lemon had something that would bring his past colliding with his future, would show him something that the Colonel knew existed but had forgotten all about.

A picture.

———◆———

You wouldn't expect to find the Colonel at a church somewhere. A JBS meeting, to infiltrate the enemy, yes. A VFW bar on the wrong side of town—out back puking in the alley, stinking drunk—yes. Any number of VFWs, yes. Any number of bars—for that matter—where you have the same people showing up day after day—some of them in as early as ten o'clock and not getting up off of their barstool until eleven o'clock or so that night, unless they have to take a piss or load the juke—yes. But a church? It doesn't make a hell of a lot of sense.

Antioch First Baptist. On the corner of Ross and Pearl. A little white clapboard of a church. Haggard. Weeds grown up around the sign, this little haggard church in need of care. Not that they don't care, but the congregation here are blue-collar workers who work all day, play hard, and barely have the energy to make it to church, much less come up on a Saturday to make sure she looks good for the weekend.

Becky Bardow—no doubt—pulls a weed or two. Spruces the place up from time to time. But when you're out there saving weary souls and feeding the homeless and caring for those with AIDS and any number of diseases—and you're pretty much doing it by yourself—you've got to prioritize these kinds of things.

But she's all about keeping the inside of Antioch as clean as she possibly can. Becky Bardow would tell you that it doesn't matter what you look like on the outside, it's the inside that counts.

We find her in the foyer of Antioch—down on her hands and knees with a bucket of Pine-Sol and a rag—scrubbing her heart away, working up a sweat.

"Soup's not on for a couple of more hours, fellows," she says.

"That's good," Lemon says, "because I just ate lunch."

We must look like a couple of homeless guys. Becky Bardow's mistaking us for wanting a handout.

Lord knows, Lemon's probably been here a time or two after one of his binges. I ask him later if he had ever been to the place and he seemed offended, getting all ticked off because I would insinuate such a thing. No, he's never been there before for a handout. Of course—he tells me later—the place, and Becky Bardow, seemed vaguely familiar.

———◆———

Becky Bardow talked about the Colonel. But it didn't come easy. It was like she was digging something up out of the past even though she admitted that she had seen him a little over a week ago.

It's hard for her to give us an exact time—as he always stops by unannounced—but it's usually closer to the weekend. He'll stop by to help her in the soup kitchen. He'll stop by to work on the serving line. Sometimes he'll stop by on a Saturday to fix a leaking roof or whatever needs fixing around the church.

I ask her if he's a churchgoing man. That's not the impression I get from him. According to Becky, my impressions are right. He's skeptical. Almost as skeptical about religion as he is about the government.

She starts talking about the past, says she's not necessarily ashamed of any of it—she often throws her stories of the past into her Sunday sermons—but at the same time, it's not something she wants to dwell on. That was thirty-five years ago.

By the way she talks, it doesn't seem like it was thirty-five years ago. It seems like it was only yesterday. She gives us the quick rundown on getting into trouble when she was seventeen or so— kicked out of the house by her mom and dad—didn't really have anywhere to go. She shows up on the front steps of the Carousel, and Jack takes her in.

She didn't dance at first. She helped run the register. She helped Jack with the books. She ran drinks when they were super busy. At Jack's suggestion, she finally started dancing.

She brightens a bit while talking about it—with only a slight hint of pain—and I can tell that she doesn't mind going back in her memory. Starts talking about the friends she made, even mentions Mary and goes off on a little tangent about their friendship. But they weren't close. That kind of life doesn't bring closeness. That kind of life forces you to keep everyone at an arm's distance. It's the only way you can protect yourself.

She talks about drugs and booze and men and the fact that she was always trying to fill that empty hole. She did it with drugs. She did it with booze. She did it with men.

One was never enough, which she understands now. She knows now that one or a hundred is never enough. Only Jesus satisfies your soul. She stays in that line of work for fifteen years or so—jumping around from club to club after Jack was convicted of killing Oswald, went down the street to the Colony Club, did some other clubs that she barely remembers—and was so messed up on drugs and drink that she couldn't care for herself any longer.

She tells us about a night that she woke up naked in an alley behind one of the clubs, beat up, lonely, destitute, with no real place to call her home. There's a point that we all reach—if we're lucky enough to have the chance—when we realize that only Jesus satisfies. Lying there naked, beat up, lonely and destitute, she calls out to God for salvation. If he'll give her one more chance, she'll change all of her bad living and the rest of her days will be spent in his service.

That was a long time ago, she says.

She's still kept her promise.

———◆———

We stick around long enough to help Becky on her evening shift at the soup kitchen. Lemon's doing it for purely selfish reasons—hoping that the Colonel will show up—but he's doing it regardless. We're putting large pots of stew on big burners and wiping down the serving line and mopping the floor of the large dining room and setting out long tables and chairs and taking loaves of bread out of the refrigerator and getting things all set up for their arrival.

Pretty soon they all start lining up—these people of all shapes and sizes—filing through with their empty hearts and empty stomachs. They take their seats and Pastor Becky walks to the center of the room and tells them that man cannot live by bread alone. But she's happy that God has given her the opportunity to serve some up. The bread and the stew is free. It was provided by God. It was God's free gift. But if they should ever tire from doing the same thing over and over again—expecting different results—if they should ever tire from living one moment to the next without feeling safe and secure, then she would like to offer up a simple prayer.

She prayed this prayer when she was naked, lonely, and destitute, lying in that alley. God if you'll help me, I'll give you everything. What's funny about that, she says, is that I had nothing to give, but yet that's all God wanted. So many of us are unwilling to give God what we don't have. We don't have anything in this pitiful life that we live, yet we're unwilling to give *that* to him. But if you reach that place of willingness—and want to give up what you don't have— turn to Jesus, because only he can satisfy your soul.

Pastor Becky gave us the address of a boarding house off of Haskell. We drive up and down a series of streets—containing rundown apartment buildings and little shacks that are weary and desolate— and we're about to give up on the whole deal when we find the street and the address that we're looking for. We get out of the car, walk across the street and up to the porch of this boarding house where the Colonel supposedly stays on occasion.

A woman in her late forties is sitting on the front step smoking a cigarette.

She's not interested in talking to us.

"We're looking for Colonel ███████."

"I'm not the information desk," she says. She blows a cloud of smoke our way. She doesn't move from the middle of the step. We have to climb around her.

"Worthless bitch," Lemon says.

"Watch your mouth," I say.

The screen door opens into a hallway with doors on either side. The hallway opens up into a living area and a small kitchen. A large black woman is seated on the couch watching television.

"Hi," I say.

"Hello," Lemon says.

"Do I know you?" she says.

She doesn't move her eyes away from the television.

"It's doubtful," Lemon says.

"Then have a nice day," she says.

"We're looking for Colonel ███████."

"I don't give out information on residents," she says.

"So he lives here?"

"I didn't say that—"

"But you said that you don't give out information on residents—"

"I know what I said," she says.

"Jesus," Lemon says. "These people are too goddamn friendly."

We are about to cross the street when the woman on the front porch smoking a cigarette calls out to us.

"So you're looking for Colonel ██████?"

"Yes," Lemon says, looking back at her. He walks across the grass and up to the porch. I follow him.

"So do you know where we can find him?"

"I sure do," she says.

"That would be great," Lemon says.

The woman takes another cigarette out of a sequined cigarette case, pops it between her lips and lights up. She blows her first mouth of smoke in our direction.

"So where can we find him?" Lemon says.

"It's going to cost you," the woman says.

"Jesus," Lemon says.

"I already told you," the woman says, "that I'm not the information desk. If I happen to have some information that you need—and I don't get paid to work here—then I guess you're going to have to pay me. If you don't, walk your skinny white asses back to your car."

"How much are we talking?"

"Ten bucks."

"Jesus," Lemon says. He pats his pocket and then looks at me.

13

GAVIN THOMPSON COMES into the bank at a quarter past ten. Something's wrong. He's sweating. His charcoal-gray hair is matted at the temples. His forehead's glowing. His eyes are shifty—busy—looking all over the bank for Maggie. He won't find her.

Maggie Smith doesn't exist. At least, the Maggie Smith as she appears on the surface. It's hard to know a mirage. Hard to understand a dream. All of this surface area dissolving in front of you. All of the layers peeled away. And the Maggie Smith you think you know is someone totally different. The Maggie Smith who counts your money back to you—smiles and tells you to have a nice day—is a figment of your imagination. She isn't real. Reach out and touch her, and she'll disappear.

You may be okay with that. You may be fine with doing transactions with a ghost. You walk away with a fold of money bulging in your front pocket, and you think to yourself, *Now that's a nice young woman*—stroll across the lobby and into the Crescent Office Building hallway—and you forget about her. You don't think of her again until the next week when she counts your money back to you and tells you to have a nice day and you walk away with a fold of money bulging in your front pocket and you think to yourself, *Now that's a nice young woman*—stroll across the lobby and into the Crescent Office Building hallway—and you forget about her. Ad nauseam.

You like it that way. You get what you need, and you stuff that satisfaction into your pocket and move on to the next thing that you need. These faceless entities who exist only to serve you. You're okay with that. These faceless servants might as well be the same person. The guy who washes your car. The woman who serves you your Starbucks Venti Red Eye. The man who dry-cleans your suits. Blah blah blah. You have no desire to connect with these people.

But I'm not okay with this.

I'm not willing to exist in a world where Maggie Smith's just another faceless entity. That's where your needs end and mine begin. I *need* to know her. I *need* to know what makes her tick. And don't put her in the category of all of the past women in my life. This one's different. Relationship or not, my need to uncover the truth beyond the mirage is much deeper than what I stand to gain.

It goes beyond obsession. Obsessive, yes. But love's all of these things and more. That's what it is. I love her. I've loved her from the moment I laid eyes on her. And before. Before I knew that Maggie Smith existed, I wanted to know her. There was that one woman out there who would help me understand who I was and—know her or not at the time—I knew I would find her. Maggie Smith's that person. I'm not about to let her go. I'm not about to let her slip away. I don't exist without her. Without Maggie, I'm a ghost.

Gavin barely looks in my direction.

But I'm the only one at the counter—Maggie stepped across the hall to the bathroom—so he has no choice but to step up and deal with me face to face.

"I was hoping to talk to Maggie," he says. He still barely looks in my direction. I can't tell if he's guilty of something or if he feels that I don't warrant respect. He looks at me, and then looks away. Looks at me, looks away.

"She's stepped away," I say.

"Do you know when you expect her?"

"Could be five or ten minutes," I say. "Can I help you with something?"

"Maggie usually helps me," he says. "If you don't mind, I'd like to wait."

He turns and walks toward a small couch in the lobby. And that's when I notice—clenched in his right hand—a rolled up manila envelope.

You scumbag. You've got balls the size of Texas. No wonder you're holding on to that envelope so tightly. It's your whole fucking career. All of it. The governorship of Texas. No wonder you're sweating like a stuck pig. No wonder you're so nervous you're shaking, you motherfucker.

I don't take my eyes off of him. I stare him down just to let him know that I'm on to him. I know what you're doing. I know what you're up to. No wonder you don't want to deal with me, you worthless motherfucker.

He picks up a magazine from the table in front of him and thumbs through it, thumbs through it like he gives a flying fuck about reading, like he gives a fuck about where to eat when you're staying in Dallas, like he gives a fuck about where to shop and where to get your groove on. He doesn't give a flying fuck about any of it, but if you didn't know any different, you would swear that he was an out-of-towner wanting to take in the Dallas experience.

I'm no moron. Gavin Thompson's afraid out of his goddamn mind. I enjoy watching him squirm. All of the money in the world can't calm his nerves.

He realizes that he has left the manila envelope on the table in front of him—realizes that he has separated himself from something that could ruin his whole political career—but he dare not grab it too quickly for fear of giving something away.

I'm on to you. I'm way on to you.

"I'm sort of in a hurry," he says, tucking the envelope under his arm. "Please tell her I was here."

He turns and walks through the lobby and disappears.

You're finished. As soon as those pictures leak out to the press, you're done. You might as well kiss your ass goodbye. All of those years you've spent honing your image as a man who stands by his family—all of those years you've spent hiding the fact that you are a degenerate motherfucker who doesn't think twice about getting a blowjob from a girl who's young enough to be your daughter—are over in the blink of an eye.

You deserve it, you worthless sonofabitch. You fucking deserve it.

———

"Gavin Thompson was here," I say.

"Sorry I missed it."

"He wanted to talk to you."

"Is that so?"

"What would he want to talk to you about?"

She gets that I'm defensive right away. I'm doing my best to hide my disgust. I don't like that he even asked where she was, not even counting the fact that she would have ever wanted something to do with the guy. It makes me want to break something. It makes me want to punch someone in the face.

"I don't know. Me sucking his cock?"

"Excuse me?"

"What do you want me to say? How am I supposed to know why he wanted to talk to me? I don't care about Gavin Thompson. Is that what I'm supposed to say? Because I don't. I don't care about Gavin Thompson. I don't care about Gavin Thompson."

———

I'm not sure what you call what we're doing. We don't talk about it. Fucking. That's what we're doing. It happened overnight. It just happened. Of course, I wanted it all along. During phone sex— when she told me that she was touching her clit and asked me if I wanted to fuck her—I fantasized about fucking her every which way, licking her, touching her. But it was only fantasy. It was not the kind of thing that I thought would happen, not in a million years. Because Maggie is beautiful. Maggie didn't want anything to do with me outside of our friendship. She never acted like she was attracted to me outside of the occasional phone sex, and it felt like she was doing me a favor. I felt like the phone sex was somehow payment for being her friend. She knew that I liked her for more than a friend, but I really never thought that we would make love.

And then, out of nowhere, Victor's gone and we make love in the middle of her bed. At times I wake up, and it feels like a dream. One giant fantastical dream. The kind of thing you fantasize about but never comes true.

Making love to Maggie's everything that I imagined. I thought about it for so long—one of those things that I built up to such a level—it seemed next to impossible that Maggie would exceed my expectations.

Anytime I set myself up with some idea of how it's going to be, things never quite turn out right.

But that isn't true concerning sex with Maggie.

It's part brute force, part angelic.

One second we're caressing each other's faces, and the next, we're throwing each other all over the apartment.

The ease of going from sheer romance to nails down my back— bleeding through my shirt, pulling hair out by the roots—is seamless.

We had probably been thinking about this for weeks. Hell, months. The phone sex late at night—stick your cock in my ass while I finger my pussy—and then silence at work. Phone sex at night, and total denial the next day. And then, finally, that chance to do what we've been wanting to do all along. This buildup finally reaches its climax.

The first time we were together, it was inevitable that we would be all over the apartment.

I knew we would fuck before it happened.

She teased me all day long.

The usual *ignore the fact that we have phone sex and deny it all day at work*, was just not happening. As soon as I got to work—with Maggie dressed in a short skirt and a tight blouse—I knew that we would barely make it through the day without fucking each other's brains out.

It wasn't that she said anything, but the little things gave it away. The way she brushed past me in the break room. The constant connection when we happened to be talking between customers— both of us practically blocking out the rest of the world—as we fucked each other with our eyes.

Even Debra sensed that something was going on and did everything in her power to keep us apart. She had me working on some

God-awful filing project in one of the senior vice-president's offices—had me doing all kinds of odds-and-ends bullshit—in an effort to prevent me from fucking Maggie Smith in the break room when nobody else was around.

But regardless, the dance continued.

Around three in the afternoon, Maggie let me know that she had made arrangements for her mother to pick up Tyler from daycare. Tyler was spending the night at her mother's house. I should meet her at her apartment as soon as we got off of work.

We rode the garage elevator down to the fourth floor. There were several other women on the elevator with us. Maggie looked at me like she was about to stop the elevator—take off her clothes—and fuck me between floors while the rest of the women watched.

She'd stop the elevator—kick off her skirt, slide her panties around her ankles—and I'd take her from behind. We wouldn't bother kissing. That'd distract us from fucking.

———◆———

She comes to the door in a pair of red panties and a bra and kisses me and leads me down the hallway to her bedroom. We don't make it that far because she's tearing at my shirt and tearing at my pants and sucking me off in the middle of the hallway. I'm pulling at her bra. Chucking it across the floor. Pulling at her panties. Dry humping her until we can't stand it any longer. Fucking so hard we feel like we're about to come undone.

———◆———

Maggie's in the back counting her drawer when Linda comes into the bank.

Debra's in her office talking on the phone.

I'm the only one up front.

I see her immediately and I want to tell her that we are closed but there's nothing I can do.

She looks like death, this woman. It's been years since I've seen her. She's been dead to me. I have the same kind of reaction you

124

would have if you were looking into someone's coffin and they suddenly opened their eyes.

It's like seeing Sam, only older. It's like seeing Sam if she had gotten the chance to age, if she had gotten the chance to grow old.

I shouldn't be shocked out of my mind—shouldn't be surprised that I see her here—because this is the bank where all the richer-than-shit people do their banking. It shouldn't surprise me at all.

But it's like getting hit in the face.

You might as well have walked up and bare-knuckled me in the nose. You might as well have walked up and pushed my nose into the back of my skull.

"It's her birthday you know."

I don't know who the hell she's talking about. We're not on the same page.

"Well, it would have been her birthday. If you hadn't killed her."

It rushes in loud and clear.

"This is where I work, Linda. Perhaps this isn't the most appropriate place for this conversation. I would be glad to sit down and talk with you about it. In fact, I have sat down and talked to you about it. I've already asked your forgiveness—"

"You stole her birthday from her. When you killed her."

What do you say here? What do you do?

You get defensive. That's what you do. You get really defensive.

"Fine, Linda. Fine. Say what you will. But I didn't steal her birthday from her. Dead or not, it's still the day she was born. Even I can't take that from her—"

"You're going to get what you deserve," she says. "Hal Scott is going to get what he deserves."

For once, I believe her.

———◆———

"Are you ok?"

"I'm fine."

"You don't look ok."

"I'm ok."

"Ok. As long as you're ok."

"I'm ok."

"Why don't you come over? I'll cook you dinner. We'll put Tyler to bed early. It will be fun. You deserve it."

I'm not certain what I'm expecting here. It's not like I expect us to set up house anytime soon, not like I expect us to get married right away. The divorce proceedings have barely even started. With a child involved, nothing's going to happen overnight.

But with Maggie cooking dinner and me sitting at the kitchen table, it brings with it a longing for the familial side of things. I wonder if that's what Maggie's doing. Setting up a family. Out with the old, in with the new.

She doesn't even talk about Victor.

Overnight, it's as though he doesn't exist.

And Tyler. He doesn't know the difference. He sits on my lap and goos and gaws like I've been with them from the start.

Maggie's going on and on about work. She deserves a raise—but at the same time—she knows better. Lone Star Bank is a dead-end job. Debra is incompetent. She is a moron who got the job based on her bloodline, based entirely on the fact that her father's a bigwig with the bank. I'm enjoying the sound of Maggie's voice, enjoying the smells of her kitchen, bouncing Tyler on my knee and wondering when it's all going to collapse. When is it all going to fall apart?

Tyler's asleep. We finally have some time to ourselves. And Maggie leads me into the living-room—rummages through her television cabinet—and pulls out a videotape.

She explains that things between us have been out of order. She goes off on a long rant about how our relationship is somehow different, because we were intimate before I got to know the others. "But it's a good thing. I don't want you to be like the rest. But you still need to see them. You need to get to know them. It's part of the process of getting to know me."

"Watching videotapes of the men you've slept with?"

"Trust me," she says. "This is sacred, Hal."

She pushes the videotape into the VCR and sits back down on the couch.

I'm surprised that she doesn't pop popcorn.

She watches the videos like she's watching them for the first time. It's disturbing. There's nothing normal about this. I'm amazed that I don't object.

Instead, I lie back and enjoy the show.

———◆———

Rod's favorite color is blue.

Peter likes orange.

Reuben likes black.

Victor likes brown.

Owen likes green.

Rod lost his virginity to his sister when he was in the eighth grade. She was four years older than Rod. Her name was Mickey. She sort of forced herself on him. Rod cried when he talked about it.

Peter was in the ninth grade when he lost his virginity. He slept with his fourth-period English teacher in her hotel room when they were on a Debate Team State Competition. She later killed herself because he wouldn't drop out of school and marry her. She cut her wrists one evening when her husband had already gone to bed. She told him she was going to take a bath. Her eight-year-old daughter discovered her—in a bathtub of her own blood—when she was getting ready for school.

Reuben lost his virginity to his high school sweetheart—Jackie. She was the only woman he ever slept with. Outside of Maggie. They got married their senior year in high school when Jackie got pregnant. He left Jackie when he caught her in bed with another woman.

Owen lost his virginity in Las Vegas. He was eighteen. The summer after graduation. He lost it to a prostitute with a wooden leg. After they had sex, she spanked him with it.

Victor lost his virginity to Maggie. Or so he says. They met at Maggie's best friend's wedding. Maggie was the bridesmaid. The video was taken after the wedding. Victor's drunk out of his mind. Maggie tells me later that Tyler was conceived on the first night they made love. They were married one month after Maggie found out she was pregnant.

———◆———

There's one more video that she wants to show me. And then we'll be done. I'll have seen all of them. She's searching. Going through a stack of videotapes in the television cabinet. A stack of videotapes clearly labeled. She knows what she's looking for but she isn't finding it. A panicked look spreads all over her face—spreads into her body—leaves her filled with tension.

"It's not here," she says, looking at me like I should know what she's talking about. "It was here with all of the others."

"What are you looking for?"

"It's here," she says. "It has to be."

More searching. More nervousness. Maggie running her hands through her hair.

"It's gone," she says. "Gone."

"We'll find it. It has to be here with the others."

I get down in the floor with her and help her rummage through the videotapes. I ask her what I'm looking for. I ask her for effect. I don't need to ask her what we're looking for. I know. I know what we're looking for. And I know we're not going to find it.

———◆———

I have this general sense of unease hanging over me.

It doesn't help that my punk of a neighbor won't turn down his stereo. My framed serenity prayer—hanging above my television—is taking so much bass it's about to fall off of the wall.

My punk of a neighbor's playing the Ramones or the Clash or whatever—probably about to get into his girlfriend's pants—and I'm forced to suffer the consequences. Play it as he must, he doesn't have to play it so loud.

I slam the palm of my hand against the wall to give him a hint that I'm about to lose my mind, but the scumbag doesn't hear it because Joey Ramone wants to be sedated.

I hit the wall again with the palm of my hand. Charlie tucks his tail between his legs and heads off for the bathroom.

I find a cigarette on the kitchen counter, light it up and take in the smoke. I want to be sedated. Another deep drag, taking the smoke into my lungs. I want to be sedated.

I picture my punk of a neighbor ripping off his girlfriend's panties with his teeth. She's running around in a pink jersey-style halter top with the number of some imagined basketball player skintight against her boobs. My punk of a neighbor'll chase her around until he corners her in the kitchen, and they'll fuck each other silly on the kitchen counter.

She's not bad, my young punk of a neighbor's girlfriend. Every time I see her—which is when she happens to be doing laundry and I happen to have the urge for a can of soda—she has a different hair color. She has a tattoo that starts at the top of her shoulder and runs itself around the center of her neck. She's made some mother somewhere a nervous wreck. She's made some father somewhere a basket case. She's the kind of girl who dropped out of school when she was in the eleventh grade to work at a gentleman's club to pay the bills. She drinks all day and parties all night. She's as friendly as she can be—probably stoned out of her mind, her boyfriend at work at a video store somewhere—doing a load of her vivid neon thong underwear. She'll say hello as I get my soda—Charlie pacing outside of the laundry room, waiting for me with his leash in his mouth—and I'll say something about nice weather we're having. She'll say something like groovy. She'll hold a pair of her thong underwear in front of her so that I can see them, sniff the crotch and say I just love freshly washed panties or something like that. She'll giggle and say don't you?

I'll go back to my apartment and bang the shit out of my dick for a half hour.

But regardless of how great she is—regardless of how sexy she is, regardless of how much I would want to jump into her freshly washed panties—when I'm trying to get a little serenity, I don't need to listen to a soundtrack of your need for sedation while you get laid on the top of your boyfriend's kitchen counter.

I turn on the television.

There's a still-shot of Gavin Thompson posing with his wife and daughter and a voice-over that says if you want someone who cares about God and Country—if you want someone who cares about family values—then you'll vote for Gavin Thompson for Governor of the State of Texas.

I need to get out of the apartment.

I need to clear my head.

14

WHEN HE ISN'T SHOOTING HEROIN in the back of an empty, dilapidated apartment building—catching rusty rainwater dripping through the sagging ceiling on the tip of his tongue—or isn't in a mangy apartment somewhere getting the Devil cast out of him, Ben works for Two Forks Catering Company.

Which is how Lemon hears about the *Thompson for Governor* fundraiser.

Which is how we end up at the Crescent Hotel Grand Ballroom in tuxedo shirts and black slacks.

Lemon says anybody who's somebody's going to be here.

That includes Gavin Thompson, who's throwing this shindig in the first place. If you know anything about politics, you know that it takes a lot of money.

Lemon says going to the event will help us find Celia Povicov, says going to the event will help us find Bob's killer.

I know better than that, but I owe him.

We can't just walk up to Gavin Thompson and tell him that we have some pictures that might catch his fancy. We know that you've been unfaithful and we have pictures to prove it. Not that we want to put a damper on your little campaign for governor of the State of Texas, but it's definitely something you might want to take a gander at.

The chances of us getting information on Celia's disappearance or information on Bob's death would be greater if we went and stood in front of the algae-inspired apparition of the Virgin Mother—under the Triple Underpass—than finding out any information at this shindig to raise money so Gavin Thompson can live in the Governor's Mansion.

But try telling that to Lemon.

I tell him not to get his hopes up if this doesn't solve the world's problems.

He accuses me of being sarcastic.

A man named Rawls comes over and looks at us suspiciously, leaning close to us like he's trying to smell booze on our breath. He tells us that we don't speak until spoken to. We go only where we're told. We follow the Captain's orders to the letter. And we don't drink the booze.

Booze is the last thing that he should be worried about. I feel like telling him that there's a pretty good chance that Lemon'll pull his dick out of his pants—while the waiters are serving the second course—and give all of these rich fucks a run for their money. More than likely, Lemon will get a load off before they tackle him and throw him out the door.

Ben just got off a four-day meth binge, and the sound of horse's hooves that old Rawls thinks he hears is the sound of Ben's teeth clacking together because he needs to do a bump every fifteen minutes in order to make them stop.

I haven't had a drink in over a year, but he doesn't have to worry about me drinking anything at this piece of shit hoedown. What he should worry about is my penchant for violence. I feel like kicking the holy shit out of a bunch of rich old men and fucking their girlfriends. I feel like telling him that every once in a while I find myself lashing out at people for no apparent reason. Regardless of my being small in stature, there's a pretty good chance that someone's going to get their nose broken.

I feel like telling him all of these things.

But I don't.

The guests aren't due to arrive until well after eight o'clock. We're basically standing around with our hands in our pockets, finding ourselves with nothing to do but crave cigarettes, so against Rawls's strictest orders, we sneak out front and chain-smoke while the fancy guests in their fancy cars start pulling into the circular drive.

They all look the same: the rich. All stretched tight from their plastic surgery, fake boobs pouring out of their designer gowns.

Even their cars look the same. You can't tell the difference. The latest model Lexus sedan. The latest model BMW. The latest model Mercedes Benz. The Bentley.

These lawyers. These doctors. These entrepreneurs. These CEOs. These stock brokers. These basketball players. These hockey players. These football players. Old money. New money.

They all look the same.

Our Captain pokes his head out front, and we scramble to put out our cigarettes. We don't care if they fire us or not. We don't plan on a repeat performance. All we want to do is scan the place for clues and get the fuck out.

———

There are no clues to be found.

But there's money everywhere. These people are rolling in it. They have it plastered all over their bodies in the form of strings of pearls, diamond rings—the size of golf balls—and Rolex watches that bleed Benjamin Franklins.

These people don't think anything about flying to L.A. to eat lunch and then on to the Big Apple for a nice dinner. These people don't think anything about spending thousands of dollars on a tux that they might wear a couple of times a year. They don't think jackshit about sending their young wives halfway across the world to get their nails done while they bang their nanny in the middle of a ten-thousand-dollar bed covered with a five-thousand-dollar bedspread. They are more than comfortable throwing down a thousand dollars for a bottle of Cristal at the Lodge while stuffing fifty dollar bills in the thongs of eighteen-year-old crank addicts who sniff cocaine off of their balls after these old men are through getting their two-hundred-dollar lap dances.

These people are rolling in it.

As much as I wouldn't mind having enough money to pay my rent, this shindig is enough to turn your stomach. It's hard to understand how these people can tolerate their own phoniness—all hobnobbing, trading phony smiles and business cards, wheeling and dealing, selling each other on their latest tax-avoidance tricks—hard to understand how these people can live with themselves. The women talk about their children as if they picked them out of the Neiman Marcus Dream Catalogue. The single men and women knock themselves over to look as uninterested as they possibly can. They might as well be wearing signs that say they're here to hook up with someone as rich and as snobby as they are.

They don't give a shit about politics. No doubt, they would like to get their man through the door so they can visit the Governor's Mansion, so they can bend his ear when they've gotten themselves into a jam. They want credit for having gotten him there in the first place. But at the end of the day—whether Gavin wins or loses—they don't give a shit. They're still winners. And it would take a hell of a lot of Democrats to take it away from them.

But they'll spend plenty of time visiting that scenario. They'll go on and on about how important it is to keep a Republican in the Governor's Mansion. Those bleeding-heart liberals are bursting at the seams to take all their money away from them and give it to the poor.

They talk about illegal immigrants pouring into the country in droves. If we don't do something to stop them, they're going to take over and convert the official language from English to Spanish if you give them half the chance.

All this wealth—all this nonsensical jibber jabber—makes me sick to my stomach.

And the government wants to know why we're so apathetic. Like we don't care one way or the other. That's wealthy-horseshit talk. We care. But we know good and well that whatever we do doesn't make a goddamn bit of difference. It's all a scam. With the kind of money it takes to get a position in the government—spending most of your first term paying back all of your favors so that word gets around that it pays to give to your campaign—only the filthy rich make it into office in the first place.

We can go out there and march until we're blue in the face, but if they do anything that even suggests that they're listening to what we have to say, there's something in it for them.

Politicians are so assured of getting what they want these days—from the Mayor to the President—that they can pretty much tell the people they don't give a fuck what we think, they're going to do what they want to do whether we scream or not. So short of total anarchy—short of a total revolution—our hands are tied.

These wealthy fucks are so arrogant, they'll throw their no-good opinions right in your face. They don't give a shit what you think about what they're doing. That's one of the plusses of being wealthy. They know that they're above the law.

Which is why I don't understand why they act like they care about what's going on. They have everything they need—are pretty much guaranteed that their gravy train isn't running out anytime soon—so why would they even show up to these things anyway? They should send their check in the mail and stay the fuck home.

These people make me so nauseated I can barely speak to them.

Of course, I can't speak to them unless they speak to me first.

Rawls's Golden Rule.

I don't give the tiniest fuck. Neither does Lemon. And Ben doesn't know if he gives the tiniest fuck or not, because he's been downing shots of vodka for the past ten minutes. They never should have put him in charge of restocking the liquor.

Lemon should tell Ben to slow down.

He's close to making a fool of himself. If Lemon wants to stay at this little shindig for more than twenty minutes, he'd better nip it in the bud.

But Rawls beats him to it. Rawls reassigns Ben to collecting empty wine glasses and gives him one of those *you better shape up or ship out* glances, and it seems to snap Ben out of it. At least for a moment.

It looks like this deal's going as smooth as it can, and suddenly, I'm face to face with Cynthia Thompson. She hasn't even made it to her table, and she's drunk out of her mind. Of course, Cynthia

Thompson's *drunk out of her mind* is really quite composed, if you don't know any better. But I know better. And Cynthia Thompson's drunk out of her mind. It's not that she's slurring her words. She's got that glassy stare. That slight tremble of her upper lip when she asks me if she knows me.

"Lone Star Bank. You're my teller. You're my teller." It's like she's discovered a long-lost friend.

She grabs me by the arm and trails me around the room introducing me to anybody that we come across as her favorite banker. They all nod and smile their fake plastic smiles as I pray for the night to end.

I tell her that I should probably get back to my station. I really shouldn't be mingling with the guests. Nonsense, she says. I *should* be mingling with the guests because I *am* one of the guests. I shouldn't be watching my station when I'm her favorite banker. We can't have her favorite banker handing out drinks when he should be sitting at her table. Before I know it, I'm sitting at the table with Cynthia Thompson and a few of her favorite friends.

I'm sitting at the table with Gavin Thompson.

He almost chokes when he looks up and sees me sitting next to his wife.

Whether it's because he knows that I could very well bring his hopes of being the next Governor of Texas to a standstill, or if he's just abhorred that the service staff is seated at his table, it's hard to tell. It's this look of revulsion that these types have when the *help* decide to sit down with their employer for a Sunday dinner. As long as they know their place, things are A-OK, but mix and mingle with the help for too long, and they might forget their place in the ultimate scheme of things.

It really doesn't matter either way. I don't care what Gavin Thompson thinks. I'm not an expert on things political, but win or lose in his race for Governor of the State of Texas, he'll still be an asshole.

He's just another condescending-arrogant-rich prick who thinks that he can fuck everything that moves no matter who it hurts and all he's going to get is a slap on the wrist.

Not that I'm vindictive, but he's messing with the wrong guy if he gets the impression that I'm going to sit back and watch him fuck women who are half his age. Sometimes you have to play the cards you're dealt.

I'm holding a full house.

But with that said, I'm no more comfortable sitting here with Gavin Thompson than he is with me sitting here. I'm no fool.

I realize that Cynthia Thompson's playing a game.

I'm not her favorite banker.

I'm not even her favorite teller.

I'm her pawn.

I'm her answer to the woman seated next to Gavin. A tall, thin-but-curvy blonde with pouty lips, blue eyes, and a pair of silicone breasts that demand attention from the eyes of men and women alike. Gavin Thompson's answer to a campaign manager. It's perfect for Gavin. It really is. He can spend inordinate amounts of time with this woman, lavish her with fine wine and diamond broaches—all paid for out of the Gavin Thompson for Governor Campaign Fund—and justify it to his wife by saying that the only reason that this curvy blonde—with pouty lips, blue eyes, and a pair of silicone breasts—is hanging around, is because they're working on the campaign.

If you call getting blowjobs in the back of his limousine "working on the campaign."

Let's not kid ourselves—Cynthia is smarter than that. She knows better. But what's she going to do?

Exactly. What she's doing now.

You've got yours. I've got mine. So there. Two can play this game.

How one can go from being entirely invisible to a man of power and prestige in the eye of the beholder is at once baffling and incredibly disturbing. As soon as I sit down at the table—served my salad by one of the waiters, my napkin fluffed and placed in my lap, my tea glass filled with care—my status as a waiter only moments ago, disappears in a liquid-filled flash.

I instantly become interesting. Everything I say is snappy and humorous. The old ladies in their Chanel gowns hold onto every word I say. The old men in their Ralph Lauren tuxedos lean forward as if I'm a bearer of great wisdom.

I tell them of my excursions into the world of exorcisms, and they beg for details that I can't remember. Not wanting to disappoint, I embellish my stories to the point of placing myself in Ben's position. I'm the one convulsing on the floor. I'm the one whose body is possessed by darkness and shadow.

I'm a celebrity. My stories make me victorious over life and death. They reach out and touch me as if my flesh has mystical properties and I have the capacity to raise the dead.

I've been shifted into something of the miraculous. I'm expected to perform miracles. I'm somehow expected to turn the water into wine. I'll reach out and take the crystal pitcher filled with water and—through my touch alone—the molecules will change in front of our eyes into a vintage Chardonnay.

They'll clap softly and praise my name to one another. Isn't this man from Galilee? They'll brush this away and forget where I come from. They'll treat me like royalty. They'll treat me as if I am a prophet.

The only skeptic at this point is Gavin Thompson. He's still asking himself where he knows me from. He has flashes of memory—glimpses in his mind's eye—of me asking him if he would like to do another transaction and if not, I hope he enjoys the rest of his day.

He's not so easily swayed.

However, his campaign manager is doing a superb job of distracting his wandering thoughts with a squeeze of his leg under the table. Once he's taken to a place of arousal, Gavin Thompson forgets me altogether.

But Cynthia Thompson won't forget. I'm the only thing on her mind. And she can't get enough. She begs me to tell my stories over and over again. She can't believe that I'm not married. She can't believe somebody hasn't already snatched me up. I've got to be pulling her leg. She grabs my hand, looking for a ring. She waves my hand around to everybody at the table and says something like maybe she should take me home.

Out of nowhere, Gavin looks at me and asks how Maggie Smith is doing. You two seem to be close, he says.

Gavin Thompson has Texas-size balls. I had no idea. His question nearly knocks me out of my chair. And then, of course, my surprise continues when it doesn't seem to faze Cynthia at all. There should be something close to jealousy easing across her face. At least a slight flinch.

But nothing. No low arching of the back. No twitch of the eye. Nothing.

The whole table looks at me for my answer.

I'm caught off guard. So caught off guard that I don't know what to say.

"Maggie," he says. "At Lone Star Bank. You work with her. You're bank tellers."

Is he calling me out? I know who you are. You are not wanted at this table. You don't belong in our midst.

He's throwing the miraculous on its ear. He's reducing me to what I really am. He's pulling the proverbial carpet out from under me for the amusement of the guests at his table.

"Maggie is a great girl. She needs to model. I tell her every time I see her. She has such a pretty face. I have friends. I know two talent scouts off the top of my head that would kill for her pictures."

Before I'm able to respond, a man in a dark suit walks up to Gavin and tells him that it's time for him to begin. Gavin excuses himself from the table—kisses the back of Cynthia's neck—and makes his way to the podium.

———◆———

"So what you're telling me," Lemon says, "is that you got nothing. You sat at their goddamn table. Why did we even go to the trouble?" he says. He takes a last drag of his cigarette and pitches it out the window.

Ben's making groaning noises in the backseat.

"Next thing I know, you'll be voting for family values."

"Hey. This little excursion was your idea. I knew it was a waste of time."

"If you call finding Celia Povicov a waste of our time."

"Say what—"

"Well, I didn't really find Celia Povicov. But I found out who she's not."

"I'm not getting you."

"Lucky for us, the receptionist at the Maddox Foundation got stuck at the coat check."

"And?"

"Let's just say that she had her fair share to drink."

"And?"

"I asked her what she thought about Celia Povicov's disappearance."

"Nosing around like that's going to blow our cover."

"I don't know about blowing our cover," Lemon says. "But it certainly complicates things."

"What do you mean by that?"

"She had never heard of her."

"That doesn't make sense."

"Yeah. This girl's been with the Maddox Foundation for six years. She's never even heard the name Celia Povicov. And, in an office with fifteen employees, it seems that she would have crossed her path by now, being the *receptionist* and all."

"I'm just going by what Bob told me."

"As far as the receptionist knows, Celia Povicov doesn't exist."

15

EVER SINCE LINDA CAME into the bank—looking like death and cursing me in broad daylight, this psychic beating, taking memory and pushing my nose into the back of my skull with it—I can't get Sam out of my head.

Even now, as Lemon leads us on a wild-goose chase to find the Colonel at some bar right outside the State Fairgrounds. Outside of casing the Daisy Chain Motel, this is our last lead.

Although I'm tired of searching for the Colonel and turning up empty—and my past weighs heavily on my mind—the cool breeze against a clear sky leaves me feeling optimistic. It has nothing to do with the Colonel. Who knows if tonight will be the night we find him, and if we do find him, who knows if it will solve anything. But regardless, everything's going to be okay. Things are going to work out. I don't have anything to worry about. It's good to be alive.

———◆———

Outside of a pair of young punks playing chess, the bar hasn't had a chance to wake up. It's still sleeping. But they'll come. Soon the glasses will be clinking, the dartboards humming, the pool balls clicking, the music from the jukebox mixing with the cigarette smoke in steady increments of a dollar.

The bartender—a young woman in a black Velvet Underground T-shirt and pink hair—barely looks at us. She's busy getting things set up for the night shift. She hasn't been here long—barely long enough for a smoke—and she's got plenty to do before the place fills up.

But this isn't one of those places where the bartender chats you up, anyway. This is the kind of bar where they don't know your name. You can get lost here. That's its charm.

We can walk around this bar asking each and every one of these drunk bastards if they've seen the Colonel in the last day or so, and each and every one of them will give us that same look. I don't know who you're talking about. And by the way, I don't care.

The bartender finally gets around to taking our order.

Lemon cuts to the chase. "What time does the Colonel usually show up?" he says.

"I don't know any Colonel," she says. She turns to straighten the bottles on the shelves behind her. Her back is covered with tattoos, a green vine stretching up out of her shirt and shooting up the sides of either arm, ending in the head of a snake on either wrist. I watch the snakes as they glide across the shelves filled with bottles. I watch their heads turn with each flick of her wrist. Their red eyes brighten as they scan bottle after bottle, as if they've spotted danger.

"That's strange," Lemon says, "because he told us that he would meet us—"

"Then you don't need me to tell you when I expect him."

She pours a drink for a customer at the end of the bar. I watch her pour it. She fills it to the brim with ice and whiskey. How many worlds would collide if I ordered one of my own? How many lives would spiral out of control due to that first drink? It would go down smooth and crisp, filling me up with its warmth. How long would I retain my sense of normalcy? How long would it take for everything to fall apart?

We pay the bartender for our sodas and move over to a booth in the corner of the bar—away from the noise of the jukebox, away from the couple playing darts, away from those who might be interested in what we have to say—and wait for the Colonel.

Lemon's nervous. He's second-guessing himself. He's going over and over in his mind whether he's doing the right thing. He's second-guessing whether he should be meeting the Colonel at all.

Because—let's face it—if the Colonel was going to come out and tell the truth about what he knew about the assassination of John F. Kennedy, he would have already done it.

Something's holding him back.

Anybody who talks gets their throat cut. Anybody who talks ends up hanging themselves with the shower curtain. Taking a handful of pills. You name it, they've done it.

And we're supposed to believe this shit? People who don't have a death wish—people who don't show any signs of suicidal tendencies cutting themselves open with a large butcher knife, right down the center of their chest. And it's self-inflicted. Shooting themselves in the mouth with a .38 using their right hand when they're lefthanded.

You've got to admit there are some talented suicides out there. People who know anything about the assassination of John F. Kennedy—people who were there—die in the most random ways.

But regardless of how they die, they have one thing in common: they knew too much. They're all dead. Except for a handful of very lucky individuals. Which explains why the Colonel's living the kind of life he's living. Drinking first thing in the morning. Never staying too long in one place. Sleeping under bridges. Homeless shelters. Boarding houses. Rooms by the hour at the Daisy Chain Motel. The Colonel has all the signs. He's doomed. He's waiting—at any point in time—for them to come in and kill him. Kill him for the kinds of things he knows. That's why he has faded into oblivion. That's why you don't hear about him on the news. That's why he hasn't written a book. He knows the end result.

Lemon knows all this. Pretty much lays it out just like that in the corner booth of the bar—jukebox playing in the background—while we wait for the Colonel.

I ask him how he thinks he's going to make the Colonel talk after all these years. Lemon pulls the manila envelope out of his army jacket and waves it in my direction.

"I'm going to give him some incentive."

It's incentive, I'll tell you that much.

This picture makes the pictures of Gavin Thompson getting his dick sucked by a woman other than his wife look like child's play. The picture in Lemon's manila envelope is the Holy Grail of conspiracy theories.

There are a lot of people who would kill to keep Lemon from leaking this picture to the press. There are a lot of people who would kill to keep Lemon from showing this picture to anyone. They would take out whole families to make sure that this picture never saw the light of day.

And here Lemon is, waving it in my face in the middle of a crowded bar.

"You might want to put that up," I tell him. "This might not be the appropriate time to be waving that around."

"I'm going to be waving it around soon enough. When the Colonel gets here."

"If he gets here," I say.

"Oh, ye of little faith."

———◆———

The Colonel won't show up. It's all for the best. I can't imagine how meeting with the Colonel's going to solve anything for Lemon. I say take the picture to the press.

Call a press conference and get this thing out into the open. Who needs a retired Colonel recluse to be involved when you have the Holy Grail of all conspiracies in your possession? But maybe he's right. What do I know?

While Lemon is going on about the reasons he quit going to his court-appointed psychiatrist, thereby violating his probation— while we wait for the Colonel to show up—I am obsessing about death. I have pictures in my possession that are going to get me killed.

Gavin Thompson is on to me.

He wants me dead.

He has too much to lose.

Someone who's running on a slogan like *Family Values*, *Family First*. Someone who's running on a slogan that says one thing and then lives their life in a totally different manner.

Photographed at some fancy schmancy charity event arm-inarm with his wife, Cynthia Thompson, in her pearls and her Chanel gown. Raising their glasses and smiling for the cameras.

Ten minutes later—after sending his wife home early to take care of the kids—he's getting a blowjob from his assistant in the back seat of his limo. He'll dump the assistant and hit every topless bar that he can possibly hit. He'll get lap dance after lap dance from women who are fifteen years his junior, women who are not his wife. He'll sniff cocaine off of the hard, young bodies of eighteen-year-old strippers and then show up for Sunday Service the next morning at Highland Park Methodist for a photo op.

Still smelling of the latest stripper fragrance, his cock still numb from lines of cocaine sucked off it by strippers with names like Desiree and Lacy, Gavin Thompson will pose for a picture with his family that'll end up on the front page of the *Dallas Morning News*. It will find its way into the pages of *Paper City*. It will find its way into a commercial encouraging Texans to vote for the man who has family values at heart.

And I have evidence.

I have pictures of this cocksucker fucking someone who isn't his wife.

And Gavin Thompson wants those pictures. He'll kill me for them, if necessary. His people will put a bullet in my skull. Whatever it takes to protect Gavin Thompson from himself. They'll put a bullet in my skull if that's what it takes to protect Gavin Thompson from showing who Gavin Thompson really is.

I'm not safe.

My friends and family are in danger.

Whoever wants these pictures won't stop at anything to achieve their goal. I have a vision of my mother being strangled with a rope and then left lying on the couch in her pale-blue bathrobe. I have a vision of my father with a bullet in his head, still lying on the couch, the television droning on in the background.

It'll be days, even weeks before they're found.

They'll rape Maggie first, and then they'll kill her.

They'll slice Lemon's throat and leave him lying in a puddle of his own blood.

Gerald.

Debra at Lone Star.

They'll kill them all.

They won't stop until they have what they're looking for. They won't stop until every last one of us is dead.

I'm going to turn myself in. I'm going to take the pictures to the police station and tell them the whole story. I'll tell them why I really went to see Billy Joe Harris. I'll tell them about Maggie. I'll tell them about Rachel. I won't leave out any details. I'll give them the pictures and let them know that I'm willing to do whatever it takes to get this behind me. I want to move on. I'm tired of running. I want my old life back.

16

THE DOWNTOWN PRECINCT is right across the street from the old red-brick courthouse—the very place where Jack Ruby shot Lee Harvey Oswald in front of a nation glued to their television sets.

From here, I can see the Grassy Knoll and the Triple Underpass and the Texas School Book Depository building—which has now become the Sixth Floor Museum—where tourists still come to witness a barrage of information detailing that fateful day in Dallas.

I can see Conspiracy Books. I wonder how long it will be before it's a luxurious hotel and a high-rise condominium. How long before young, rich, lawyer types and young, rich, broker types with their fancy briefcases and their MBAs—driving their fancy BMWs and their high-end Lexus SUVs—stink up the place with their expensive furniture and their fancy paintings and their fake girlfriends with their fake boobs and their fake noses and their waxed eyebrows and their French manicures? How long before they invade the place, doing blow on the balconies of their expensive condos, talking of hedge funds and start-ups and stock options? How long before all talk of conspiracy—all talk of government cover-ups—will be lost forever?

As soon as I walk into the downtown Precinct—and see officers in their dress blues, plainclothes detectives with their holsters under their suit jackets, lawyers being buzzed in to talk to their clients, hear the ringing of phones and the rustle of paperwork—I have the urge to turn my ass around, walk out to my car, and drive home.

But, at the same time, I'm anxious. I'm tired of running. I need to fess up to what I know and start my life over. I need to start living. I need to get my act together.

So I can get the girl.

I want this saga to end well.

I want this picture to fade out with a kiss and a happy ending.

I want *And they lived happily ever after* to scroll across the screen, and then a slow fade, and then the credits to roll.

The only way that this is going to happen is for me to walk up to the desk clerk and tell her that I need to speak to a gentleman named Officer Cohen. I need to walk up to the desk clerk and tell her that I need to speak to a gentleman by the name of Officer Jacobs.

They'll take me back to a room with white walls, adorned with a table and two chairs, and I'll tell them all I know. I'll tell them everything that I've left out. I'll fess up to everything I've done. And then some.

———◆———

"May I help you?" says the clerk. She's a woman in her mid-thirties. Her hair wrapped tightly in a bun. Bright pink lipstick. Wearing a business suit. All business and no pleasure. Piercing blue eyes. The kind of eyes that look right through you. The kind of eyes that have you confessing before you know what you're doing.

"I would like to speak to Officer Cohen."

"Cohen?" she says.

"Officer Cohen. And Officer Jacobs." I slide her Cohen's business card. "He told me to contact him here."

"Wait right here," she says. She turns around and walks down a long hallway.

I follow her with my eyes. She walks into an office and returns a moment later with an officer in his dress blues.

"Maybe I can help you," he says.

"I wanted to speak with Officer Cohen. Or Officer Jacobs."

"I'm Sergeant Dan Riley," he says. "Why don't you come on back?"

The clerk buzzes me through, and I follow Sergeant Riley down a long hallway and into his office.

He motions for me to have a seat.

He sits down behind his desk and looks at me.

"How can I help you?"

"I hate to be rude," I say, "but I really want to talk to Officer Cohen. Or Officer Jacobs. They told me to give them a call."

"How do you know these gentlemen?"

"They came to my apartment."

"Hmmm," he says. "Why did they come to your apartment?"

"To ask me some questions," I say.

"What kind of questions?"

"Questions regarding my recent contact with a private investigator. They were asking me questions regarding my visit to Billy Joe Harris Investigations."

"Hmmm," he says. "What did you tell them?"

"I prefer to talk with Officer Cohen and Officer Jacobs. I would feel comfortable talking to someone who already knows the situation—"

"There are no officers by the name of Cohen and Jacobs," he says. "I don't know where you got this card, but it's bogus."

"Bogus?" I say.

"I don't know who they are," he says, "but they're not officers in this precinct. It's doubtful that they're officers at all."

He holds up the business card.

"This is not a Dallas Police Officer business card. This is fraudulent. I don't know what you told them. I don't know what they were after. But they're not cops. Plain and simple."

"This must be some kind of mistake," I say.

The dread eases into the pit of my stomach. I can't hear him when he asks if there's some way he can help me. I can't hear anything as I stagger out of the downtown police station and stumble to my car.

———◆———

I'm on the way up to my apartment when Lydia is walking down the stairs with a load of laundry. She's wearing a pair of yellow shorts and a tank top that says *Stop staring at my nipples.* She lowers the basket as I walk by so I can read her shirt.

I'm fumbling for my keys when I realize something's wrong.

The door's unlocked.

I don't leave my door unlocked.

It's slightly open.

I check around the doorjamb. I look carefully around the doorknob. It wasn't forced open.

Although my gut tells me to run, I ignore it. I almost never go with my gut. I've had a long morning. I need to drink less coffee. I'm being ridiculous. I'll laugh about this later, when I realize there wasn't any reason to be afraid.

Charlie's skittish. He's waiting for me by the door—as usual—but something's wrong with him. He's in that low, crouched position, like he's been kicked. He's afraid.

I don't have to fear the worst. I don't have to run.

Nothing's disturbed.

I'll take a nice long shower. I'll take Charlie for a long walk. I'll masturbate while thinking of fucking Lydia in the backseat of her Ford Mustang, in the hot tub by the pool, in the laundry room while she sniffs the crotch of her vivid neon thongs. And all of this will go away.

I walk down the hallway—stopping to grab a towel, Charlie following closely behind me—and walk into the bathroom.

It's funny, getting myself worked up this way. It's old behavior, this paranoia. I need to let it go. I need to have faith. I need to accept the fact that I'm safe. I need to let go of my fear.

When I turn on the bathroom light and the tiny mirror hanging above the tiny sink with little or no space for clutter is free from any sign of blood, I'm relieved.

But the relief's temporary. An image of a man standing behind me appears in the mirror.

He's familiar, but menacing. He's angrier than I remember. That rough-but-friendly demeanor—that yellow tooth grin that just wants to ask me some questions—has disappeared.

A gun. An arm raised. An arm lowered. Fast. Heavy. Everything I know is lost.

She appears. She's wearing her yellow shorts and her tank top that says *Stop staring at my nipples,* and she's walking down the apartment stairs with a load of her laundry, and she lowers the basket so I can read her shirt and she smiles and licks her lips and says that the shirt doesn't apply to me and says that she hates doing laundry, says that the only thing that would make it all worth while is if I would follow her to the laundry room and fuck her on the folding table while she washes her vivid neon thongs and her yellow shorts and her tank top that says *Stop staring at my nipples.*

The folding table becomes a blue high jump mat, and Lydia becomes Katie, and I'm fucking her, and Katie becomes Sam, groaning, and it's the first time we made love, and it's after a concert or something, and I realize that I'm going to spend the rest of my life with her and there's no way that anything can come between us, and Sam becomes Cheryl, and I'm fucking her, and we're lying on the bed smoking cigarettes, and Cheryl's worried about Sam getting home from work, and I tell her that there's absolutely nothing to be worried about because she's working late, and Cheryl says what if she suspects something, and I say she would never suspect that I'm fucking her sister and Cheryl becomes Rachel, and I'm fucking her on her couch shortly after she arrived home from a date with Bob and we're all over the couch and all over her bedroom and all over the kitchen fucking like we've never fucked before, and Rachel becomes Maggie and she is riding me with Tyler sleeping soundly in the next room—

——◆——

I have no movement in my arms and legs.

I have a hard on.

I'm tied to a chair in the middle of my living room.

I have guests.

Cohen and Jacobs.

The figure in my mirror was Cohen. With a gun. Which he's still holding.

They're both smoking cigarettes.

They're not smiling.

"Ok," says Cohen. "Playtime is over."

"Yes," says Jacobs. "Playtime is over."

"Where are the goddamn pictures?" Cohen says.

"What pictures?"

"You know what we're talking about."

"What are you going to do if I don't know what you're talking about?"

"The same thing we're going to do if you *do* know what we're talking about."

"We're going to stick a gun in your mouth and pull the trigger. You're going to die like your friend Bob French. You're going to die whether you talk or not."

"Then I don't guess it matters."

"Oh no, it matters. It may not matter to you, because you're dead either way. But it matters to Maggie Smith. And her son. It matters to them."

"They don't have anything to do with this."

"They have everything to do with this."

"Then I don't know what you're looking for."

"Of course you do."

"What are you looking for?"

"Pictures of Gavin Thompson in a compromising position."

"I don't know what you're talking about."

Jacobs punches me in the face.

He punches me so hard that it topples me over.

He breaks my nose.

All I can see is the ceiling.

It's shifting, spinning. The throb in my nose shifts to my brain. I implode. The crack reverberates, rings in my ears in rhythm with the throb in my brain. It burns. It stings. It's a hot brand to every nerve ending in my entire body.

"Let me tell you a story, you moron. I guess you know by now that we're not cops. But it goes deeper than that. How many years you done in the pen, Jacobs?"

"I don't know," Jacobs says. "I've lost count."

"Fair to say you've done over ten?"

"That's fair."

"So what did you do your time for Jacobs?"

"Nothing. I was innocent."

"Tell the truth. He's a dead man."

"I killed a man."

"That's good to know. And what did you kill this man for? He do something stupid? He sleep with your wife?"

"No," Jacobs says. "Nothing like that."

"How did you kill him, Jacobs?"

"I cut his throat with a potato peeler. And as he bled out of his throat, I stabbed him in both eyes."

"He must have done something pretty bad."

"He screwed someone over and they paid me two thousand dollars to do him in his kitchen. While his girlfriend was taking a long hot bath."

"You did that to someone you didn't even know? For two thousand dollars?"

"I would have done it for free. With the kind of tip I got when his girlfriend got finished with her bath. How bout you, Cohen? How much time you spend in the pen?"

"Twelve to be exact," Cohen says. "And I'm not going back."

"What'd you do, Cohen?"

"Armed robbery."

"Armed robbery. Twelve years for armed robbery?"

"I also took out a teller."

"Took out a teller?"

"I thought she was getting ready to push the button."

"So you shot her."

"Right in the face."

"In the face?"

"She was such a pretty thing. Really pretty."

"Anything else, Cohen?"

"A security guard on the way out."

"A security guard. Now why did you have to go and do a thing like that?"

"He was in my way."

"Couldn't you just ask him to move?"

"Oh, I moved him."

"I'd say you did."

"As much fun as I'm having letting Hal in on a few of our secrets, I'm afraid that we're wasting precious time."

Cohen reaches down and grabs me by the throat.

"Are you ready to talk?"

I'm not ready to talk. I'm not ready to move. I'm not ready to breathe. I'm not ready to do anything but deal with the slow burn.

"Just kill me."

"Fine with us," Cohen says. He grabs a handful of my hair.

"I don't know about any pictures," I say.

Jacobs reaches into his pocket and brings out a knife, which he opens. It's the largest blade I've ever seen.

"I'm going to cut out your eyes."

I think of Maggie. I think of Tyler. I'm not ready to die this way.

So Tyler. Maggie's baby. Sometimes I would forget that he was there. Other times, he filled up the apartment. When I look at him, I see her. I see her whole life mapped out in his eyes. When he smiles, it's like seeing into her soul.

I want him to like me. I want to connect with him. I'll win her heart through her child. He'll like me so much, she'll never let me go.

But he ignores me. I'm not there. He blinks me away into oblivion. All of those picnics together, those walks in the park, those little league baseball games, those trips to Six Flags, those concerts, those Dallas Cowboy games, those trips to the State Fair of Texas, fade away into nothingness.

I panic. I want another chance. Let me ring the doorbell one more time. Let me stand there in anticipation, waiting for Maggie to open the door in one of those cute little sundresses she always wears, holding Tyler in her arms—

"You'd better talk," Cohen says. "You'd better talk."

"I don't know what you want."

"You're lying. Billy Joe Harris was following your girlfriend. And he stumbled onto something really big."

"I don't know what you're talking about."

"We know about the pictures. We don't know who hired him. We don't know if he was in on the blackmail or if he stumbled into the middle of a conspiracy and realized he could make a lot of money if he double-crossed you and took the money for himself. What kind of money can you get for pictures of the next governor getting a blowjob?"

"I don't know about any pictures—"

Jacobs punches me in the face. Right in the ragged bridge of my nose.

I'm numb to the world.

This isn't happening. Blood isn't gushing out of my face like a fountain. My brain isn't spewing pyrotechnics. I'm not here.

All I'm thinking is that Lydia should be done with her laundry. She'll walk back to her apartment, turn on Oprah, sit back and relax.

If I'm lucky, she'll hear the commotion going on through these thin walls—walls so thin that, on occasion, I can hear her and her punk-ass boyfriend fucking all over the house—and she'll get an idea that something's wrong.

Regardless of how much pot she has been smoking—if she hears Cohen slap me upside the head with his revolver—a little bell might go off in her head and she might have the sudden insight to call 911.

Right now, she's sitting on the edge of her couch, loading up a bowl, listening to Oprah tell one of her lucky audience members— some poor lady who has raised sixteen kids and has never owned a new car—that she's the lucky winner of a Cadillac Eldorado. She'll hear Cohen slap me upside the head with his revolver. She'll take a hit off her pipe, stick her head up against the wall and hear Cohen tell me that if I don't tell them where the pictures are he is going to put a bullet in my skull.

Lydia will think to herself, maybe I should call 911. It sounds like my neighbor might need a little help.

Through the bloody haze, I see Jacobs flashing his blade. This guy looks serious. He means business. He's going to—

"—Cut your eyes out, you cocksucker." He waves his blade in front of my face like he's a psycho killer, gets only millimeters from my retina—

"—but first," Cohen says, "we want to show you something."

Cohen walks over to my television, turns on my VCR. And presses play.

Praise be to God. I think I'm about to take a blade to the eyeball and these assholes decide to watch a movie.

But I know what's coming. I don't know how I know. I just know.

But before the movie starts, I imagine punching Jacobs with a hard right to his face and as he falls back toward the couch, grabbing his right hand—the one holding the knife—and snapping his wrist back until it breaks with a nice, loud crack and stabbing him in the throat with his own blade. He'll gurgle blood as he curses my name—blood pouring down his chest, the blade still poking out of his throat—and I'll grab the knife, pull it out of his throat and throw it at Cohen as he starts to shoot me with his tiny, black gun. The blade will pin his hand to the wall, and I'll walk over to Cohen and pummel him into a deep sleep. He'll be pinned to the wall by Jacob's knife, and I will pummel his face until you can't recognize the sonofabitch. I'll unstick him and pummel him some more. By the time I finish, Cohen will be dead, or will wish that he was dead.

But before I finish him off, he starts the movie.

I know what's coming.

A close-up of a naked man.

All I can see is his face and his bare shoulders, but I've been there. I've done this. I know how this one ends.

He says that he's happily married. A wife and two kids. Says that he's blessed.

"Then why are you here?"

"You're married too."

"I never said happily married."

"Semantics," he says.

"Do you have any secrets?"

"Everybody has secrets."

"What's your wife's name?"

"That's none of your business."

"Do you think you're a good husband?"

"I do my best."

"That evidently isn't good enough."

"I'm human. I've never said I was perfect. All have sinned and fallen short of the glory of God."

"What do you do for a living—"

"That's none of your business, but you know what I do anyway. It's not like I haven't been honest."

"Does it make you feel hypocritical, running a foundation that preaches morality? Does it make you feel hypocritical attending all of these charity events with your wife and posing for the camera and then hanging out at strip joints?"

The camera lens catches a glimpse of a mirror behind his head and you can see Maggie holding the camera—topless—wearing a pair of white panties.

"Yes, I feel hypocritical. But God understands. God knows my frailties. And forgives them."

"Would your wife approve of you going to strip clubs? Would your wife approve of you sitting here?"

"I don't like being judged—"

"If you have such a good marriage, why are you here?"

"My needs aren't being met. She's been pregnant through most of our marriage. She's got her mind on other things. But if she needs me, I'll be there."

"What if she needs you now? Maybe you should call her. Maybe you should check in—"

"I'm not going to call her."

Maggie gets him to talk about his sex life with Cynthia. Maggie gets him to talk about their children. Their hobbies. Their ages. What they want for their birthdays. Their baptisms. Their communions. Their report cards.

Gavin masturbates on camera—right in front of her—the red light going off in his face. He masturbates on camera and tells her that he would be willing to trade it all in—each and every birthday, each and every baptism, each and every communion, a life with his wife and family—for just one minor indiscretion.

Gavin calls Cynthia and tells her that he's going to be late again. He knows that they had a special family outing planned with the kids. He has some campaign business to take care of. It's all going to be worth it, he says. It'll take some sacrifice, but it will be worth it. He starts talking in baby talk. I wuv you too, my little pipsy fipsy. I wuv my wittle pipsy fipsy.

Maggie's hand comes into the frame to jack him off.

Gavin cries. The camera gets closer until the frame is filled up with tears.

The tape's over.

I'm empty.

"Don't act all shocked, Mr. Scott. We know you're in on this."

I don't say anything.

"We know you're in on a plot to blackmail Gavin Thompson."

"You're wrong," I say.

"Bob was in on it, too. A nice little threesome."

"You're wrong," I say.

"I don't think so," Cohen says. "We know everything. We know that Gavin met Maggie at Obsessions. He has a fondness for strippers. We know that Mr. Thompson was a frequent visitor. Gavin felt sorry for her. A stripper with a heart of gold. And Billy Joe Harris took the pictures. And Maggie took the video. We have the video. Now we want the pictures."

"None of this is true—"

Cohen pulls the hammer back on the gun and sticks it in my mouth.

Please God don't let me die like this. If you'll give me one more chance, I'll do everything better the next time around.

I decide to get back in the here and now. I'm tired of living in the past or living somewhere in the future. If I'm going to die, I want to be smack-dab in the present. When Cohen pulls the trigger and the back of my head splatters on the wall behind me, I want to be here for it.

17

I SEE COHEN'S TRIGGER FINGER—that tiny little spasm before you kill a man—and the spasm stops and Cohen has my death centered in his eyes and I thank God for the day he has made, and—

Lemon knocks on the door.

I know that it's Lemon because of his nervous rap. Three or four quick raps on the door. Silence. More raps. Finally, continual knocking. And Lemon, in his nervous voice going on and on about knowing that I'm in here, he knows because he sees my car. He really needs to see me so I need to quit masturbating—need to quit whacking off to my goddamn pictures—and get up and answer the door. And something about knowing who Celia is. He knows that Celia is not the one in those pictures. He knows that it's Maggie in those pictures. He doesn't know if I know but he knows and that's all that matters. Oh, Goddammit, Hal. Open the goddamn door.

"Don't know anything about the pictures, huh?" Cohen says.

Lemon raps on the door again, tells me to put down the pictures and answer the goddamn door.

"Get rid of him," Cohen says. "Before we kill him too."

I guess they forgot that I'm tied to a fucking chair.

"What am I supposed to do—"

"Get rid of him. Tell him you have the flu, tell him whatever you want, but get him out of here," Cohen says, getting right up in my face.

That's easier said than done.

Lemon won't go away.

I tell them as much.

"Well, you'd better give it a goddamn try."

"Go away, Lemon," I say. "I've got the flu. And I'm not getting off of the couch."

"Don't give me that shit," Lemon says. "You don't have no goddamn flu."

I picture Lemon leaning up against my door, his whole body twitching out of its need for some crank, a bump, a snort, a drink, anything that will quench this thirst.

"Open the door."

"I'm telling you, buddy. You need to do what I'm telling you. I've got the flu. I'm contagious. I'll call you later."

"I'm not leaving—"

Jacobs walks over and opens the door.

"Then I guess we're going to have to kill you too," he says. He pulls Lemon into my apartment by his hair.

"Jesus," Lemon says.

Lemon forgets he needs some crank, a bump, a snort, a drink, anything that will quench this thirst. Lemon forgets how much he wants to die. Lemon has a reason to live. Lemon doesn't want to die. His eyes are filled with that crazy wide-eyed fear—like he just walked into his dealer's house and there's a hulk of a man standing there with a loaded gun, like he walked into his dealer's house and there's a room full of cops with their semi-automatic weapons aimed and ready—that expects the worse. Things are so bad he can't find time to react.

Jacobs throws him over the arm of the couch, pulls out a long black gun and sticks it in his face.

"Jesus," Lemon says.

Lemon shrinks into the couch, burrows down—like the further he shrinks down, maybe they won't see him.

"You so much as even breathe, and I'm going to shoot you in the mouth—"

160

"I can't help but breathe—" Lemon says.

Jacobs bounces the gun off of Lemon's forehead.

"Jesus—" Lemon says, holding his head. "What am I supposed to do? Hold my breath?"

"Shut up," Cohen says. "Before Jacobs puts a bullet in your skull—"

"Ok," Lemon says. "Ok. Enough of the macho shit. I've got a headache. Hitting me doesn't help."

"—Please, Lemon," I say.

———◆———

They tie Lemon to a chair in the kitchen.

I'm still tied to a chair in the living room, and I've totally lost feeling in my arms and legs. Wish I could say the same about my face.

Jacobs is pacing in front of me.

Cohen is stationed in the space between the living room and the kitchen with his gun trained on me. And then Lemon. And then me.

Lemon's doing this little whimper thing—sounds like Charlie—and this little whimper thing's getting under Cohen's skin. It annoys Jacobs. It annoys me.

I feel sorry for Lemon. He got hit pretty hard upside the head with the barrel of a gun. His head can't be feeling too good right now—his T-shirt tied around his head to stop the bleeding—but at the same time, I want to tell him to shut the fuck up. We've really gotten ourselves into one gigantic mess and these two fuckers—waving their guns—are irritated. The last thing we want to do is piss them off. It's clear that the whimper thing's getting under their skin, so get your goddamn wits about you and get it under control.

"Would you shut the fuck up?" Cohen says, pointing his gun toward Lemon in the kitchen.

Lemon whimpers some more.

"Because if you don't, I'm going to shut you up. I can goddamn guarantee you that you don't want that."

"My head hurts—" Lemon says.

"I don't give a goddamn," Cohen says.

"I'm nervous. This is what I do when I'm nervous. It's a tic," Lemon says. "There's nothing I can do about it—"

"You'd better find a way," Jacobs says. He pulls the gun out of his belt and walks into the kitchen and shoves it into Lemon's mouth.

Lemon continues to whimper, but the muzzle of the gun muffles the sound.

"Don't make me shoot you in the goddamn mouth," Jacobs says. "If you don't shut up in three seconds I'm going to blow your brains out of the back of your goddamn skull."

Lemon whimpers.

"One—"

Lemon whimpers.

"—Two."

Lemon stops whimpering.

Jacobs pulls the gun out of his mouth and walks into the living room. Lemon starts whimpering again.

"You goddamn numbskull!" Jacobs says.

He walks back into the kitchen and punches Lemon in the mouth so hard it almost snaps his neck.

Lemon throws his head back and starts crying. I'm not talking those little annoying whimpers, I'm talking *baby got colic* crying. Crying like a little girl.

Cohen walks into the kitchen and sticks his gun to the side of Lemon's head. Jacobs jams his gun into the middle of Lemon's forehead.

Lemon's either goddamn clueless because of all the drugs he's done—is absolutely off of his rocker crazy—or he's the bravest man I've ever met in my whole goddamn life.

He starts singing "Tis So Sweet to Trust in Jesus."

It's the craziest thing I've ever seen.

They're about to blow his brains out of his ears from both sides, when there's a knock at the door—

"You've got to be kidding me," Cohen says. He storms into the living room and waves his gun in my face.

"Go to the fucking door," he whispers. "Go to the door and look through your peephole and tell me who it is. If you make a goddamn sound—"

He cuts the rope that binds me to the chair and pushes me toward the door.

"It's Gerald," I say.

"Sit on the couch," Cohen says. "If you say a word, I swear to God I'm going to blow a hole in your face."

Gerald knocks again and I'm praying under my breath that he'll go away. I'm about to give these fuckers what they want and they'll beat me around a little more—maybe beat the shit out of Lemon a little more—and then they'll leave. That's what I'm hoping.

If I'm wrong—and they kill me and Lemon and leave us in a pool of our own blood—it's not going to help for Gerald to stick around and get caught up in it too. He shouldn't have to die for the sins I've committed.

Thankfully, Gerald leaves.

I'm sorry that I dragged Lemon into this mess. He doesn't belong here. He's got enough going on in his own fucked-up world to get dragged into mine.

But this is how it's always been.

I'm not content to suffer on my own. I have to get all of my friends and family involved. If I'm going to suffer—by God—they're going to suffer too. That's just how it is. I'm tired of it. I'm tired of dragging everybody down with me.

"Let him go," I say, pointing to Lemon. "Let him go, and I'll give you what you want."

"Yeah," Lemon says. "Let me go. He'll give you what you want."

"You," Jacobs says, sticking his gun in Lemon's face, "shut the fuck up."

"Nobody's going anywhere," Cohen says. "Until we get the pictures. And frankly, I'm running out of patience."

"I can't believe y'all are getting so upset over a few pictures. As much as that cocksucking conservative gets around, you know that there are hundreds more out there. Maybe thousands—"

"Shut up, Lemon," I say.

"—Did you not goddamn hear me? Did you not hear me say that I'm running out of patience?" Cohen slaps Lemon upside his head.

"Ouch," says Lemon. "Why'd you have to go off and slap me? I'm not the one who has the pictures. I'm just stating facts. Thompson's a sleazebag. He makes you guys look like saints."

Cohen slaps him again.

"You are a goddamn numbskull," says Jacobs.

Lemon's about to smart off with *It takes one to know one*—

163

So I intervene. "How do we know you're not going to kill us once I give you the pictures?"

"You don't," Cohen says. "But you know what we're going to do to you if you don't. Your chances are better if you just give us the pictures."

"They're in the trunk of my car," I say.

"Keys," Jacobs says.

———◆———

If you've ever looked in the face of death—if you've ever been on the brink, if you've ever realized that you might not make it out alive—you'll know what I'm talking about.

There's a certain moment—if you have any time to reflect, while you're facing whatever it is you happen to be facing—that you feel absolutely nothing. I'm not talking about numbness. I'm not talking about sheer fear. I'm not talking about feeling a sudden peace, a sudden warmth that overflows you like a sunlit stream.

I'm talking about feeling absolutely nothing.

You don't feel empty. You don't feel filled up. You don't feel nauseated, lonely, hungry, tired. You don't feel sadness, loneliness, helpless. You don't feel angry, bewildered, hopeful. Not to say that there aren't moments—while you're facing death while looking in the barrel of a gun—that you don't feel all of these, sometimes all at once.

But there's that moment in time—a moment that you don't see coming—where all feeling is suddenly lost. It's like looking down on yourself, almost like an out-of-body experience. You're looking down on your life as though you are an observer. What you're looking at is entirely unfamiliar. You have no associations with whatever it is that's going on, and you're able to watch your death—or what may soon become your death—with absolute detachment.

———◆———

I'm looking down on me as I'm sitting down on the couch, looking down on Lemon as he's tied up to a chair in the kitchen, looking down on Cohen as he paces from the living-room to the kitchen, looking down on Charlie as he huddles in the bathroom tub, can see all of these things at once. Can pull up and go completely through the roof and see the whole apartment complex from the air. I'm not connected to anything. I'm a floating, sentient being.

I see Jacobs walking down the stairs and then down the sidewalk, past the laundry room—where he'll give a second glance to my punk neighbor's girlfriend, Lydia, folding her thong underwear—and then down the sidewalk to the parking lot to my car where he'll open the trunk and rummage around looking for the pictures.

Well before he's found them, I rise higher into the late afternoon sky—the light slowly squeezed out of the atmosphere—rising higher and moving across Dallas—spread out in multicolored squares, the city lights starting to twinkle, the sun being replaced by soft yellow lights spreading across the city—and I hover over the Grassy Knoll. Only a few stragglers are paying their last respects at the edge of the road—looking at the X that marks the spot—and I lower myself so that I can get a glimpse of the small line of pilgrims snaking under the underpass, waiting to get their miracles. I hover over Claire as she counts the register—walks over to the front door and turns the open sign over to closed—done with conspiracies for the day, locks up and walks to the Sixth Floor Museum parking lot, unlocks her car and drives toward home. She'll eat a light dinner and then go to a movie with friends, and make out in the car with a guy she just met—the cousin of a friend of a friend—who has quick hands, hands so quick she'll have to slow him down, have to push—whoa mister, not quite ready for that, we just met—him back.

I hover over downtown Dallas and catch Thompson's limo weaving through traffic, while his campaign manager gives him a blowjob, the stereo blaring Pearl Jam. He's sipping Cristal out of a long-stem glass. I follow them into Javier's and watch the maître d' hustle off to get a table for them. I watch the manager rushing over to take their coats. They're kissing Gavin's ass like he's already the Governor of Texas.

This kind of spectacle makes me sick to my stomach.

I move on across the night sky and penetrate the roof of Maggie's apartment. She's getting Tyler ready for bed. She bathes him, feeds him, and rocks him to sleep, returns her mother's call—I just need a favor, need you to watch Tyler for a while—and she starts getting ready for work. There is money to be made.

———◆———

I settle back into my body once again and all of my feelings return as Jacobs returns from his trip to find the pictures. He opens the manila envelope in the kitchen—drops the pictures on the kitchen table—and spreads them all out.

Lemon looks over—trying to get a glimpse of his favorites—with Cohen watching from the living room, looking satisfied.

"You've done a good thing," Cohen says. "These pictures were going to get you killed. But you've saved yourself," he says. "But if either one of you ever breathe a word of this little ordeal, just know that as soon as you get those words out of your mouth, we're going to be all over you like stink on shit. Just know that."

"We hear you, brother," Lemon says.

"Let Maggie know," Cohen says, "that the rules are the same for her. If she breathes a thing to the press or to her family or to a goddamn stranger, we'll kill her so fast she won't know what hit her."

"We'll kill her goddamn son," Jacobs says. "Let her know that too—"

"That's uncalled for," Lemon says. "You should be ashamed of yourselves—"

"Shut up, you goddamn moron," Jacobs says, slapping Lemon upside the head one more time for nostalgia's sake.

"You're a terrible man," Lemon says.

"Consider yourselves lucky," Cohen says. He takes the pictures, the video, and my pack of cigarettes.

Jacobs follows him. Just like they had appeared, they are gone.

"That bastard took our smokes," Lemon says.

"Shut up, Lemon." I say. "Shut the fuck up."

18

IF YOU TELL A LIE LONG ENOUGH, you start to believe that it's true. There's so much I don't know anymore. There's so much that I thought I knew, but now I realize that most of it are things that I made up out of the clear blue—things I invented—to protect Maggie.

What am I protecting her from?

Herself.

It's impossible.

"Can I get you something to drink, Hon?"

My waitress is half naked, and I don't even notice. I'm not here to get my rocks off. I'm not here to satisfy some urge that isn't being fulfilled at home. I'm here to see it for myself. I'm tired of ignoring the truth—hoping it will go away—pretending like this side of Maggie doesn't exist.

"Can I get you something to drink, Hon?" She doesn't flinch when she sees my face. My nose. My swollen lip. My puffy left eye. She doesn't ask what happened. Secrets are honored here. She doesn't want to know anything about my life. Her only obligation is to give me what I ask for.

"A Dr. Pepper," I say, when what I really want is a Jack and Coke. I need something to take the edge off. I need something nice and smooth to send me off into oblivion.

It would be easy enough.

———◆———

It all starts with that one drink. And one drink's never enough. And then, insanity. Doing the same thing over and over again expecting different results.

I find myself at bars watching television with a Jack and Coke sitting in front of me. I find myself counting my straws knowing that I should be home healing the wounds that I created the day before.

But with this kind of pain, healing's not an option. My only option is another drink. And in turn, my mind—that aching universe—gets a much-needed rest.

I erase all of those things that have brought me to this very moment—Jack and Coke sitting in front of me, four or five straws laying on a wet napkin—with another drink.

I don't talk to anyone. Outside of asking me if I need another drink, they don't talk to me. It's a stupid question, really. *Do I need another drink?* Do I look like I need another drink? Sitting here—numb, careless, angry, absent—unaware of everything. All of this spread out on my face like a rash. *Do I need another drink?*

Absolutely.

I've been married for less than a year.

At this point, I really should be at home enjoying Samantha's company. There are fences to mend. To keep the wolves at bay.

But she understands.

That's what I tell myself anyway. Samantha didn't walk into this blindly. She knew precisely what she was getting herself into.

Truth be known, our marriage is the thing that saved her. She needed someone who would never be there for her. Samantha spent a lifetime convincing herself that this was all that she would ever get. This is what she deserved.

So really, all I'm doing—sitting here with my Jack and Coke—is giving her what she's always wanted. Nothing. That's what I've got to offer. Absolutely nothing. And I give it freely.

It's in the wee hours of the morning, the bar starting to close. The bartender's about to cut me off. I need one more drink, and I'll weave my way home.

"No more drinks for you, buddy," he says.

I'm belligerent. I give him a long list of reasons—including that he is a sonofabitch—why I need another drink.

And, of course, the bargain.

This bargain is the source of my anguish.

"You can have one more drink if you let me call you a cab."

"I don't need a cab."

"That's the offer," he says.

"What if I call someone?" I say. "What if I get them to pick me up?"

He hands me his phone.

I call Samantha.

I tell her I'm drunk.

"I'm tired of this," she says.

"Then never mind, goddammit," I say.

I hand the phone back to the bartender. He talks to Sam. He tells her that I'm in severe need of a ride. I'll end up killing someone if I try to drive home. I'll appreciate it in the morning. I'll owe her one.

He hangs up the phone and pours me another drink.

This last drink is important. This drink is the kind of drink I'll never forget. It goes down like water. It calms every last nerve. It goes down easy and leaves me warm and comforted. I want this feeling to last forever. This is a drink that I'll take with me to my grave.

———◆———

"One Dr. Pepper coming up," she says.

She swishes off—shaking her ass—looking back at me to see if I've fallen into her snare.

She's pretty enough to occupy my thoughts late in the evening when I've got nothing else on my mind. But she's not why I'm here.

I scan the room. I go from stage to stage, watching the skinny, scantily clad women as they arch their backs and pose. They hump and grind the floor and then slink to the front of the stage to collect crinkled dollar bills with their mouths. I watch them swish their asses in their customer's faces, watch one woman grind her crotch into the face of an expectant older man, watch one woman flail her boobs in her customer's face and then push him away when he takes things too far.

I watch men in their business suits walk to the front of the stage with their twenty-dollar bills. I watch the girls swarm to their tables when their dance is over. I watch men in their business suits buy round after round of expensive drinks for everybody at their table.

A deejay in a hidden booth tells us to give it up for the angel of Dallas. This angel sent from God.

Angel saunters onto the stage in a white negligee with enormous wings attached to her shoulders by a harness. Wearing high heels, she practically flies across the stage. She twirls. She spins. She gyrates around the pole.

I'm in the Carousel. There's a jazz band in the background—*tssss tsssss tsssss tttssss tsssss*—and it's smoky and an old black man who has gray fuzz for hair is standing behind the horseshoe-shaped bar. He leans forward—a cigarette dangling from his mouth, smoke drifting off in the neon air—and points to a row of bottles behind him.

"What's your poison?"

A woman sitting on a stool at the bar says that I've got to try some of Jack's champagne. It's the best in Dallas.

I ignore her and ask for a Jack and Coke.

The old man puts it in front of me.

I take it and sip it down about halfway—looking around the place at the usual cast of characters—before finishing it off and slamming it on the bar.

I'm not afraid of these people. These small-time criminals. These seedy characters into drugs more than crime. A couple of guys who look like they stepped out of the pages of a Mafia novel. A couple of cops ogling the girls dancing around on small stages spread around the room. Sailors in their dress whites.

And a man in a T-shirt and a pair of brown pants—who I recognize as Lee Harvey Oswald—staring at the stage, expecting a miracle.

Jack walks over—leans down—says something to him.

Lee signals a cocktail girl who brings him a drink. Jack is satisfied, now that Lee isn't sitting here for free.

Jack walks over to a table and starts talking to a military man—who could very well be General Edwin Walker—as Colonel ███ walks into the room. The Colonel takes one look at the General, and the tension builds. But the Colonel doesn't want to cause a scene. He walks over and sits at the table where Lee is sitting—neither acknowledging the other—both staring attentively at the stage as Angel works her magic.

As the second song plays, Angel unhooks her wings—slides them to the back of the stage—and disrobes. Maggie stands in the middle of the stage in a red thong. Topless. Shaking her tits to the rhythmic beats of a song that she doesn't hear.

I hardly recognize her. She's not Maggie. This isn't the same woman who I've worked with day after day, isn't the same woman who talks to me during our lunch breaks. Phone sex in the wee hours of the morning. Sitting naked with me in the middle of the living-room floor. This woman didn't read my mind, didn't connect with me in a way that I never dreamed possible. This is not even the same woman who films me before we fuck each other in the middle of her bed, while Tyler sleeps soundly in the next room.

She doesn't see me sitting in the corner smoking a cigarette, taking the smoke into my lungs and then blowing a steady stream into the cold air. Fumbling for the money in my pocket. Taking one last drink of Dr. Pepper in an effort to calm my nerves. Her mind—her attention—is elsewhere. I walk down the stairs to the lower level—approach the stage and patiently wait my turn—as she grinds her crotch into the face of a young man wearing a baseball cap and a Dallas Mavericks jersey.

She tucks her money in her G-string—does a spin around the pole in the middle of the stage—and looks directly at me.

I'm standing right in front of her.

The music stops. I'm holding my dollar bill. She turns and walks away. She doesn't acknowledge my presence. She doesn't take my money. She leaves me standing here.

I won't move. I'll stand here drenched in sweat. I'm oblivious to everything around me. There are a million things flooding my mind at this exact moment, but the one thing that I know for sure, is that I'm in serious need of a drink.

———◆———

The Virgin Mother visits me in my dreams. She's a starry trail of blue light—a halo of color spreading across my room—lighting up the shadows in ribbons of gold.

I lie there in her heavenly light, her whispers filling me up with warmth. Everything's going to be ok. God is in control. Let go and let—

—when I hear Charlie barking at the front door. It's unusual for Charlie to bark. He's not that kind of dog. So I get up, put on a pair of jeans. The knocking continues. Okay, okay, give me a goddamn minute.

———◆———

Lemon's drunk. He has a lit cigarette in his mouth, a long teetering ash. Which of them will fall first? I've got to work tomorrow. It's not a good time.

I look at my watch. I look back at Lemon. He's wondering if I'll take the chain off of the door and let him in. Why would anybody in their right mind knock on my door at three o'clock in the morning? Of course, Lemon's not in his right mind.

"I can't do this anymore," he says.

He moves his hair out of his eyes and staggers backwards. He catches himself before he falls down the stairwell to his death.

"I can't do this anymore," he says again.

"You're right. You can't do this anymore," I say. What I mean by this is that he can't show up on my doorstep at three o'clock in the morning—drunk. Not when I've got to wake up in three hours.

"This isn't a cry for help," Lemon says. "This is goodbye."

"What are you saying?"

"I'm tired of living."

"Jesus, Lemon. This really is a bad time."

"You're telling me."

"I've got to work in the morning."

"Am I supposed to feel sorry for you? At least you have a decent job."

"Right," I say, removing the chain and opening the door. "That's not what I meant. But you're right. Why don't you come in for some coffee? I've got all the time in the world to sleep."

"I'm not in the mood for coffee."

He collapses on my couch.

"Whoa," I say. "Watch your cigarette."

"I've got it. I've got it," he says. "I'm not in the mood for coffee—"

"Sorry, Lemon. That's all I have. Since you're sitting on my couch at three o'clock in the morning—disturbing my sleep—it should be my call as to what we're drinking."

"I'm tired of talking," Lemon says. "I'm tired of feeling my feelings, pausing between the thought and the action. I'm tired of coming back because it works if I work it. I'm just tired. Tired. Tired. Tired."

"You and me both."

"Do you want me to leave?"

"That's not what I said. But if you stay, you're going to drink some coffee."

"I just want to die."

———◆———

"So talk to me," I say to Lemon. He's sitting at my kitchen table with his head in his hands. He's tired. He's drunk. He's not in the mood to talk.

"I'm tired," he says. "I'm drunk. I'm not in the mood to talk."

"Then why are you here?"

"I came over to tell you goodbye."

"What do you mean by that? Are you about to kill yourself? Is that what this is all about?"

"Not exactly," he says.

"Then what are you talking about?"

"I was hoping you would do me a favor."

"Do you a favor?"

"Shoot me in the head—"

"I'm not going to shoot you in the head."

"I thought you were my friend."

"I am—"

"Then shoot me in the head."

"I don't have a gun—"

"Then throw me off your balcony."

"It wouldn't kill you."

"Then cut my wrists. Please, Hal, I'm begging you. Here," he says, holding out his wrists. "Let me help you."

"I'm not going to help you kill yourself."

"I can't do it by myself. I'm too chicken. I need a little help."

"Why do you want to die anyway?"

"I'm thirty-five-years old. I've never been married. I can't control my urge to jack off in public places, and the bank's threatening to file charges because I can't pay them the ten-thousand dollars up front. They said I have another week left to pay. I don't have that kind of money."

"Did you tell them what happened? Did you tell them you got scammed?"

"Yeah, I told them I got scammed. Told them that I thought I won the Canadian Lottery. Told them that I got conned."

"What did they say?"

"If it's too good to be true, it's probably not."

"Ok, things are bad. But regardless, Lemon, it's not enough to kill yourself over. You just need to get sober and everything else'll fall into place."

"My mom has two more weeks before she's out. That means that everything she's worked so hard for is gone. That bookstore is all she has left."

"How can they do that?"

"They just can. And they will. I thought I would be able to come up with a plan to make some money, Hal. But it's not working out. And I don't have the balls to kill myself. What's my choice?"

"Get sober."

"I don't know how."

"Sure you do. You just have to do a few things differently."

"Like what?" Lemon says. "What do I have to do differently?"

"Everything."

"That's so revolutionary," Lemon says.

19

"—I REALIZE I'M NOT DOING IT one day at a time," says a girl in a white tank top. "I'm busy living in the future. Or I'm busy living in the past."

Do you want me? Do you want to rip off my white tank top, tear off my tight jeans? Because if that's what you want—

"—hard. It's just so hard."

"Thanks for sharing," we all say in unison. "Keep coming back."

Gerald walks into the meeting and sits in the seat beside me.

"How are you?" he whispers.

"Fine," I say. "Everything's fine."

"You look like you got hit by a Mack truck."

"I'm fine," I say. "Everything's fine."

———◆———

Gerald doesn't buy that. He knows something's wrong. On the way out to the parking lot, we talk about it. Actually, Gerald talks about it. I listen. I need to tell him who pummeled me. I need to tell him who turned my face into pulp. Secrets breed sickness. When he realizes I'm not going to talk about it, he moves on to Maggie. He forgets her name. He goes through a list of guesses.

"Maggie," I say.

"Ah, yes. Maggie."

He asks me how we're doing. I tell him about my fantasy to marry her and start a family.

"You're at that point," he says. "You've done the steps. You're turning your will and your life over to the care of God as you understand him. God gave us a brain to use."

He points down to my crotch.

He laughs.

Gerald laughs at his own jokes. Constantly.

He asks me if I've ever told a lie. Have I ever hidden a part of my life from someone else out of fear of rejection? Have I ever hidden a part of my life because I'm afraid of the repercussions? I should treat Maggie the way I want to be treated.

And he talks about anger.

"Nothing is more palatable than anger," he says. "That's why it's so powerful."

That makes sense to me. That's why it's so hard to let go. As bad as it makes me feel, I feel. I feel through it. It gives me those nerve endings that had been ruptured, soldered out of my very being.

It holds me over. It fills me up. It held me over for ten years. I heard nothing. I saw nothing. My life was a mirage. I felt hollow. I felt filled up. All in the same breath. I was nothing but one giant contradiction. Contradictions made me whole. They gave me something to live for.

Before the anger was a definite numbness. An inability to feel anything. I watched my whole world fall apart with the death of my brother. I watched my mother turn to the bottle. I watched my father fade into his own brand of nothingness.

It left me empty.

Gerald tells me that you have to be empty to be filled up.

That's why I drank.

I needed something to fill that hole.

Who knew that I would fall into a world where everything that seemed random and entirely coincidental was instead a world where a patch of mold under an underpass was transformed into the Virgin Mother with the power to heal. A world where miracles blossomed all around us. Where living in the here and now was an absolute joy.

Gerald tells me that I can believe or I can refuse to believe. But regardless whether I believe or not, God works in mysterious ways. The world of miracles won't vanish into oblivion. It will always exist.

"You don't have to believe," he says. "But that doesn't alter the universe of miracles."

———◆———

"Tell me about Sam," Gerald says.

"I'm not really comfortable talking about this," I say.

"Then you really need to tell me about Sam," he says.

———◆———

We met at a funeral. I had forgotten. We were all drinking at a pool hall—had been drinking all afternoon—shooting pool, when John's buddies stop in and remind him that his grandmother's funeral is at four o'clock that afternoon. He's already drunk as shit, so we go with him to be supportive.

We don't know this woman from Adam, but we're there for John. We're all drunk—sitting on the back row—and we look around and see everybody crying. People are saying all of these nice things about her, and we just start crying. All of us. It starts with a guy named Quentin. He gets choked up, and then my friend Jessica starts in. And then Bradley. I'm doing my best to hold it all in, and then it's the granddaughter's turn to speak.

It's John's cousin, Sam. The first time I saw her.

She says the most moving things. What she says is absolutely beautiful. She tells a story about her grandmother's birdbath. It was this little, old, blue number. Her grandmother kept fresh water in it. They would sit in the back yard in these yellow metal lawn chairs watching the birds.

Sam's telling the story in such detail. She never says a word about her grandmother, but she describes every little detail of that birdbath—this old blue ceramic number—describes the kind of birds that took a bath in that old blue birdbath, how the water glistened on their feathers. They would dip their beaks in it and in just the right light—the light would catch the tip of their beaks and the water would glisten—you could see God.

Sam closes her eyes. Right there at the funeral. In fact, she gets everybody to close their eyes. She tells us to search our mind for a picture of this old blue birdbath, the sun glistening off of the beak of a little tiny bird. By the time she finishes, I'm crying like a baby.

And then, I threw up right there in the church. I threw up on an old gray-haired gentleman with a really bad toupee. My buddies had to carry me out of there.

She was wearing a red dress. A bright red dress. A beautiful, bright red dress.

———◆———

We go to a restaurant with the family after the funeral. Chili's on lower Greenville. There are eleven or twelve of us. It's crowded. We're waiting for a table. They're telling stories of their grandmother. It feels like I knew her. At that moment, it felt like I had just buried my own grandmother.

Sam's mother pulls her aside like she has something important to say—one of those things that, even if it isn't the most appropriate time, you're afraid you'll forget. So she pulls her aside. She whispers, but we can hear what she's saying. She tells Sam that she did a wonderful job with her eulogy. It was absolutely the most beautiful thing. But she says she had only one correction to make. She pauses—all dramatic like—and tells Sam that she got one thing wrong in her description. The birdbath was red. Not blue.

She says, Honey, I can't believe you forgot.

And Sam—without flinching—says, Oh, I know.

Then why on Earth did you say blue? says her mother.

And Sam—without apology—says, Blue is my favorite color.

That's when I knew I loved her.

———◆———

"Tell me your secrets."

Maggie's standing in the doorway to her bedroom, holding her video camera.

I tell her what happened to Samantha.

———•———

Samantha comes to the bar, and I'm passed out cold. I'm sprawled out on the bar. The lights are dim. The bartender's wiping the place down—mopping the floors—and Samantha shows up. She's disgusted. She's embarrassed. She wonders why she ever married me in the first place. But she doesn't say this. She's quiet. They carry me out to the car. They strap me into the front seat. Samantha drives into the night.

That's what the bartender tells me. Later. I'm having an iced tea. I sit there for a good part of the afternoon. I want to know everything. I want to know everything she said. What she was wearing. Blue jeans and a white tank top. Her hair was wet. Like she had just gotten out of the shower. She had been asleep probably. Had probably showered to wake up.

I ask him if she looked happy.

He tells me that she looked disappointed.

"Yes, yes of course she did. But underneath all of that. Did she look happy?"

He doesn't say anything. It saddens me to the bone. That's all I wanted. To make her happy. That's the truth. I just didn't know it at the time. You don't know things like that until it's too late.

We were two blocks from our apartment when Henry Garnett ran a red light. A man I've never met. Coming home from a bar. I find his name in the police report. I read about him in the newspaper.

He broadsides us going fifty miles per hour. Samantha's not wearing her seatbelt. She dies from blunt trauma to the head. Instantly. Samantha always wore her seatbelt. Always.

I survive.

I survive.

I survive.

———•———

"This won't last," I say, after making love.

"That's one way to look at it."

"No, really," I say. "I don't mean that in a bad way. Just the way it is."

"And what makes you say that?"

"Just a feeling I get."

"Does it have something to do with the others?"

"No. At least not that I know of. Well, maybe."

"It shouldn't."

"But I'm no different. We may have different favorite colors, different hobbies, different likes and dislikes, but in the end, I'm just another guy in your collection."

"That's not true."

She eases herself off of the bed, walks over to her dresser, retrieves the video camera.

Everything stops.

I know the drill. I needn't continue the conversation until she's ready. If I do try to get a few words in before the red light appears, she'll only ask me to repeat myself.

"What will you think of me when this is over?" she says.

"I haven't really thought about it."

"But you said it wouldn't last."

"That doesn't mean I know what I'll think of you when this is over."

"What if I were to tell you that you're different?"

"I don't know."

"Try to know."

"I don't know."

"But if you did know."

"I can't say I would believe you."

"That is so unfair. I've been nothing but honest with you."

"Maybe. But then again, I know nothing about you."

I get up from the bed and walk over to her.

"What are you doing?"

"Let me have a turn."

I turn the camera on her. She shrinks up. Now that the tables are turned, Maggie climbs into herself. Watching her through the lens—watching her—is like watching a wall, watching paint dry.

She's a sculpture. A painting. Something to be admired, but giving nothing in return.

"Talk to me."

"It doesn't work that way."

"It should work that way. Tit for tat."

"What do you want me to say?"

"What you say is not important."

"Then why should I say anything at all?"

"If you want this to work, it should work both ways. I've opened up. Now it's your turn."

"I have a recurring dream," she says.

I zoom in on her face. It softens. It's remarkable what is happening here. In front of my eyes. It's simply remarkable.

"What kind of dream?"

"There is a house. In the dream. Always the same house. But when I wake up, I can't really remember the details. But a pretty house."

"Continue."

"Every dream is the same. A man walks into the house. And this is where the dream changes. Every time it's a different man."

"Ok."

"He walks into the house. Oh, and something I forgot to tell you. The house is totally empty. No furniture. No nothing. Nothing but clean, white walls. The man walks into the house, walks over to the back wall. And writes his name on it. I never can remember their names. But he writes his name on the wall and leaves. And the last thing I remember before waking up is how many different names are on that wall. The wall is covered with them."

And in the lens that is her face, a tear.

"I'm done," she says.

And I turn off the camera.

We climb into bed. And hold each other. We hold each other for a really long time.

I gather my clothes and slowly put them on.

She turns on the camera and watches me.

"Are you really leaving?"

"Yes."

"This is so unfair," she says.

I put on my shoes and walk down the hall.

She doesn't follow.

I stop at the front door of her apartment and call to her. "Maggie?"

"Yes."

The camera moves toward me, down the hallway.

I look closely into the camera. So close that I see my reflection in the lens.

"You're the house," I say.

20

THE CITY IS ANGRY.

We drive up Greenville Avenue, past the bars, past the couples eating wings and drinking beers and margaritas on the patios. They chain smoke. They laugh at people walking by. The men stare at girls in short skirts when their girlfriends aren't paying attention.

Lemon fumes.

Gerald drives.

I look out of the window.

We pass Whole Foods Market, the Blockbuster. We pass through neighborhoods of little houses with wooden shutters and groomed flowerbeds. We pass men watering their lawns and smoking their cigars. We pass children swinging in their swings in large backyards. We pass a woman in a short skirt walking her miniature poodle.

The class is conducted in a small room in the office of a therapist in a building off of Mockingbird Lane. A multitude of therapists— specializing in dysfunction—have their practices there. If you want a twelve-step group, you can find it in this building. If you need grief counseling, you can find it here. If your wife ran off with your best friend and you're feeling suicidal, you can pretty much bet that you'll find someone else in your condition, chain smoking out front, waiting for their class to begin.

This isn't my first time.

I come with Gerald on occasion. It helps me deal with my anger. And he thinks Lemon might find it useful. Gerald says that if Lemon's going to stay sober, he needs to get rid of some of his anger.

Try telling that to Lemon.

It was like pulling teeth to get him to come along.

———◆———

"Identify it. Listen to it. Let it go."

"Identify it. Listen to it. Let it go."

We sit in a circle—cross-legged—on blue yoga mats. This is our mantra. *Identify it. Listen to it. Let it go.*

Paul, the guy leading the session—a balding psycho killer with a goatee—has told us ahead of time what to do. He goes as far as to give us an example, with one of us in the middle of the circle— surrounded by the rest of us sitting cross-legged on blue yoga mats— our hands resting on our knees. The person in the middle does a free for all. A rant on all of the things that make him angry, a free association exercise. The person in the middle screams at the top of his lungs. When he's finished, the circle chants its mantra at him. *Identify it. Listen to it. Let it go.* When the circle has chanted it enough times— allowing the maniac in the middle of the circle to calm down—the chanting circle will stop. The maniac in the middle of the circle chants *Identify it, Listen to it, Let it go*, and points to the person who he wants to be in the center of the circle—they switch out—and this continues until we've all had a turn. We stand in a circle at the end, say the serenity prayer, and walk around and hug each other.

———◆———

"It freaks me out," Lemon says, when we're walking out to Gerald's truck.

"What?"

"Hugging everybody."

"It's good for you," I say.

"It's useless."

"What makes you say that?" Gerald says.

"The whole time that Paul guy was explaining things to us—telling us to Identify it, Listen to it, and Let it Go—I thought how nice it would be to cut his throat."

"You should do something about your anger, Lemon," Gerald says. "Before it eats you up."

———◆———

Lemon should listen to Gerald.

Gerald knows.

It was at the bar at the Dixie House, where Gerald first told me his story. Gerald exposed himself—opened the book on his life—so to speak. He told me everything there was to know about him.

Gerald got ten years in prison for shooting his brother-in-law in the face. At this point in his life, Gerald was drinking every day. It was the first thing he did when he woke up. Every day. Like clockwork.

On this Saturday, it had been earlier than usual. Seven o'clock. All he had was a six-pack of Schlitz malt liquor. He finished two of them before he had his breakfast, which was a piece of stale cornbread dunked into a glass of milk. By nine o'clock, the six-pack was gone, and Gerald decided it was time to start his day.

Which meant doing his sister a favor. He had promised her that he would fix her fence. Her dog kept getting out. He kept putting it off and the dog kept getting out and she kept calling him and begging him to stop by the house. How big of a deal can it be? It'll only take you a couple of hours. That no-good husband of hers couldn't fix it because he had a bad back.

So Gerald takes a quick shower—already feeling slightly inebriated, already feeling like going back to bed—and drives over to his sister's house.

Gerald's brother-in-law probably wishes that Gerald would have gone back to bed. But of course, he didn't. The rest of the story made the papers.

Gerald arrives at their house and is greeted at the door by his sister. Her lip is cut. Her left eye is swollen shut. Her husband—Ronnie—is passed out cold on the couch. Tracy tells Gerald that it isn't a good time. Maybe he should wait until later to fix the fence. Maybe he should just leave and not cause a scene.

Gerald's never one to avoid causing a scene. Maybe he should do things differently. Maybe he should sober up first. After all, he's heated up from the inside out from drinking a six pack of Schlitz Malt Liquor first thing this morning.

So he tells his sister to call him if she needs him. He walks out to his truck, pulls out of the driveway, and heads for home.

He makes it four blocks or so before he turns his truck around.

He gets his Ruger 9mm from out of the glove compartment of his truck and walks back up the sidewalk to teach Ronnie Franklin one hell of a lesson.

Ronnie isn't in the mood for an education. He comes out screaming. He comes out flailing his arms and legs.

Gerald puts a bullet in his head.

Gerald does ten years. Ten hard years.

That's what anger will get you.

———◆———

Lee Harvey Oswald had his share of issues. But when Mary hooked up with Lee, she certainly wasn't thinking of starting a family. And as it turned out, he already had one.

Mary never gave any thought about Marina—never gave any thought about Lee's children. In fact, during the first few weeks, Mary didn't have a clue that Lee was married.

When she found out, she quickly forgot. Unless you see them on a daily basis—unless you see him interacting with his family—they cease to exist. If they don't exist, it's impossible to do them any harm.

If he was getting what he needed from Marina, he wouldn't have to be stepping outside of the boundaries of his marriage. He wouldn't be spending most of his free time hanging out at the Carousel.

It's not like Lee talked about them.

To be fair, Lee didn't talk much about anything.

But if he'd shown her a picture of his kids—or if he'd gone on and on about how bad things were at home—it might have weighed heavier on her mind. As things went, Mary forgot about them.

Before she knows it, she's pregnant, and then she has her own family to worry about. She has to worry about who's going to take care of her and her baby boy.

When Lee gets killed, none of this really matters.

Until she sees a photo of Marina on the news. Or reporting on her testimony before the Warren Commission. Or the handful of interviews Marina does throughout the years. And then all of that heaviness that she'd forgotten returns. She can barely move.

That's how she looks when I drive over to Lemon's apartment to check on him, and his mother's sitting on the couch.

That's how she looks when we drop Lemon off at her house. Lemon wants us to come in and tell her that he is doing better.

She doesn't seem convinced.

She's drinking a glass of iced tea, smoking a cigarette. Her grief— her memory, the heaviness of all of those past mistakes—weighs her down. She looks catatonic.

She drinks her tea and smokes her cigarette in slow motion. She nods to me when I say hello, and the nod takes forever. Her head's still in its slow nod many minutes later, when conversation has moved on to Lemon and how he's doing.

Mary looks at him—this son who has suffered, who has had one setback after another, who has put her through hell—and she has that look that says maybe this is her penance for sleeping with a married man. This is her just reward. What she gets for breaking up a family.

It's almost more than she can bear.

———◆———

Lee isn't who they say he is. Not that what she thinks is important. They wouldn't give Mary the time of day, would dismiss her as a total kook.

That's why she hasn't said anything. Every one of Jack's girls who spoke out ended up dead or in a mental hospital, locked up for all eternity.

One by one, they spoke to the press, and weeks later, they would find them dead of a suspected heroin overdose or killed by a john in a rented room on the outskirts of town.

Not that these girls were perfect—none of them were above giving a guy a blowjob for some cash to help out with rent at the end of the month, and yes, she had known a few of them to smoke dope on occasion—but these girls weren't prostitutes, these girls weren't addicts, that was the kind of thing that Jack prohibited.

But regardless, one of them decides to tell her story and weeks later, dead or locked away for good.

Mary was convinced the government was involved. They didn't want the word to get out. If it did, they would do everything in their power to discredit whoever it was who had the balls to speak up. Discredit or kill them.

Mary had Lemon to protect. So she remained silent.

They must have gotten to Marina. Or she was sorely mislead. One of the two.

Because when she talked about Lee, it was like she was talking about someone else. She said that Lee didn't drive. But more than once, Lee showed up in a light green Impala and drove them both over to her apartment. Marina said that Lee didn't drink. But Lee was always drunk. There wasn't a time that Mary can remember when Lee didn't have a drink in his hand.

So either Marina was lying or Oswald did one hell of a job of living a double life.

Which wouldn't surprise Mary a bit.

Because there were things going on that didn't make sense. Lee was always on the go—always traveling, telling Mary that he couldn't tell her what he was up to, telling her that there were things she just couldn't know—and he would be gone for weeks at a time. And when he returned, he would have very little to say about where he had been.

He had very little to say in general.

But she didn't have any expectations. She wasn't going to nag him and beg him to start a life with her. And she felt the same way when she found out she was pregnant with his child. Who knows if she even wanted him to be a part of their child's life. And even if she did, he had another family.

The closest she got to telling him she was pregnant was when Lee brought home a copy of the Montgomery Ward catalog. He was holding on to it like it was the Holy Bible. He had dog-eared pages, but now—try as she might—she doesn't remember what he had been looking for.

He pointed out clothes that he thought would look good on her. He talked about things—new appliances—that would make her life easier.

And, as if he were looking into the future for a brief moment, Lee pointed to a cute little outfit for a baby boy and chuckled.

Little Lee, he said. Little Lee.

And that was the end of things. He would be dead before Lee Montgomery Pickens was ever born.

She should have known that he was short for this world. She never really knew him.

Lee was an enigma.

But one thing she knew for sure was that Lee was a different person when he drank whiskey. When he was drinking champagne, he would laugh and crack jokes—and although never boisterous and loud—he would have a really good time.

But when he drank whiskey, everything changed. He would become seriously quiet, and the smallest thing would set him off. It was like daylight and dark. He was *that* different.

When Lemon was under the influence of drugs or alcohol, he behaved exactly like his father. He got all quiet with this intense look in his eyes and you never knew if he was going to punch you or break a piece of furniture.

Mary saw this downward slide into drug and alcohol addiction, that slow decent into madness. She told him that he was going to have to stop drinking and drugging. If he didn't find a way to stop his drug and alcohol abuse, something bad was going to happen.

But he didn't listen to her.

The one thing she didn't dare say—but was always thinking—was that if he didn't stop abusing drugs and alcohol, he was going to end up like his father.

———◆———

Gerald tells Mary that Lemon's going to be fine.

I don't know if I believe it.

Lemon doesn't get it. There is this disconnect and no matter what you say to him—although he tells you he's listening—it doesn't seem to sink in.

I know if he doesn't stop drinking, things are going to get bad. If he doesn't stop drugging, he's going to end up dead, or worse.

He's going to end up hurting someone.

He's going to end up raping some woman on the street and is going to spend the rest of his life in prison.

Lemon wouldn't make it in prison.

Lemon would never make it out alive.

Of course, Gerald thinks prison might do Lemon some good. It certainly saved his life. Before Gerald's stint in prison, he couldn't stop drinking, he couldn't stop drugging, and he didn't even know if he wanted to stop.

But if he didn't stop, he would die.

When he went to prison, Gerald thought his life was over. And then he met Henry G.

———◆———

I never met Henry G. He died in prison.

I would have liked him, Gerald tells me. Hank had one sick sense of humor. Funny as shit.

Smoked Marlboro reds until the day he died of lung cancer.

He didn't apologize for it. We're all going to go when it's our time. According to Gerald, he would say things like that when they were out in the prison yard—Henry's cigarette bearing its two-inch ash, Henry flicking it away from him, sucking in a full lung of smoke and blowing it in rings above his head.

His face and hands were like leather. His voice like gravel. One of those voices that sound more like a cough.

This killer saved Gerald's life.

As simple as that, Gerald tells me.

He could drink you under the table, Henry. The last ten years of his drinking career had started well before the sun came up.

Henry had a gulp of vodka before his feet touched the floor. It was how he greeted each new day.

By this time, Henry had been divorced two or three times and was living all alone. Nobody could live with him. Not with the kind of drinking he had to accomplish just to start his morning. He would drink all day, doing whatever it was he did for a living. Odds and ends. Painting. Fixing up places. Whatever it took to pay the rent. But whatever it was he did for a living at the time, he drank right along through it.

Did his share of honky-tonks. Spent a good part of his evening in little bars with smoke-filled rooms and jukeboxes and pool tables and waitresses missing half their teeth. Bars filled with men who threw darts and played cards and gambled away their paychecks. They would drink and drink and drink into the wee hours of the morning, get into fights—punching each other in the face for sleeping with each other's girlfriends—and then buy each other a drink in an honest apology. This kind of man. This kind of life.

Henry G. didn't give two hoots about driving home drunk as a skunk. Driving home with one eye closed so he could manage to stay on his side of the white line. He didn't think this kind of thing was out of the ordinary at all. He thought that everyone drank like he did, that blacking out at a party and doing things that he wouldn't recall the next day—which on at least two occasions were reasons for his divorce—was perfectly normal.

He could pass a roadside sobriety test with his eyes closed. He couldn't remember a day when he hadn't been drunk to the gills on vodka or bourbon or tequila. He had gotten off going to jail more times than he could count—to the cops' dismay—because he functioned so well when he was drunk out of his mind.

Which comes in handy when you drink like Henry drank. But with that said—with all of the many times Henry had avoided the cops on his way home from a bar or had cleanly passed a roadside sobriety test—you're bound to fail on occasion. Which means spending time in the drunk tank. Calling your wife to bail you out. Attorney fees. Getting your car back from the impound lot. Appearing in court in front of a judge in your suit and tie that you didn't wear for anything other than weddings, funerals, and court appearances. And, of course, the occasional stint in the county jail when probation didn't seem like a viable option.

Henry does this deal four times—ends up with four DWIs—and still gets out of jail on good behavior due to crowding problems in the prison system. Within hours of getting out of the county jail for his last time, Henry makes it back to his local bar, shoots some pool, drinks entirely too much vodka—or bourbon or tequila or scotch and his fair share of beer—and decides that he really needs to get home. He walks out to his truck. Runs a red light. Plows into another car and sends a woman on to meet her maker.

You know the story.

They basically throw away the key.

Henry dies in prison.

But not before he saves Gerald's life. And he saves Gerald's life by showing him how to forgive. He saves Gerald's life by showing him how to give without thought of receiving something in return. He saves Gerald's life by showing him how to live.

21

SHE HAS LEFT ME MESSAGE after message, and I don't have the balls to call her. As far as I'm concerned, whatever she has to say can wait. I don't say this with a certain sense of callousness—not at all—I'm just weary. Regardless of what she has to say, there's nothing I can do.

I would be lying if I told you I don't think about her. I think about her more than I should. But I move on. If we were supposed to be together, we would be together. If you look at it any other way, it's enough to drive you crazy. I don't have far to go as it is, so I ignore her calls and move on to something else.

I should have known that she would stop by.

I'm surprised it hasn't happened sooner.

"Rachel," I say, when I open the door.

"Why aren't you taking my calls, Hal?"

She walks in without an invitation, flings herself on my couch.

"Have you been drinking?"

"What do you think, Hal?"

"Jesus," I say. "Jesus, Rachel."

"It's eating me up, Hal. I don't know what else to do."

"I can't believe it," I say. "I can't believe you're drinking."

"Believe it."

"I don't."

"You should. Don't worry. You'll be next. You can't keep the kind of secrets you're keeping and stay sober."

She's wearing one of those short little sundresses she wears and her hair's platinum blonde. Flung out on the couch like she is—extremely distraught and vulnerable—I remember why I liked her, remember why I was willing to risk a friendship. When she pulls up her dress and she isn't wearing any panties, I remember even more, and—although I know it's not the right thing to do—the only thing going through my mind right now is that I want to fuck Rachel all over the apartment. Why do I get myself into these situations?

"You know you want me."

"You're going to have to leave—"

"I'm not leaving."

"This isn't right—"

"Isn't right? Isn't right, Goddammit! You thought it was right when you were fucking me when he was alive. This isn't right? Don't give me your holier than thou shit."

"You really should go."

She pulls her dress over her head and throws it on the floor.

"I'm not leaving."

It dawns on me. This was the dress Rachel was wearing the first time we fucked.

———◆———

She was having a hard time with her grandfather's death—was having a hard time dealing with her father's cancer—and she told me she needed to talk. We had coffee. Ended up doing dinner and a movie. She said I ought to come up for a few minutes. And everything in my head told me that it wasn't the right thing to do. Fucking my best friend's girlfriend could only lead to trouble. But what would going up to her apartment for a few minutes hurt?

She walks into the kitchen to grab us a couple of waters. She walks into the living room holding a bottled water in each hand, totally naked. She's beautiful. She's tan. Her platinum blonde hair's in direct conflict with her tan body and she's beautiful and I can't control myself and we fuck all over the apartment.

I forget who Bob is.

Just fifteen minutes before, I was standing at the foot of the stairs to her apartment thinking this probably wasn't the best thing to do.

———◆———

"Fuck me," she says.

"You've got to leave," I say. "Get dressed and go home and sleep it off. I'll call you tomorrow, and we can talk about it."

"You won't call me tomorrow. I know you better than that. You won't call me because you're getting fucked by someone else."

She puts on her dress and stumbles toward the door.

"I'm sorry," I say.

"I killed him," she says.

"Jesus, what are you talking about?"

"I killed Bob. There's no other way to say it."

"Don't go," I say. "Stay for a minute."

I push her toward the couch.

"I killed him, Hal."

"We both know that isn't true. He killed himself."

"Yeah. Yeah. But why? Why did he drink? Why did he kill himself? Haven't you been asking yourself that? Surely you've been feeling guilty yourself."

"Yes," I say. "Yes, I've been feeling guilty. But drinking isn't going to help."

"I told him, Hal."

"What are you saying?"

"I'm saying I told Bob we were sleeping together. I told him the night he killed himself."

"Jesus."

"Yeah," she says. "Now do you understand why I had to get drunk? Do you get it now, Hal?"

"Why?"

"I was feeling guilty. I was tired of hiding our relationship."

"We didn't have a relationship."

"Is that what you think? It's not true, and you know it."

"It's all I have," I say.

"That's why he shot himself. He couldn't deal with us sleeping together."

"Yeah. I imagine he couldn't."

"Do you care? Do you care at all?"

"Of course I care," I say. "Of course I care. But what can I do about it now?"

"So you're just going to move on?"

"What am I supposed to do?"

"He was your friend."

"Yes. Yes, he was."

"So shouldn't you be mourning or something?"

"I'm mourning. Don't you worry about that. I'm mourning enough for all of us."

"It doesn't seem that way. Off fucking whoever the hell it is your fucking."

"That's my own business."

"Yes it is. That's your business. Just throw me away. Throw it all away, Hal. Throw it all away."

"I'm not throwing anything away. It's too much. That's all."

"So run, Hal. Run away."

"There's no running away, Rachel."

"You sure seem like you're doing a pretty good job of it."

———◆———

I've crossed many lines that I thought I'd never cross, found myself on the edge of the precipice and suddenly threw myself off without fear of repercussion.

I never thought it would end this way.

I can turn the events over in my mind—can pick apart each and every event that led to Bob's death—and say truthfully, I never saw it coming.

Not that it starts off where it ends up.

It never does.

It starts with the little betrayals. Those incidents that you justify to yourself and say that you won't let them happen again. You tell yourself that's something that you would never do. And then you tell yourself *Well, I didn't think I would do that, but I know for sure that I'll never do it again.* And then it happens again, and you barely know you're doing it. You have allowed yourself to get caught up in your own web of lies, and you really do believe that whatever it is that you're doing isn't really happening at all.

———◆———

The whole Rachel thing's more complicated than it seems on the surface. It wasn't anything more than an innocent friendship. I was her confidant. She and Bob were having problems, and I was able to help her see through the cloudiness of their relationship. I was able to help her understand Bob, in all of his complexities.

I knew him better than anyone.

You don't have the kinds of conversations that we did—in the late evening, smoking cigarettes on his balcony, watching the sun go down, listening to the last echoing chirps of the birds as they fluttered around the large branches of the trees outside his apartment before settling in for the night—and not know someone. Those conversations that come out of nowhere. Those discussions of your hopes and dreams. Your fears. Conversations that come out of the darkest places of the heart, the warm part of joy and the steamy stories of love between the sheets. You talk about anything and everything.

These conversations make me uncomfortable, conversations that go into the most private moments that they've shared. The night she found out her father had cancer. Secrets she wouldn't want anyone knowing. Like that she pees the bed on occasion, and that's since she's been sober. Conversations that traverse the deepest, darkest secrets of her past. She got so heavy into crystal meth that she started giving blowjobs to total strangers to raise the cash for her next score.

I already knew most of it. I've heard her share her story in meetings—in bits and pieces—so I probably don't feel as uncomfortable as I should, but a part of me wonders if I should know these kinds of things. She would be horrified knowing Bob and I were smoking cigarettes on his balcony—listening to the birds chirp before settling in for the night, watching the moon rise up into the sky—while talking about her past indiscretions.

Although it makes me feel uncomfortable, I start to look forward to these conversations. You really start to care about a person when you hear about their secrets. You start to really love someone when you hear their secrets, and identify.

It helps you know that you're not alone.

Conversations like these.

He told me that he loved her. He really loved her. At the same time, he was thinking about leaving her. You can love someone without making a lifetime commitment. That's what he said to me. I remember it vividly. You can love someone without devoting your life to them.

But Bob had never been good at walking away. Instead, he would stay in a relationship that wasn't going as perfectly as he wanted— would hate himself for not having the balls to walk away—and be miserable.

He didn't want to do this with Rachel.

She deserved the truth.

I listened intently. I didn't allow myself to get in the middle, didn't allow myself to offer a lot of opinion about something that I didn't know firsthand.

But I did tell him that I thought he was making a mistake.

I did tell him that there was something different about Rachel.

She was the kind of girl worth sticking around for.

I could say—in all honesty—that she was one of those women who come along once or twice in a lifetime.

But regardless how many times I cautioned him against walking out on Rachel, Bob was going to do what Bob was going to do.

It was my job to be supportive. My job as a friend.

I did my best, considering the circumstances.

But I never thought it would end up like this. I never thought that violence would creep its way into something so averse to such a thing, never thought that viciousness would weave its angry self into a place called love.

The heart is deceitful above all things.

22

LEMON ISN'T READY.

He opens the door like he just got out of bed.

"Do you want to go to jail, Lemon? Is that what you want—"

"What do you think?" he says. He turns and walks into his apartment, and I follow him. He gets a pack of cigarettes off of the top of his television and lights one up, takes the smoke into his lungs like he needs it to breathe.

"—Because if you want to go to jail, being late for court is the way to do it."

"I'm not going to be late for court."

"You haven't even started getting ready."

"I don't have much to do," Lemon says. "I just need to freshen up."

"You need to do more than freshen up," I say. "You need a serious shower. And a serious shave."

"Back off," Lemon says.

"I'm not going to back off," I say. "I'm trying to help you out."

"You're not my goddamn mother."

"Someone has to do it," I say.

"You're not that someone."

"Why don't you get ready?"

"I'm going, I'm going."

He continues smoking while he puts on a pair of dark pants and a white shirt. It's wrinkled. It looks like he's slept in it for days.

"Aren't you going to iron that?" I say. "It's wrinkled. It looks like you've slept in it for days."

"It's fine," he says. "I'm not trying to win a beauty pageant, I'm going to court."

"If the judge feels like you haven't met his requirements, you'll be going to jail. I don't guess what you're wearing will matter then."

"Jesus," Lemon says. "Jesus Christ."

———◆———

Lemon hasn't been going to his court-ordered therapist. And I don't understand it. He's lucky that they're giving him a chance.

They frown upon exposing yourself in the park in front of a troop of Girl Scouts.

They lock those guys up as sex offenders, and they throw away the key.

Lemon doesn't get it. Lemon doesn't understand why he's considered a threat, why he needs rehabilitation.

"Society is afraid of sex. That's what it is. They use people like me as the poster child of bad behavior while they go about their daily lives doing the same or worse. These people should quit using me to justify their own behavior. Yes, they're sleeping with their personal assistant—but at least they're not streaking in the city park."

"It's more than that Lemon. You can't justify your behavior by saying society is afraid of sex."

"I'm not afraid of my sexuality."

"But they are, Lemon. They're afraid of your sexuality. They're going to lock you up if you don't keep your clothes on in public."

"How about the homeless? Are you telling me that not only do we have the right to deny them a roof over their heads but we have the right to deny them the simple sexual pleasures that God bestowed on us at birth? Criticize me all you want—I'm fighting for civil rights. As a progressive citizen of these United States, I can't apologize for archaic laws that shouldn't be on the books in the first place. Call it civil disobedience."

"I call it denial."

"Call it what you will, I'm a freedom fighter."

—◆—

The courtroom is filled with degenerates. Overflowing with them. A man with his third DWI—swollen from all of his years of drinking, beet-red face and nose pocked with thousands of tiny busted blood vessels, gray hair shooting out of his nose, decked out in a fancy suit and a pin-striped tie and cuff links—wondering why all of the money that he has in his bank account can't save him when he puts a drink in his hand. A couple of girls charged with prostitution, in clothes that show way more cleavage than the court allows. Skintight skirts and fishnet stockings and the reddest red lipstick that you have ever laid your eyes on—the kind that never washes off collars. In deciding what to wear, they weighed their options—wondering if they should go with something conservative—but their street clothes won out. The best way to win the judge over was to give him an erection and then offer to give him a blowjob. Of course, they wouldn't charge. And they wouldn't swallow. They have their dignity. A young man charged as a minor in possession of alcohol. In trouble with the courts. In trouble at home, his father and mother refusing to speak to him until he gets it all behind him. His future is threatened. What kind of school is going to accept you when you have trouble on your record? Speeding violators and drug offenders and a smattering of sex crimes. Young men caught flashing in the park. A couple caught naked in the back seat of the boy's car. An eighteen-year-old man who has been fucking his fourteen-year-old neighbor.

I feel right at home.

Like all of the others, Lemon's not guilty. He's here by accident. I tell him—over and over—on the way to the courthouse that he must be honest and forthright with the judge. The only way that he's going to beat this is by accepting responsibility. He can lie and cheat his way out of it and get out of doing any jail time, but—at the end of the day—if he lies and cheats his way out of it, he'll get it in the end. That's how the universe works. I have myself as an example.

Try telling that to Lemon.

As we sit in the courtroom, Lemon starts to fidget. Playing with his hands. Making smacking noises with his lips. Twirling his thumbs. Crinkling his gum wrapper. Pulling out his library card. Folding his money in various shapes. Making a small tear in George Washington's mouth and moving it, making George talk along with the words of the judge.

The man with the beet-red face and the pocked nose.

George Washington says: Guilty.

The girls arrested for prostitution in their clothes that show way more cleavage than the court allows. And skintight skirts and fishnet stockings and the reddest red lipstick that you have ever laid your eyes on, the kind that never washes off collars.

George Washington says: Not guilty.

"Jesus," Lemon says, "they bribed him."

"Stop, Lemon," I say.

"Did you see them? At the end. When they walked up and whispered in his ear. They offered to give him a blowjob."

"Stop," I say.

The judge moves on to the minor in possession.

George Washington says: Guilty.

The speeders and drug offenders and the smattering of sex crimes, the young men caught flashing in the park, the couple caught naked in the back seat of the boy's car, the eighteen-year-old man who has been fucking his fourteen-year-old-neighbor.

George Washington says: Guilty. Guilty. Guilty.

"Jesus," Lemon says. "Isn't there any justice here?"

"This is justice," I whisper. "You'd better be on your best behavior. This guy's not easy on anybody."

"Unless you offer to give him a blowjob."

"How about not mentioning that you're a freedom fighter for the sexual revolution," I whisper. "Promise me that."

"You don't have to worry about that," Lemon says. "I'm not crazy."

———◆———

The judge has a shock of white hair and bushy eyebrows and wrinkles that run across his face like red-dirt roads, with bumps and crevices and well-worn divots that have been washed by wind and rain and embedded in a red earth.

When the bailiff calls Lemon's name, I realize that Lemon's days of freedom are over.

Lemon straightens his tie, squeezes down our aisle, and makes his way to the bench.

The judge looks down at his court docket, looks at Lemon, and then looks down at his court docket again.

"Defendant Pickens?"

"Yes, your honorable," Lemon says.

"Says here in my records that you have violated your probation. This is your opportunity to show cause as to why the judgment in front of me should not become final."

"Guilty, your honorable," Lemon says.

"Fine," the judge says. "That's easy enough."

"Guilty as charged," Lemon says. "But I have a higher authority, your honorable—a higher judge to which I submit my authority. It's an abomination to abide by an earthly court of law in direct conflict with the Lord God Almighty."

"I hope this isn't long," says the judge. "I have a good forty more defendants to stand before this court today."

"I respect that, your honorable. I wish I weren't standing here before you. But many are called, few are chosen."

"Tell me this, Mr. Pickens," says the judge. "Why did you find it necessary to miss your meeting with your probation officer on two separate occasions? Why did you find it necessary to miss your meeting with your court- appointed therapist on three separate occasions?"

"By his stripes I am healed, your honorable. I will not waste the time of this court—being that it is of great and uttermost value—by postponing the inevitable in explanatory utterfication. In my time of fasting and prayer during my most recent spiritual retreat, the Lord God Almighty wiped my slate clean and told me thou shalt have no other gods before him. With that said, may you enter your verdict with a clean and perfect heart, knowing that your judgment will be thoughtfully and gratefully accommodated with my utter and full participation. I bless you in the name of all that is perfect and holy."

"Guilty," says the judge. "With a sentence of thirty days in the Lew Sterrett Correctional Facility, effective immediately."

"You've got to be fucking kidding me," Lemon says.

"What did you say?" says the judge.

"What do you have to do to get an innocent verdict around here? Would it help if I gave you a blowjob? Do you want me to come around there, hike up your robes, and blow you off? Because if that's what it takes, I'm willing to go down on you for the cause."

"Sixty days."

"You're one sick bastard, you know that?"

"Ninety days."

"Fuck you."

"One hundred and twenty days."

"That's all? Well, goddamn. That's a hall pass."

"One hundred and fifty days."

"How about you drop my sentence for exposing myself in public, and I'll drop the fact that you're a fuckwad. Does that sound like a deal, your holiness?"

"One year," says the judge.

"Fuck you and the horse you rode in on," Lemon says.

———◆———

People—judges in particular—are not fond of being told *fuck you and the horse you rode in on*, and particularly not in a courtroom filled with petty criminals.

There's a point at which one must set an example.

Mr. Judge here, is no exception.

Lemon goes from thirty days to a year in jail, in microseconds.

But the fun doesn't stop here. He calls his bailiff and a smattering of other law enforcement officers who happen to be in the vicinity—this being, after all, a courthouse—and they yank Lemon out of the courtroom like he shot the judge in cold blood.

Lemon doesn't go without a fight. Not only does he curse each and every officer, each and every felon in the gallery—and of course the judge—but he curses their children and their children's children, and their children's children's children. By the time it is over, I feel like I'm in the middle of a bad dream.

It is surreal.

I should have seen it coming.

After all, we're talking about the bastard son of Lee Harvey Oswald.

———◆———

It seems that Lemon knew all along that he would be spending some time in jail. He knew this ahead of time.

Lemon sent me a package in the mail. Scheduled for next day delivery, it was waiting for me by the time I got home from court.

It was a manila envelope. Inside it contained a rambling three-page letter and the picture that seemed to have started Lemon's descent into madness in the first place.

With Charlie whining at my feet to be taken for his walk, I sit down on my couch and read Lemon's note. He wants me to know that although all of this seems arbitrary, there is much more than it seems on the surface.

They have been wanting to take him down for years.

Cohen and Jacobs. The judge. Gavin Thompson.

This all ties in together. Bob's murder. Lemon's arrest for public indecency. This isn't something haphazard that just happened. This was well planned.

Take for instance, the judge. Classic John Birch Society Member who has been wrapped up in a campaign from the early 1960s to do away with the government as we know it, and get one of their own into the White House. Running a campaign behind closed doors—accusing LBJ of having something to do with the assassination of President John F. Kennedy—and in public, showing his support of the incoming President. Talk about contradiction. Preaching too much government on one hand and—in the other—participating in a government that's working toward enslaving its citizens and turning the U.S. of A. into a goddamn police state.

It seems old Judge Habersham was a young federal prosecutor who ran around with old LBJ around the time LBJ was sworn in after that fateful day in Dallas. If you look close enough, you can see old Judge Habersham in several of the swearing-in pictures.

Seems like the judge was connected to LBJ at the hip. But behind closed doors, he ran a smear campaign against him. He's a man who can't be trusted. Turns out he ran with a certain General by the name of Edwin Walker. Turns out these guys hung out at a certain burlesque club on the weekends. These guys have big secrets they're covering up. They're worried that Lemon's going to expose them.

Lemon doesn't want me to think of him as a hero. He's an ordinary American citizen thrown into extraordinary circumstances. He's willing to fight until he has no fight left.

What do I think Lemon's father was trying to prevent in the first place? Lee Harvey Oswald had infiltrated the very web of deceit that they would later accuse him of masterminding. The JBS was out to kill the President of the United States because they felt he was in bed with Fidel Castro. They let Oswald take the fall. Or they set him up, who knows. But tell me this, why would Oswald—a supposed defender of communism—set out to assassinate a president who was in bed with Fidel Castro, after attempting to assassinate a general who was an avid communist hunter?

Of course, you and I both know that Oswald didn't attempt to assassinate General Walker. That was a young Colonel who was tired of Walker sleeping with his girlfriend.

Who knows if the JBS carried out the assassination of the President of the United States or not, but they certainly had the ways and the means. They certainly had an agenda. Passing out literature the day Kennedy came to Dallas, calling him a traitor. Although they've changed their tune in the public eye, they're still a powerful force behind the scenes. It looks like they're about to usher in one of their own into the position of Governor of Texas. And then the White House.

I'm telling you, Hal, they'll stop at nothing. It's not like you know who they are, being so famous for their secrecy. You may not know it, but they're everywhere. He gives me a list of everybody who's anybody who has direct ties with the John Birch Society. The list alone takes up two pages of Lemon's three-page tirade. Which includes Mr. Gavin Thompson, CEO of the Maddox Foundation and the future Governor of Texas. Don't be surprised here, Lemon says. The Maddox Foundation is in deep. One can argue that The Maddox Foundation *is* the John Birch Society. Founded by oil tycoon August Maddox, the Foundation has pretty much funded any and every activity that the John Birch Society has been involved in, from the past to the present. Who do you think funded General Edwin Walker's efforts to disseminate JBS into the United States' military? The Maddox Foundation. Who do you think funds surveillance cameras in downtown Dallas and the surrounding cities? The Maddox Foundation. Who do you think funded the surveillance project on the Texas-Mexico Border that has surveillance cameras spread across a third of the border? The Maddox Foundation. Of course, they're not turning them on the border, they're turning them on the American people. They don't really care who's crossing our border, but they do care what we're doing. They found a way to get us on tape without the American public coming unraveled.

Don't kid yourself, anything going on—of any consequence—is heavily connected with the John Birch Society, funded in large part by the Maddox Foundation. And Cohen and Jacobs? JBS Operatives. Gavin Thompson? JBS. Running for the Governorship of the State of Texas. Give him a few years: Presidency of the United States of America. You watch, Lemon writes. You keep your eyes open. As soon as he occupies the White House, that's when all hell will break loose. That's when they start lining us up and marching us into concentration camps if we don't march to the beat of the drum they're playing.

He explains that the picture—which is included in this envelope—is the first step at uncovering the conspiracy. If I will leak this to the press so the powers that be can't suppress it, then I might be able to stop—what Lemon calls—the greatest injustice known to man.

You know what to do.

Godspeed and good luck.

Love, Lemon.

———◆———

This picture is the Holy Grail of conspiracy theories. If you believe that Jack Ruby killed Lee Harvey Oswald in a random act of violence due to his patriotism—due to his anger because Lee Harvey Oswald killed the President of the United States—then you don't give a rat's ass about the picture I have in my possession.

But if you're one of those who truly believe that Lee Harvey Oswald didn't act on his own—that Kennedy was killed by more than one assassin, not just by some crazed lunatic who wanted his day in the spotlight—but that a group of men plotted the death of an American President, then you want to see the picture that I have in this manila envelope. If you're one of those who truly believe that there was more of a connection between Lee Harvey Oswald and Jack Ruby—a shady strip joint owner—then you'll be curious to take a peek inside.

This picture doesn't necessarily prove anything, but it shows a connection. They have been trying to prove Lee Harvey Oswald was an acquaintance—maybe even an associate—of Jack Ruby since they put JFK's dead body on the plane to fly him back to Washington.

This picture is your connection.

The picture was taken by Mary Pickens. A burlesque dancer at the Carousel, dancing under the stage name Angel—at the same time that JFK took a limo down the streets of downtown Dallas, waving to the throngs of those who loved him and those who hated him. A burlesque dancer at the Carousel who fucked Jack Ruby because he was good to her. A burlesque dancer who had been cheating on Jack Ruby with another man—a man by the name of Lee Harvey Oswald—who was the father of the child now growing inside of her. A burlesque dancer who had been cheating on Jack Ruby with Lee Harvey Oswald, a man who would soon be arrested for the murder of John F. Kennedy.

So when you see this picture, the picture that Mary Pickens took of Lee Harvey Oswald sitting at a table with Jack Ruby, a young Colonel by the name of Colonel ████, and a General by the name of Edwin Walker, you're bound to get an idea that there was more going on than the government is telling us. There was more going on than Jack Ruby killing Lee Harvey Oswald because he wanted to get his picture in the papers.

But what you don't know is that Jack Ruby killed Lee Harvey Oswald because he knew that Lee was sleeping with the woman he loved.

Jack Ruby couldn't stand that. He couldn't stand that this woman—who he had bought and paid for, this woman who he had cared for as if she were his own daughter—had been fucked right under his own nose by a no-good loser who pretended to be a Russian spy one week and a CIA covert operative the next.

If you know anything about Jack Ruby, you know that that's something he wouldn't stand for.

Walking into the county courthouse and killing Lee Harvey Oswald was more than an act of patriotism. It was an act of love.

23

INSANITY IS DOING THE SAME THING over and over again, expecting different results.

Sometimes the miracle is as simple as having the ability to change.

It's not something you're going to do on your own. You have to turn it over to a power greater than yourself.

You have to want to change.

It's not something that's going to sneak up on you—something that's going to come out of nowhere. It's going to come from taking action.

It all starts with a step.

Driving towards Lancaster—going down 45 towards 20 and then cutting west, the sun barely making its way into the sky, my little blue Saturn zigzagging down country roads, away from the City that had pretty much eaten me up and spit me out—I have no idea where I'm going. I don't know what's about to happen, but I'm excited for the chance to do things differently.

It's not that I don't have an idea where I'm going. I have an idea what's about to happen. I'm just going to take a little action and leave the results up to something outside of my control.

I'm driving back into the places in my past in order to change my future. I'm going back to the town—that little town outside of Dallas that birthed my childhood—that shaped who I am today. This is where it all began.

I pull over at a gas station across from my old high school and thumb through the phonebook.

The buildings are run down and slowly falling apart.

I strain my eyes, and if I look out far enough, through the morning sun, I can see joggers, runners, mothers pushing their jogging strollers around the old track, where—on a moonlit night—I lost my virginity and betrayed a friendship all in the same evening.

It's been downhill from there.

It may seem like there's nothing that I can do about it now, but that's not true. I have to do something about it. My future depends on it.

I think of Bob's death. The night he called me. He knew that I was sleeping with Rachel and he wanted to talk to me about it.

The night that changed everything. The night that my future collided with my past. If I wasn't careful, the night that would destroy all chances of my survival.

Twenty miles outside of Dallas, and it looks like a nuclear wasteland. Your occasional housing development going up with identical houses dropped on identical lots with identical shrubs and identical trees—grass planted in squares—but everything around it bare for miles. A bomb was dropped here, and these housing developments are the only things left. I drive through the bends and turns in the road and then miles and miles of wasteland. Two men stand next to their mailboxes by the road. They wave as I pass, as if I know them. I've just left them, and they are wishing me well on my journeys through the wasteland.

My parents are not comfortable living in the city.

They don't want to be close to anything.

Their only connection to the outside world is their occasional chat with the neighbor—did you hear about so-and-so, or little Kimmy had her baby, yes it's so nice to be grandparents again—and the television.

My mother has already been sipping on a glass of wine. I smell it on her breath. She uses it to brush her teeth. She grins when she opens the front door and discovers that her prodigal son has come for a visit. Flinching when she notices my face. Flinching because it hurts her—even in her drunken state—to see me in this condition.

She asks a million questions. What on earth happened to you?

I tell a million lies. I fell down the stairs when I was taking Charlie for a walk.

She finally settles down and grins again because she's glad to see me. Her teeth are shiny red rubies coated in wine. She could pluck them out and make a nice little necklace. Little bloody pearls.

She's already doing that slurring thing. Her words drip out of her mouth in slow motion. They tiptoe out and occasionally stall in her mouth before stumbling out of her lips. Her words are too drunk to stand up.

That's fine. It really is. It has to be.

I'm not here to tell my dad he watches too much television. I'm not here to tell my mother to check herself into a rehabilitation clinic. I'm here to let them know that I'm still alive and that I'm proud to be their son.

It's doubtful that I'll put that into words.

They wouldn't believe me if I said them.

I'm stopping in for a little conversation. And some coffee. That's all.

My dad hardly realizes I'm here, but he does turn away from the television long enough to ask me if I'm ok—says something like, I hope you put up a fight, his attempt at a joke—when he sees the mess I've made of my face. He turns away from the television long enough to acknowledge that I've gotten into some kind of jam. And then he's back to his program—some news show—stopping between commercials to complain about so many goddamn commercials and then back to his program again.

We sit listening to the chatter of the television and my mother stumbles into the living room to ask me if I need more coffee. I fight off saying something about her drinking so early in the morning. I don't say anything to my dad about him standing by and watching someone he loves spiral like this. I'm afraid of his answer, so I don't say a thing. I'm afraid he'll say he's standing by her the way he stood by me as I spiraled. I'm on the defensive, and I haven't even said anything. I'm preparing my rebuttal—at least I got sober, at least I'm trying—but I won't go there.

I hold my tongue.

Because saying something goes against the very reason that I'm here. I'm not here to live their lives for them. I'm here to let them go. I'm here to absolve them for their past mistakes—here to absolve them for all of the things I think they've done wrong.

"They found her," says my dad. "Turns out she wasn't lost after all. Just turns up. Ran away with her boyfriend and didn't bother to call."

"Who?"

"The girl who was lost. Sixteen or seventeen. That girl in your neck of the woods. That girl in your neighborhood. Celia. Or something like that. Celia Povicov. Hungarian or something. Sure as shit—you think she's been kidnapped, think she's in some kind of mortal danger—and she just turns up, out of the blue. Case closed," he says.

———◆———

I find Travis Haley in the phone book. A Mr. and Mrs. Travis Haley.

He hasn't moved far. Maybe a mile or two away from the house where he grew up.

When I arrive, I am astonished at the niceness of his house—the way everything's so shiny and new, kept up, cared for.

When he answers the door, it's like looking into the eyes of somebody else.

Travis doesn't look the same.

He's feeling the same way. Almost doesn't recognize me. That has nothing to do with my swollen face, has nothing to do with my nostrils caked in dried blood, nothing to do with my face a multitude of blacks and purples. He backs up for a second and then moves toward me.

"Hal?" he says.

"Travis," I say.

———◆———

I meet his wife and two daughters.

We go out on his deck to smoke.

We drink coffee and talk about old times.

I tell him that I have something to tell him. I have to tell him to get better. So I won't go absolutely batshit crazy.

He already knows.

I tell him I slept with Katie. I betrayed him.

"We were in high school," he says. "That was a long time ago."

"It feels like yesterday."

I tell him I'll do anything to make it right.

"Take care of yourself," he says. "That's what you can do to make it right. Fall in love. Get married. And start a family."

He tells me I look startled.

I tell him that's the last thing I expected him to say.

He says it worked for him.

I tell him thanks, wave to his wife and two daughters, and drive away.

———•———

I want what Travis has. I guess I always have. But now, it's not the teenage cheerleader girlfriend with the perky boobs and the winner smile, but the wife and two daughters. A family. A home. Something to be proud of.

Travis is happy.

In my lifetime, happiness has been hard to come by. Let's face it, that's all we really want. All of us. We want something to come home to. We want a wife and two daughters. A family who loves and respects us. A family who thinks we hung the moon.

It's something you have to work for.

That's something I was never willing to do.

Until now.

I was content trying to find happiness by taking a shortcut. By sleeping with someone else's girlfriend. Shortcuts have their price tags.

I knew from the beginning that I had no right sleeping with my best friend's girlfriend. I knew it in high school, and I knew it when I was seducing Rachel out on the balcony at my AA club on a moonlit night. Everything about it was wrong. But I didn't think there was any other way. I was too restless, irritable, and discontent to find happiness the hard way. By working for it.

I wanted the easy way out.

I didn't think the consequences were too high a price to pay.

I was wrong.

———◆———

Rachel answers the door.

This is not the Rachel I fell in love with.

Fell in love. Who's to say that's what it was. Love's such a complicated thing. That's at least what I thought it was. It was one of those things that you don't have any control over. You know you shouldn't do it but you find yourself doing it anyway.

The Rachel I fell in love with—or whatever it happened to be—was filled with vigor, energy, light.

This is not that Rachel.

She doesn't look good. She hasn't slept. Wired out on meth or something, it looks like she's been up for days. Death, with a pulse.

"It isn't a good time," she says. She's propping herself up in the doorway. But she's not all droopy like she's been drinking for days. Her joints are stiff, like she's been snorting speed. Wide-eyed and buggy. And bloodshot. Her blonde hair, dirty and greasy. Fingernails grimy with dirt. This is not the Rachel I fell in love with—the Rachel who had a new lease on life, the Rachel who learned from her past mistakes—but a Rachel who's doing it over and over again expecting different results. This Rachel's crazy. This Rachel doesn't want to talk to me.

"This isn't a good time." She takes a drag from her cigarette and spews smoke all around me. She's lost in the cloud for a moment. I know she's there, but I can't see her.

"We need to talk."

"I've got nothing to say to you."

"No," I say. "I think you do."

She turns and walks into her apartment.

My first impulse is to turn and walk away. I don't have to be here. I don't have to witness this, don't have to be a participant in her slow dance with death. I can turn and walk away.

But I follow her.

She's on speed. Her apartment is spotless. She has been cleaning for days. What else do you do when you don't sleep? Everything's dusted. Wiped down. Neat and orderly. The books on her bookshelves are in alphabetical order. Everything's in its proper place.

But she's all in her head. She hardly knows I'm here. She sits on the edge of the couch like she's about to break. She's fragile. If I reach out and touch her, she'll crumble in my hands. I'd have to clean her up off of the floor—scoop her into the dustpan—and throw her out with the trash. You wouldn't ever know that she had been here.

Her apartment's quiet.

An uncomfortable quiet.

I can hear myself think. In audible tones. All of this shit going around in my head—wondering what I should do next, if I should try to talk some sense into her, should tell her that she needs to get sober, if only she would check herself into rehab then maybe we could try to build some kind of life together—and I don't know whether to stay or to go.

I should leave. I should drive over to Maggie's apartment and tell her that I made a big mistake. I shouldn't have walked out on her like I did. I want her to give me another chance. All of these things going on in my head all at once. All of this rattling and rumbling. Yet it's so quiet in Rachel's apartment that I can hear her heart beating. I hear the minute hand on a clock in her kitchen. The drip of the faucet in her bathroom. The slow whir of a ceiling fan in her back bedroom. Our past selves lying in bed—the leopard print bedspread in a heap at our feet, both of us sweaty from making love, smoking cigarettes—and listening to the soft whir of the fan. I hear the burning of her cigarette as the tip turns to ash, hear the smoke as she blows it out in a messy cloud, the sounds of cars as they pass by her apartment. I can read her mind.

That kind of quiet.

But her head is abuzz. There are some serious conversations going on. And they have nothing to do with me. They're not real. They're the kinds of voices you hear when you've been snorting meth for days.

She's not in any shape to hear what I have to say.

I don't need her to say anything. I don't need her to tell me that I'm right. It's one of those things that I need to say because I need to hear myself say it. I've known it all along but was afraid to face it.

I'm not leaving until I've got it off of my chest. I'll confront her. I'll tell her all I know.

"I miss him," she says.

"I know."

"Do you?" she says. "Do you know?"

"Yes," I say.

She slides a cigarette out of its pack and puts it to her lips—leaves it there for the longest time—lights it, takes a drag and blows a cloud of smoke over her head.

What is she thinking? Is she trapped in her meth- induced frenzy, or is she having coherent thoughts and memories? Or is it all lost? Regardless of what I have to say, she won't hear me.

She reaches across the table and grabs a small, framed picture of Bob. She rubs her fingers across the frame. This silent anguish. Crying with the sound muted. She's crying—swinging her head from side to side and then running the frame across her face and through her hair—but I can't hear her.

"What do you want?" she says.

I can't tell her the truth. I can't ask why she hired Billy Joe Harris to follow me. Why she hired him to take those pictures. Why she left the pictures of Gavin Thompson and Maggie Smith at Bob's apartment.

"You said you needed to talk to me," she says. "What do you have to say?"

"It's not important," I say.

It's really not. I know she hired him. I know he took those pictures. I understand. I really do. I did her wrong by sleeping with her in the first place. But especially, sleeping with her and then walking out of her life. And then sleeping with her again.

Rachel hiring Billy Joe Harris to follow me because she didn't trust me isn't important. Of course she didn't trust me. I'm not trustworthy. So she hired Billy Joe Harris to follow me.

He followed me to Maggie's apartment—one of the many times after work when I went to her apartment for dinner, being supportive because she was going through a difficult time—and takes a shitload of pictures.

Rachel didn't like it. When Billy Joe Harris brought her his findings—that I was spending time at Maggie's apartment—she was furious.

She went over to Bob's apartment and told him that we were sleeping together. So he would move on. So he would forget about her. And then she would be able to date me without his interference.

That night—while she was there—Bob called and confronted me. He had something to tell me. He wanted me to come over.

But I didn't get there in time. Instead, Bob blew his brains out with her standing there.

Rachel knew I was on my way over, so this gave her the perfect opportunity to plant the pictures of Maggie and Gavin. I would recognize Maggie, end our relationship, and come running back to her.

But all efforts on her part to scare me away from Maggie didn't work. I wasn't going to walk away.

But what good will it do for me to tell her this? I won't say anything at all.

"Why aren't you saying anything?" she says. "I thought you wanted to talk."

She hasn't been looking at me at all, and now—for whatever reason—she sees me.

"What happened to your face?" she says.

24

DRIVING AROUND DALLAS. I'm not certain what I'm searching for—what I think that I'll find—but I needed out of my apartment. Out of my head. I have a lot that I need to process. For some reason, it feels easier in my car. Driving through downtown Dallas—the buildings blinking on either side of me—watching couples through large glass windows near the street, eating their dinner in candlelight. And the occasional businessman calling it a day, briefcase in hand. The homeless—here and there, sitting on a bench eating a sandwich. Cops on horseback, doing their routine patrols.

I find myself sitting in the parking lot of the Daisy Chain Motel, wondering what the hell I'm doing here. I do happen to have the manila envelope on the passenger seat—sitting right here beside me—but until now, I can swear to you that I really hadn't planned on showing up here. Until now.

I suppose it's because Lemon has been on my mind. I've been wondering how he's doing, locked up in Lew Sterrett, serving out his time. Wondering if he's giving them trouble. If he's been locked up in solitary confinement for masturbating in the mess hall. If he's tied his sheet to the top bunk and tried to hang himself by throwing himself off. I think about him. His crazy rants. His schemes. His many attempts at getting sober.

Panhandling off of the service road of I-30—posing as a young man with Cerebral Palsy—wheeling his wheelchair up next to cars as they're parked at the red light, asking them for spare change. Flipping them off as they ignore him, jumping out of his wheelchair and chasing them down the street. You can't help but love the guy. He made me laugh more times than I can count. It wasn't necessarily the stuff you should be laughing about, but Lemon was funny. He was the quirkiest, funniest man I had ever been around. There's simply no other person in the world like Lemon. I'm thinking of him in the past tense—like he's dead or something. I pray that I'm wrong.

But I want to do my best to go through with my part of the bargain. I want to find the Colonel. I want to give him the manila envelope and tell him to do with it what he will. Lemon put his trust in the Colonel, so that's the least that I can do.

The Daisy Chain Motel's the last place you want to be once the sun goes down. The freaks come out from the shadows, renting their rooms by the hour, shooting up while watching bad television. They take a shower to clean themselves up, but with the grime and grit that lines the tubs, it doesn't do them any good. Drug deals. Hookers giving blowjobs. Pimps counting their money.

A woman in a very short skirt approaches my window and I don't know whether I should roll down the window and hear what she has to say, or put my Saturn in reverse and get out of here.

I'm still trying to make up my mind when she puts her face up next to my window and shouts at me in an undecipherable fashion.

I roll down the window.

"Are you a cop?" she says.

"No," I say.

"Do you want a date?" she says.

"I'm not sure what you mean."

"A blowjob. Whatever you have in mind. But no tying me up. And no beating around on me like you're my old man. But anything else. Sky's the limit."

"I'm not really up for any of that," I say.

"What do you want? Dope? Crank?"

"None of that," I say.

"You got no business here," she says. "Plug's gonna get pissed as hell if you don't leave. All there is too it, my man."

"I'm here to see Mo," I say.

———◆———

Sadie walks me down a long sidewalk, with rooms on either side—rooms that are dark, outside of the blue glow of televisions. They look like caves adorned with an adobe facade. The Daisy Chain Motel is a dilapidated replica of the Alamo. We pass the ice machine, walk up a flight of stairs that seem like they're going to buckle under our weight, and down another long hallway with a rickety row of railings.

Dallas glows in the distance. There's a clear view of the Triple Underpass and the Grassy Knoll. If it were light and you could see, then you would see a small line of pilgrims lined up to pay their respects to the apparition of the Virgin Mother.

Sadie raps on the door of the room at the far end of the hall. And waits.

"It's not too late for a quick blowjob," Sadie says. "I'll blow you ten times better than Mo will."

"No, really," I say. "That's not what I'm here for."

"That's what they all say, honey," she says. "Hey Mo, open up."

"I'm not here," Mo says.

"Could have fooled me," Sadie says. "I hear you. Open the door. You have a visitor."

"I'm done for the night," Mo says.

"Hey, Mo," I say. "It's Hal. Lemon's friend. I'm looking for the Colonel."

"You're looking for trouble," Mo says, standing in the open doorway.

———◆———

Mo walks out on the balcony with her cigarette. Which is just as well. I didn't feel comfortable going in her room. It would remind me of what pigs we are. It would remind me that things—when

221

you get to the bottom of the barrel—are ugly. Our core nature—whether we're good or not—is sometimes hard to look at. What we have become.

So I'm fine, standing out on the balcony with Mo, overlooking downtown Dallas, watching the lights blinking on and off against a dark sky, smoking our cigarettes.

"You missed him by a couple of days," Mo says. "And I can't say that I expect him any time soon. He's done for awhile. Says things are getting too hot for him these days."

"What does he mean by that?" I say.

"Who knows what he's thinking," she says. "But he's got a reason to be nervous. They've been after the Colonel for a long time."

"I need to see him," I say.

"Just what do you boys think the Colonel can help you with, anyway?" Mo says.

"Lemon wanted me to give him something. Personally, I don't care one way or the other. But I'm doing it for Lemon. Lemon wanted me to find the Colonel. And that's what I'm trying to do."

A young girl walks by in a short dress. Looks like she's ready to go turn tricks or something. She's way too young to be selling herself, that's for sure. She asks Mo for a cigarette.

"When are you going to start buying your own smokes, girl?" Mo says. But she reaches into her pack anyway. Pulls out a cigarette and hands it to her. The girl thanks her, looks me up and down so that I'll notice, and walks down the long hallway.

"You be careful, girl," Mo says. "The streets are ugly tonight, sister. The streets are ugly."

"Have you ever thought of doing something different with your life?" I say. "You seem way too good for this."

"What other life is there?" she says. She's offended by my comment. I didn't mean anything by it, I really didn't. But it's the truth. I can't understand why someone as smart and as pretty as Mo would be out on the streets. Renting a room by the hour at the Daisy Chain Motel. But that's not my business.

"That's really not your business," she says.

We smoke our cigarettes, watching cars pull in and out of the Daisy Chain Motel. A carload of young Mexican boys drive by and holler. The young girl walks across the parking lot and into the street. The carload of young Mexican boys backs up in the middle of the street, and the young girl walks over. They hoot. They holler. She gets them to pull the car into the Daisy Chain parking lot and walks over and talks to them through the window. She's trying to convince them to rent her a room. She'll do them each at fifty bucks a pop. That's two hundred dollars. She'll do them two at a time. Ten minutes each. Twenty minutes total. In and out.

It makes me sad, watching this. I tell Mo goodnight. I thank her for talking to me. Tell her that I would appreciate it if she would tell the Colonel I stopped by. Tell him Lemon's locked up in Lew Sterrett and would really appreciate this favor.

I'm about to walk away from her when I see a huge cloud of flame fill up the night sky.

It's a brilliant orange that leaps out of the Grassy Knoll. The entire Dealey Plaza is on fire.

"Take a look at that," Mo says. "Would you take a good look at that."

———

I know right away that it's Conspiracy Books. I don't know how I know, but I know. I watch with Mo on the second floor of the Daisy Chain Motel, leaning on the ledge, smoking cigarettes. Neither of us says a word.

I'm grateful that Lemon's locked up in Lew Sterrett, because he would be the number one suspect. But I don't have to worry about that now. They can't blame Lemon.

I want to get closer. I tell Mo that I'm going to get in my car and see if I can get a better look. I need to be able to give Lemon the kind of details that will give him some peace. I need to be able to tell him exactly how it all went down. I invite Mo. She passes. She needs to make some money or she's going to be sleeping in the streets. I reach into my wallet and pull out a twenty. I tell her to be safe.

"You don't worry about me," she says. "I'll be fine."

I don't know it at the time, but Mo will be dead within a few weeks. Plug will be pissed as shit because he hasn't heard hide nor hair from Mo. She owes him money. And she hasn't turned in her key. He'll bang on the door until he's about to knock it down, will finally use his key and Mo will be lying face down—naked—on the bed. There will be no signs of foul play. The coroner will rule it an accidental drug overdose.

There will be a small article in the paper about a woman found dead in the Daisy Chain Motel, dwarfed by the coverage of Gavin Thompson's landslide victory for the Governorship of Texas. It will not give any details about her life, will not say that she abandoned her baby and moved with a trucker to Dallas to turn tricks for enough money to afford a room by the hour at the Daisy Chain Motel. It will not say that she drank herself silly, that she lay naked with the Colonel while he told his stories about his love for a woman named Becky Bardow. The article will not mention that she and the Colonel danced naked on the second story of the Daisy Chain Motel and that Mo dreamed of a life where she was married, was still a professor, still married to an attorney, and still the proud mother of a beautiful baby girl. It will not say that she was sad and lonely and looking for a way out. It will not say that she was empty. And hollow. It will not say that if you held her up to your ear you would hear the waves of a thousand oceans.

———◆———

They have the streets blocked off before I even get close, so I park behind the Union Station and make my way across the Grassy Knoll. The crowd's already gathering. I don't know where they came from. But they're everywhere. There's no getting close, but I want to get as close as I possibly can. I wade through a crowd of onlookers—push my way past reporters and news crews—make my way as far as I can before I reach the cordoned-off area and cannot possibly push any further.

I'm dreaming. I saw this coming. Long before it happened. Not that I had any kind of premonition, but the way Lemon's life was headed, it seemed par for the course. I saw it coming, but it still feels like I'm dreaming.

It's impossible to watch this orange and yellow consumption without a jaded sense of reality. I watch the flames curl up around the building and think of Mary, think of Lemon, think of all of those relics that are withering inside a mass of heat, smoke, and flame.

I think of all of those theories, those blueprints—as Claire put it— all of those treasures that couldn't be found anywhere else, fading away into ash right in front of me.

I experience it on a gut level, this emptiness. Lemon and Mary should have burned up inside of it. It would have been quicker than the slow shrivel that their lives will become as a result of the fire. Burning up in the fire would have been kinder than the grief that will eat them up, one piece at a time.

Never before has this building been consumed with such thoroughness, such care. Although brutal, there's a certain beauty about it, the night sky being lit up like a Summer day. Books that haven't been turned in years, leafed through by the fingers of fire. Forgotten conspiracies energized in one last fanfare. Neglected words flung into the night sky with the same excitement they were thrown onto the page, when wild eyes threw their prose down in a fiery rant against whatever ill that ailed them. These words— baptized by fire—their ashes raining down on the curious and the passersby who wonder why everything appears to be wrapped up so neatly. Surely somebody else was involved.

The firefighters will track the dust of conspiracy into their homes and their children will take it into their barefooted skin and ask them in the morning about the cover-up in Los Alamos and Area 51. They will write their eighth-grade term papers on the Illuminati, will suddenly give up on team sports and dedicate their lives to shadow governments and patsies and mob bosses who were sleeping with blonde movie stars, and—in a jealous rage—hatched a plan to assassinate the President of the United States of America.

But now, as Conspiracy Books takes its final bow, glowing bright orange in the night sky, the ghosts from all of those conspiracies stand in silence—watching it burn, watching themselves fade out.

As the smoke intensifies, all of those theories and their ashes mix one with another, and we have new theories. Jack Ruby and Lee Harvey Oswald planning to blow up the Alfred P. Murrah Building. Timothy McVeigh—the lone gunman who takes his lunch on the sixth floor of the Texas School Book Depository building—focusing his rifle on the President's Motorcade as it wraps its way through the streets of Dallas. The puff of smoke from the Grassy Knoll, the magic bullet gliding gently from the sixth floor window. Another puff of smoke, the bullet dancing with John F. Kennedy, slinging him backward and forward. An alien from the mothership at Area 51, caught near the railroad tracks—questioned and let go. Jimmy Hoffa killing Timothy McVeigh in the basement of the courthouse. Monica Lewinski and her famous blue dress, blowing upward as she stands over a grate, found dead later of a drug overdose with only brief memories of singing Happy Birthday Mr. President. Happy Birthday, Mr. President. Flying off on a cloud of smoke in the great vastness of a Dallas sky.

———◆———

The crowd, still transfixed by the fire, doesn't seem to be thinning. More news trucks arrive. Passengers getting off of the train at the Union Station filter over. Everybody wants to know what's going on. Nobody wants to miss anything.

It's over, really. There's nothing else to see. I'm about to walk across the Grassy Knoll—about to walk back over to the Union Station parking lot to get my car—when I notice a small but faithful gathering lined up at the sidewalk leading under the Triple Underpass.

For some reason, I move away from my car and move toward them. I'm not sure what I'll find, but I'm willing to try anything. Doing anything other than what I've been doing seems like the right thing to do.

As the last surviving remnants of Conspiracy Books buckles under the weight of the onslaught of water, as the last surviving remnants become consumed by flames that light up the evening sky, I suddenly have no thoughts of the General or the Colonel or Lee Harvey Oswald assembling his Russian-made rifle. I have no thoughts of Jack Ruby. I have no thoughts of secret meetings held by the John Birch Society behind closed doors, or the Mafia, planning the assassination of John F. Kennedy in the smoke-filled rooms of the Carousel Club. I have no thoughts of LBJ conspiring with Dallas oilmen for his only chance to become the President of the United States of America.

I'm here for my miracle.

I'm where I'm supposed to be.

Up ahead, as I enter the Triple Underpass, edging slowly behind a small group like we're waiting to get on the Ferris Wheel, a small scattering of colored lights flicker in contrast to the flames looming on the horizon. These small, colored lights flickering in the darkness are candles laid at the foot of the Virgin Mother—gifts placed at her feet, a simple offering so that she might bring peace to their troubled hearts. Regardless of what I expect to get from my sojourn under the Triple Underpass, despite what I stand to gain from my pilgrimage to see the Virgin Mother, these colorful gifts of flame laid at the Virgin Mother's feet in a symbolic gesture of their faith, bring me hope. I'm not the only one trying to believe. I've been on a long journey, and I'm almost home.

This journey started with my discovery of Bob, dead in his apartment. The realization that life is fragile. Sometimes life gets the best of you. Try as much to find out the answers—try as much to understand why things happen the way they do—sometimes you just end up with more questions.

But I quickly learned that Bob was not the only one feeling desperate and empty. Lemon had been on that same search. Searching for the reason behind his very existence. These things that are complicated and out of our control. Searching to fill that God-shaped hole.

Up until that moment, I hadn't been able to put a finger on it. I hadn't realized that I was in that same predicament. Empty. Consumed with a severe longing for something else.

The night that Maggie sat naked on her living-room floor— holding my hand, telling me to close my eyes and to not open them under any circumstance—I had a revelation. A sudden vision overwhelmed me and wouldn't let me go. For some strange reason— and now I think it had something to do with the miraculous—I had a realization of who Maggie was. She was this empty shell. Nothing but skin and bones. Something had hollowed her out. An emptiness you can't comprehend. A hunger. And I realized how empty I was. This vision of Maggie—empty and hollow—spilled over into me, and I realized that I was empty and hollow. Empty. Hollow.

It was horrific. At the same time absolutely beautiful. I was on a path that would help me do something about it. It would lead me to my miracle. And it would do more than that—it would save me.

As for Maggie—although I couldn't admit it at the time—she was lost, and there was nothing I could do to help her find her way out. She would have to do it on her own. There was nothing I could do to save her.

Everything that happened after that moment was an act of desperation. Watching her drown and doing everything in my power but knowing there was little I could do to help her. She had to want help.

But that didn't keep me from trying.

These random acts of desperation.

At the end of the day, I have more questions than I have answers. I don't know anything about conspiracies carried out by Generals and Colonels and strip club owners and men who may or may not be working with the government in some kind of plot to assassinate the President of the United States of America, but acts of desperation in the name of love—*that* I understand.

The small gathering of pilgrims grows quieter as we reach the apparition of the Virgin Mother. Where there had been restless chatter, the closer we get, there is a solemn silence, something that springs out of the sacredness of our situation. Drawing closer to the Virgin Mother, each of us feels that we're closer to our miracle. Whatever miracle that may be.

How beautiful it feels to be in the presence of so many people filled with longing. How wonderful it is to be a part of this gathering that—by their very presence here—admits their difficulties, their transgressions, their frailties. The silent but outward confession of the weak. Our faith will make us whole.

The air's thick with the scent of roses—as if thousands of rose petals are scattered everywhere, their petals throwing out a fragrance so sweet it's overwhelming.

The flickering flames of hundreds of candles dance in the narrow tunnel of the Triple Underpass. Gone are the lights from the lamps surrounding the Grassy Knoll. Gone are the lights from the consuming flames of Conspiracy Books. Gone are the lights from the television cameras.

I stand in front of the Virgin Mother.

I stand in the near silence of the Triple Underpass, the faint sound of cars in the distance, the small echo of tires and their low thud as they drive away from us.

I stand in front of the Virgin Mother, with my thoughts. Soon, even the thoughts are gone. I stand there naked and empty, waiting to be filled up.

TIMOTHY S. MILLER lives in Dallas, Texas with his wife and daughter. He's been a ranch hand, waiter, contract driver, professional clown, and spent over ten years working in office services for two prestigious Wall Street-based firms. He is currently a business instructor who enjoys designing board games in his spare time. He graduated with his B.A. in Literature and Writing from the University of Montana, Western.

www.ingramcontent.com/pod-product-compliance
Lightning Source LLC
Chambersburg PA
CBHW061034120726
47910CB00006B/2240